Close Relationships with Strangers

a novel

Krista Diamond

simon & schuster
new york amsterdam/antwerp london toronto
sydney/melbourne new delhi

Simon & Schuster
1230 Avenue of the Americas
New York, NY 10020

First Simon & Schuster hardcover edition June 2026

Interior design by Carly Loman

Manufactured in the United States of America

1 3 5 7 9 10 8 6 4 2

Library of Congress Control Number: 2025945429

ISBN 978-1-6682-1105-2
ISBN 978-1-6682-1107-6 (ebook)

Close Relationships with Strangers

los angeles, amid scandal

chapter one

When she asks me what I photograph, I say people, which is technically true.

We're on a first date in Los Feliz—a bar inside a bungalow, banana leaves shading the porch, blood orange margaritas. She is a teacher at a private elementary school in Hancock Park.

The cocktail is pulpy. "Famous people," I say. "I take pictures of famous people."

"For magazines?" the teacher asks.

"Sometimes."

"You're being opaque."

"Websites mostly."

"What kind of websites?"

I press my fingers against the condensation on the glass. "Celebrity websites."

"Oh."

I ease into what I want to ask her: "Your profile said you teach third grade, right? What school is it, again?"

She gives me the name in a tone that says, *Come on, I can tell you already know it.*

But I keep pushing. "You must be around celebrities all the time. Teaching where you teach."

"I really can't say."

"Do the parents usually pick them up or do the nannies—"

"No, I really can't say." She knows what I'm trying to do.

"Right," I say. "I'm sorry. I shouldn't have asked that."

She nods, stirs her drink.

"Your teeth are nice," I tell her. "Like, they're a little bit crooked."

"Sorry?"

"They're a little bit crooked in a good way, I mean."

"That doesn't sound like a compliment."

"I mean, I'm always looking at veneers. I've been looking at veneers all day. Your teeth are real and that's nice."

The teacher reaches for her ice water and starts drinking it very quickly. She sets the glass down and doesn't look at me. "I don't really want to talk about my teeth. So you're a . . . is it okay to say paparazzi?"

"Well, yeah, it's not a slur."

"It has negative connotations. You don't want to be called something else? Celebrity photographer, maybe?"

"No, I wouldn't want that."

Mentally, I compare her to famous actresses who have played teachers, trying to figure out which one she looks the most like, organizing them by the ones I've photographed, the ones I haven't yet, the ones I could be photographing right now.

I'll give you some free advice, a celebrity meditation coach once told me. *Be present*.

"You like the term *paparazzi*?" she asks.

I finish the margarita, attempt to recalibrate. "It's accurate."

"But your profile said photographer."

"That's accurate too."

"So this is a stepping stone to being a *photographer* photographer—doing something artistic." She relaxes.

Her dress is white with blue flowers, which makes me think of Ellory, who had one just like it. She wore it once, on her birthday. Sunset on a terrace. A vanilla cake. The spray from the Bellagio fountains. The opera song I recognized but couldn't place.

"I don't mean to minimize what you do," she says.

"It's okay. I get it."

A pop song is playing—it's a former child star named Roxane Alexandra, who now goes by Roxy A. *Break my heart in the moonlight, go ahead and give it to me.* Last week, after her publicist paid me to take pictures of her leaving SoulCycle, she tweeted, *I just want to be left alone like a normal teenager for like five minutes.*

I try to get the teacher to talk about her job again, the celebrity parents, but she continues to ask me about what I do. "So what is it that you like about it?"

I give her one of my prepared answers. Paparazzi photography is art, I say. I tell her about Ron Galella, who shot iconic images of Audrey Hepburn. Rino Barillari's photos of Sophia Loren. That kind of photo, I tell her, the kind that ends up in magazines, sometimes even books and galleries, creates a cultural conversation. That kind of photo, I say, is art. I wonder, when I finish speaking, if I sound like I believe myself.

"But I don't know who Ron Galella and Rino Barberella are," she says.

"Barillari."

"Exactly. I don't know who those guys are."

"But you know their work."

"Maybe."

Three girls in USC apparel sit down at the table next to us. They order Moscow mules and talk about the movie they just saw. I try to listen in. You never know; one could have a friend who served the lead actor his usual cucumber-celery-kale at a Brentwood juice bar. I could overhear the name of that juice bar and go there tomorrow and photograph him ordering that again, maybe with a new girlfriend in tow. It is impossible to predict how these things will happen. *You just have to remain open*, the meditation coach said.

"I promise I'm trying not to be judgmental of what you do," the teacher says.

"You have every right to be judgmental in your line of work. The celebrity parents must say awful things about us."

Nothing in her eyes confirms or denies what I've just said. "I like my job," she says, a warning in her voice. "I'm not going to jeopardize it by telling you—"

"I'm not asking you to."

I could offer her money, I think. I could be direct about what I want.

In an alternate reality, I might really be on this date, completely present with no ulterior motive. But I don't live in that world anymore.

The light through the banana leaves is heavy and honeyed. I can smell the Thai restaurant across the street—coconut, tamarind, lime. Maybe I will go there after this is over and eat alone.

"Tell me about your day," the teacher says. She wants to be convinced that I'm not so bad. Or she's curious, the way a person is curious about a place they'd never visit.

"Well," I say, "this bodyguard texted me, telling me that his client, a model, had just sat down for lunch in Beverly Hills. She announced her divorce last week, so, you know."

"What does that have to do with her having lunch?"

"People want to know what she's up to."

She nods but doesn't look convinced.

"So," I continue. "I drove as fast as I could, parked in a garage with free two-hour parking, and was the first one outside of the restaurant."

"Did you have to hide so she didn't see you waiting?"

"She wanted to be papped—that's what we call it. A lot of them do. Paparazzi only hide when the celebrity is doing or has recently done something bad. You know, like that socialite, Misty Wilcox, cruising around Santa Monica with a suspended license and a glove compartment full of cocaine."

"I'm not familiar with that story," the teacher says. "Have you ever done that? Hidden and secretly gotten a photo of someone who didn't want to have their picture taken."

"We all have to do that sometimes."

"What about if someone is really in crisis, or is doing something that feels very private, very personal? Have you ever photographed someone like that?"

My mind goes to the photo of Mia Luna. Everyone knows it, but not everyone remembers who took it. So I say, "No. I've never done that before."

"That's good."

"Anyway," I say. "The model came out of the restaurant, I said hello and took her picture. I sold it and I gave the bodyguard his cut. It was a good photo set."

She looks at me blankly.

"A photo set," I say, "is a set of—"

"Yes, I get it."

"It's good money," I tell her, because some people like that as a reason why. Some people want to know how much. *Come on, ballpark figure*, they'll say. And I'll smile coyly, like, *Let's just say it's pretty good*, ignoring the ghosts of paparazzi around me saying *good* is a word best applied to years ago—a decade ago. A time, they keep reminding me, that I wasn't even present in Los Angeles for. Six-figure checks. Paparazzi driving the same nice cars as the celebrities they photographed. *You had to be there*, they keep saying.

I am half listening to the teacher, half listening to the tables around me, when one of the USC girls says, ". . . Jack Whitlock . . ."

I look to the street, to the kitchen, as if the most famous actor in the world might appear. For a moment, every other noise in the restaurant goes silent and I am tuned in to the specific frequency of his name.

"Do you know those people?" the teacher asks.

"Oh, what? No, sorry."

The girls notice me staring at them and shift uncomfortably, turning toward one another. What are they saying about Jack Whitlock?

I try to return my attention to the teacher. I try not to look at the dress.

The dress on a hanger. Ellory in her underwear, running a steamer up and down it, releasing the wrinkles.

"Do you ever think about doing another kind of photography?" the teacher asks.

"I used to do something else."

"But you don't anymore?"

"No."

Her phone chimes, a sound I associate with a tip coming through from a front desk agent at the Chateau Marmont, who often texts at this time with an update on who has recently checked in.

"Sorry. I meant to put it on silent."

"Oh, no, that's okay," I say, as if letting her check her texts, her Instagram, her email, will erase how lousy the date has been, put her in a better mood, ease her into talking about the parents of the kids at the school she teaches at.

"Look at it as much as you want," I add, which sounds pathetic at best, sarcastic at worst.

The hostess appears, lacquered nails drumming on a tablet. "Sorry, guys, but I'm going to need this table for a reservation."

"No problem," the teacher says. "We'll go ahead and close out."

It's almost dinner, or at least almost time for an early dinner, and I think about asking her if she wants to get something to eat at the Thai restaurant. But I don't.

"It was great meeting you," she says outside the bar. "I parked on Prospect."

After she's gone, I stand on the sidewalk, feeling the air cool around me. When I first moved to Los Angeles, I could taste the ocean, even miles inland. Sometimes I still find myself looking for that sensation.

I imagine the teacher stopping for a burrito, a consolation prize for a disappointing evening. She'll unwrap it on her couch and tell her roommate how much dating sucks here. *Why was the date bad?* the roommate will ask. And maybe the answer will have something to do with me saying too much, or not saying enough. Or maybe it was too obvious why I asked her out in the first place. What might it have been like, I wonder, if she had liked me?

I don't think about it for long.

I think about earlier, after I got the shot of the model. I took surface streets all the way home, driving leisurely, talking to the photo agency on speaker as reflections of palm trees kissed the hood of my car. The afternoon swelled, open and abundant, and I rolled the windows down. By the time I hit Hollywood, I'd already sold the photo for three hundred dollars. It wasn't much, but it was the most money I'd made in a long time, a reminder of how things had once been.

At my apartment, I stand in the kitchen, resting my palms on the white quartz countertop. The rent is thirty-five hundred a month. It will go up when I renew.

The sun goes down. I pour some vodka into a glass with ice and sip it in the bathtub, a superstition I picked up after having the same drink the night I got the Mia Luna photo, the one that changed everything. Tonight, the vodka tastes like a prayer for a miracle. I turn on the waterproof TV on the wall. I drink and I wait. I close my eyes. And when I open them, I see Jack Whitlock's face.

"BREAKING," says *E! News*.

I am suddenly aware of every vein in my limbs, every sac of air in my lungs. My bones, my skin, my body.

I spent most of my life four hours from him in Las Vegas, wanting to get closer, and yet moving to Los Angeles—to the city where he lives—hasn't given me that. And here he is now, in a context that is so beneath him. *E! News*.

The bathwater is hot. The drink is cold. My breath hitches in my throat.

Stills from Jack's films on the TV.

The entertainment reporter gazes seriously into the camera. "An unnamed source close to the matter exclusively revealed intimate photos of the actor."

The image on the screen changes. The photo is a selfie, shot from overhead: Jack shirtless on a floral comforter—something made by Target for a dorm room—a girl with chestnut hair and heavy eyelashes on his chest, her tongue extended, licking his nipple. His smile is careless, drunk.

"The famously scandal-free actor, forty-five, is married to Jessica Hartley of the popular *L.A. Facelift* home renovation show. The couple has one child together." The screen flashes to a photo of Jack and Jessica at the premiere of his World War II epic. Then back to the shot of Jack on the bed with the girl. A sheen of sweat on his forehead. "The woman pictured with Whitlock has not been identified, but our source informs us there are more images forthcoming. We've reached out to both Whitlock and Hartley for comment and have yet to hear back. This story is developing."

"Holy shit," I say to no one.

I stand, letting the water run off me, walk to my bedroom closet, soaking the floor as I go, not caring. I get dressed quickly. The usual uniform: jeans and a black hoodie. A phone call from the photo agency, right on cue. I tell them I know, I'm already on my way, even if I don't know where I'm going yet.

This is it.

I text Eddie, even though he never responds, because he is the person who got me into this work and because I can't text Ellory. **Remember when you asked me if there was one celebrity I really, really wanted to take a picture of?**

Jack Whitlock appears on screens and billboards and bus stop ads and magazine covers in many forms: the spy sliding out of the black car, the lovesick cowboy in the red desert, the soldier reaching for his weapon, blue eyes fixed on the sky. I don't know what he does in his real life. He has no social media. He rarely gives interviews. But still. There is something in his eyes that forges an immediate connection. This, I think, when I watch him, is a person I can understand no matter what role he is playing. Film reviewers call him "the last movie star." Old Hollywood jawline. Voice like a friend entering the room. When he appears in a scene, there is the comfort of a reunion, the simultaneous connection and total isolation of a stranger who is deeply familiar. Sometimes I wonder if he even occupies a physical space, if we exist in the same universe. On nights when I can't sleep, I circle my apartment and try to see it through his eyes. I pick up the things I own and imagine him asking me about them.

Everyone says the paparazzi industry is dying, that it's a relic going the way of print magazines, that it's being replaced by social media and smartphones. People say that about Hollywood too. But here is Jack Whitlock, the last real movie star. And here I am, the guy with the camera.

Jack Whitlock is the Grand Canyon. He is a landmark. And there is no shame in capturing a landmark. It is an instinct so natural, it is accepted. It is expected.

If you saw him, you would take a picture too.

chapter two

He will lie low. But in the meantime, I can do the groundwork, talking to my sources, letting them know I'm on the hunt.

I meet a server on her smoke break behind Craig's. "You're going to be hearing from a lot of us if you haven't already," I tell her. The rest of the staff is notoriously tight-lipped; she's the lone leak inside the restaurant. "But I'll pay more than them. I just want to find him."

"Y'all don't waste any time," she says, stubbing out her cigarette on the wall. I can hear the collective voice of the patio, dining beneath string lights and vines, but I can't make out the sound of anyone in particular.

"Have the other guys reached out to you already? Which ones?"

"I'll do what I can," she says. It doesn't matter whether or not I believe her.

After, I head to The Nice Guy and catch a bartender I know counting his tips. I say Jack's name and he understands right away. "Ha, yeah, I've seen the news." He leans in. "Dude, I heard there's a *video*."

"Who'd you hear that from?"

"A buddy of mine."

"Can you give him my number?"

He folds his cash neatly and tucks it into the pocket of his apron. “I don’t know. He could be full of shit.”

“I don’t care,” I say. “Text me anytime. Tell your friend—tell all of your friends—to text too. I mean it. I don’t care if it’s four a.m. and you overheard someone in a bathroom say his name.”

“Heard,” he says. “But my rate has gone up.”

The concierge at the Edition says the same thing when I flag him down in the employee parking lot. So does Ava, a veteran dancer at Jumbo’s Clown Room. She meets my eyes from upside down on the pole and mouths the exact percentage she wants in exchange for a Jack Whitlock tip. All of them—all of us—sensing money, but also something else. *Whatever you say*, I tell them all, finding them in bars and restaurants and bathrooms and alleyways, in hotels and parking lots, in luxury apartment lobbies and weekly motel parking lots. I drive and I walk and I text and I call and I DM until every possible source on my contact list has been promised a cut.

“We’re all in this together, my guy,” the lead host at Redbird says, showing me screenshots of the car he’s saving up for. “I help you. You help me.”

“Exactly,” I say. “You get it.”

The push notifications from TMZ are coming in, calling the story “explosive” but not offering anything new. But there is a promise of more information. This is just the beginning. I can feel myself bumping up against the particular type of danger that comes from wanting something too much. The desire an infection, the dream a disease.

“He is the last person I’d expect this from,” a DJ on a local radio station says. “I mean, the absolute last.”

I stop for a cold brew and then keep driving. I don't know what I'm looking for—not yet, anyway, but I know I won't find it at home. By dawn, Los Angeles is a ghost story. Silhouettes of palm trees in the smog. The sky silvery, illusive. The streets are deserted. Vacant eyes from Emmy campaigns watch over the city from billboards. Each one with the same three letters: FYC. *For your consideration.* His face is everywhere; he has a new film coming out, a dystopian thriller set at a lighthouse in Maine. It has been getting good early buzz. I bet the studio executives have been awake all night too, pacing in high-rise offices and Beverly Hills mansions, trying to decide whether they should lean into this or ignore it. The morning air is damp, but the fog will burn off by ten.

I think about climbing Mount Whitney, those first steps on the trail, getting what the guidebooks called *an alpine start.* Every mile an act of faith. Every footstep above ten thousand feet a decision to keep going even when I couldn't breathe.

This is how I feel as I comb the streets for Jack Whitlock, the slippery start of day growing ever out of reach as the minutes pass. It is a meditation. I believe the gray daybreak hours will bring me to him. Maybe not today, but soon. I can feel it. I have always felt it. Maybe I didn't always know it, but I always felt it. Watching his movies at casino theaters, hearing his voice on TV, his name in the mouths of people around me.

Do you think the universe has a plan for us, I text Eddie.

I carry a quartz with me, *Good for wisdom and awareness*, the woman at the crystal shop said. I was just pretending to browse, keeping my eyes on a housewife from a reality show, but there was something comforting in the rows of citrine and tourmaline. I stayed looking at them, even after I got a shot of the housewife buying a money-scented candle labeled *Abundance*. In a smoker's voice, the saleswoman asked what I was looking for. I lied, picked up the quartz, and said, *This*.

Of course, he doesn't turn up, but I am unbothered. He will. I go home. I sleep. I dream of the Sierra Nevada mountain range, the granite washed pink with alpenglow.

Two days after the first photo, there's another one. The girl stands in a green-tiled bathroom that I immediately recognize as the Chateau Marmont, holding a white towel to her naked body. The entertainment reporters all zoom in on Jack's reflection in the mirror, some of them circling it, to make it clear that he took the picture.

I text the concierge: **wtf Jack was at the Chateau Marmont and you didn't tell me**

I don't work for you, he responds.

Can you at least tell me when it was

He texts me his Venmo information, which I already have. I send him some money.

Valentine's Day, he says.

On TV, *Access Hollywood* is interviewing experts on infidelity and divorce. *Could be sex addiction*, one of them says. They speculate on how an alleged sex addict might behave, ending the segment with a caveat: *The mental health professional who spoke with us has not personally treated Mr. Whitlock*. I wish that Jack had an Instagram to look at right now.

Fortunately, his wife does, and she posts frequently. A photo from her home renovation show: a backyard patio with Bermuda grass, beige furniture, and a fire pit. Caption: *TBT to this dreamy backyard transformation. The perfect setting for wine and charcuterie. I'll bring the prosciutto!*

I scroll to Valentine's Day. A photo of an antique silver tray on white sheets. Breakfast on china, a single rose. *Croque monsieur from my monsieur*, the caption reads. I try to imagine Jack cooking for her, crawling into bed with her, and then excusing himself under the pretense of a meeting, promising to be back by dinner.

I keep scrolling. Each cheerful, banal photo is accompanied by a sea of comments from strangers. Some complimentary: *looks so good wishing you much love*. Others antagonistic: *why are you posting this fake shit with everything going on wheres ur husband*

I pick up a salad from Sweetgreen and eat it standing up in my kitchen while studying the TMZ website on my phone. There's a cropped image: the lower half of a woman shown from behind. Pink bikini, manicured hands cupping her own ass, spray-tanned legs, sandals. The headline: *Who does this pert derriere belong to?* The article itself is just one line of copy—*Jack Whitlock's sidepiece!!!!*—accompanied by a gallery of images from the girl's now deleted Instagram. At a beach bar with a pink drink, on a Hollywood rooftop, at Coachella in a crop top, a close-up of the roses tattooed on her hip bones. They've identified her. Her name is Sasha.

Texts from other paparazzi, wondering who figured it out first, if anyone has gotten to her yet. Where is she? Where is Jessica? And most importantly, where is Jack?

Jack Whitlock's college coed mistress, TMZ says. *23 years his junior*. I think of the date in Los Feliz. It was a long shot, but it could have been something. The USC students. They were right there. I could have asked them what they knew.

The weighted blanket is supposed to help me relax, supposed to soothe me the way compression sweaters soothe dogs who are afraid of thunderstorms. But tonight it's not working. A podcaster who was not as well-connected as I'd hoped recommended it after a night of making out, taking our clothes off, but never actually fucking. *I can tell that you have trouble falling asleep*, she said. When I asked her if I had been tossing and turning, if I'd kept her up, she said I hadn't been moving at all. *But still, I can tell. There's something keeping you awake. Something . . . existential.* She told me about the weighted blanket and looked at me earnestly in the morning light, her face bare, the dark roots of her blond hair showing just a little. *I think it'll really help you, Ben.* I nodded. I wanted to tell her that I'd never had trouble sleeping in my life, not until Ellory left. Some previously buried emotion swelled in my throat. I thanked her, told her I'd buy the blanket. She put her hand on mine and said, *Please, if you do, use my code ALEX20 for a discount at checkout.*

Tonight, the blanket is crushing me. I grip my phone so tightly in my right hand that my bones ache. It vibrates, as if it's responding to my touch. Cocooned beneath the blanket, I hold it to my face in the dark.

Text message from an unknown number: **did you think we'd forgotten?**

In my email, similar messages.

Subject line: *we're coming for you*

Subject line: *u brought this on urself*

Subject line: *kill yourself (:*

Delete, delete, delete, delete.

The blanket feels heavier. I toss it off, get up, and check the lock on the door. I open the app on my phone that connects to the golf ball–size camera on the other side. The hallway is empty. I go to the fridge and take out a CBD seltzer. Coconut-pineapple flavor, but it tastes earthy, not tropical. *You deserve to feel chill when you chill*, the advertisement said. Through the blinds in the bedroom, helicopter lights pour over bungalows and palm trees and surfaces of pools.

I go out on the balcony and watch the helicopter navigate the night air, slow like an overstuffed bumblebee, heavy with pollen. The light lands on me, just for a second, before moving on.

An old paparazzo is telling the story he always tells, the one about the singer's dead body. She overdosed at a hotel in Hollywood. He waited outside; he took pictures of the body bag.

"The worst part," he says, "is that it wasn't an exclusive."

"Give it up," another paparazzo tells him. "That was ten years ago."

"Not even an exclusive," he repeats, picking at the butt of his jeans. The sun hits my eyes. I squint at the forest-green entrance of the Gucci store across the street, waiting for Jessica, who is rumored to be inside. I can imagine the headlines, the money. *Jessica Hartley steps out for shopping in Beverly Hills amid Jack Whitlock cheating scandal.* But that's not what thrills me. It's the thought of being a little bit closer to Jack, standing in the presence of someone who knows him, has touched him.

When I was in junior high, he shot a movie in Las Vegas. I knew he was important. I could hear the reverence in people's voices when they talked about him—adults, teenagers, men, women, kids at school, cashiers at the grocery store, tourists on the Strip, it didn't matter. Everyone loved him. Sitting alone in the living room after school, watching his movies on TV, I wondered what made a person that way.

There's a trio of cops down the street—a sure sign that someone famous is nearby. Whispers among the group of a producer and his boyfriend. We stay where we are. The others talk about Jack Whitlock. I listen.

"Dude. That sidepiece chick? That college girl? I'd cheat on my wife with her too."

"She's your daughter's age."

"Yeah, but she ain't my daughter."

"What are we thinking? Quick fling or full-blown affair?"

"You want to know what I think? I think the college girl is the one who leaked the photo. Probably sold it to *E! News*. I bet she thinks she's going to be famous now."

The cops approach the Gucci store, talking to the security detail outside. We all reach for our cameras, getting ready.

"These wasteful pieces of shit," one paparazzo says. "Shopping at Gucci. Enough wealth to end generational poverty and they spend their money on purses."

I hold up my camera, look at the store through the viewfinder. "Yeah, totally."

"Have you seen this year's list of the worst water wasters in Los Angeles?" he asks. "It's the same people who shop at these stores. We're in a drought and these celebrities are using four times their monthly water budgets. It makes me sick. No one should have a grass lawn in this city, you know what I mean? I say light these lawns on fire."

"Jack Whitlock has a water conservation nonprofit," I say.

"I bet he still drowns his lawn in sprinklers."

Another paparazzo: "I just heard she's going to go out the back entrance. She's going straight to the garage and will be coming out in her car." He jerks his thumb toward the parking garage. "I'm going to run over there. You guys text me if she comes out front. You'll text me, right?"

He dashes off.

"Amateur hour," the guy with the dead-singer story says.

Across the street, tourists pause to look into Gucci and are turned away. I can't see anything through the glass. I imagine Jessica inside, picking up and putting down leather wallets. Is she keeping up appearances? Selecting an *I'm sorry* present for herself? Is she even there at all?

The door opens. We point our cameras. It's someone else. A rapper and her sister, both in pink tracksuits, brown sunglasses. They jaywalk across the street, stopping to smile, to wave. I take one photo. It's uninteresting, overexposed. The sky behind them is white; the most unappealing Beverly Hills has ever looked. The rapper and her sister get into a waiting car and drive away.

I break off from the rest of the group, leaving them to snipe at one another, to call their photo agencies. There's a staircase I like to use as a staging area on Rodeo Drive. When I get there, I find a paparazzo drinking boba tea, waiting for an invite-only lunch gala nearby to let out.

"I hear their house is going up for sale," he says. I don't have to ask who he's talking about.

"Really? They're talking divorce already?"

"Fucking Bel Air. Twelve *thousand* square feet for two adults and a kid. Seven bedrooms and fourteen bathrooms. I live in a studio. I shit three feet from where I cook. What's he doing with fourteen bathrooms? You piss in a different one every hour or something? Unbelievable. No wonder some paparazzi end up completely insane or worse."

A man in gym clothes passes us on the staircase. We flatten ourselves against the wall to let him by. Seeing our cameras, he shakes his head.

"Disgusting," he says, looking right at me.

The other paparazzo keeps talking about Jack's house. "It makes me want to get out of this business. Get my real estate license."

"But where do you think he is?" I ask.

"We're never going to find him."

"Somebody will."

"He's probably in one of his other houses. These people own so many houses."

I list them off. "He's got one in Bel Air, one in Manhattan, one in Jackson Hole, and one in Mallorca."

"Geez, you're obsessed with the guy."

"But he's probably here," I say, manifesting it.

Later, I see an actor leaving a steak house. An A-lister, though he's never been in a movie with Jack. An unpredictable kind of guy. Sometimes, he is kind to paparazzi. Once, he put one in the hospital. He is wearing a baseball cap and has his head down. I can see his unshaven jawline. He has his phone to his ear. People pass without recognizing him, which is a thing that happens often with guys who can only turn it on for movies. Guys who are not Jack Whitlock.

The actor is yelling into his cell phone. People on the sidewalk hear his voice, start to put together who he is. I take out my camera but make no move toward him. The last time I took his picture, he grabbed my camera and hurled it into the street, chased after it and kicked it, stomped on it.

That was back when I thought the money would never run out. I bought a new camera the next day, laughed at the anecdote.

The actor paces back and forth, gesticulating with his hands. A tourist approaches him. She's tiny, draped in an oversize Dodgers shirt, carrying a paper bag from a hotel gift shop. She produces a phone and angles it so they're both in the frame. The actor flinches, steps back. He tells her to get out of his face. She apologizes and walks away quickly.

My fingers itch, wanting to take the photo, but I can't afford a new camera. It's not worth it. There's nothing newsworthy going on with him. No new relationship or baby or movie. Even his whole *pace back and forth while yelling into the phone and shouting at tourists* thing is pretty basic. There has to be a narrative; that's what everyone wants now. It's not enough for the celebrity to just be there; there has to be another layer. The celebrity can't just be getting lunch; they have to be *getting lunch amid pregnancy rumors*. Jack Whitlock could be doing anything right now and it would be *amid scandal*. I try to picture him stepping out of a glossy town car *amid scandal*, running beneath the shadow of palm trees *amid scandal*, swimming in a pool alone, looking out at the city, at me, though he does not know it yet. Both of us, circling each other, *amid scandal*.

* * *

I walk aimlessly, vaguely in the direction of Westwood. Along the way, I pass a picket line. A bunch of unionized hotel employees on strike. The same union that represents most of the casino workers in Las Vegas.

I want to be alone in the dark. I want to drink a single drink and listen to a single song and check my phone for updates on Jack. I want to text my sources, apply pressure, promise them money I don't have yet.

Unfortunately, there is no bar that matches the one in my mind, not in this part of Los Angeles. Every bar is the kind of bar that uses the phrases *sun-dappled patio* and *mixology program* on its website. I go to the least offensive one and order a gin and tonic, which is served in a mason jar with ribbons of cucumber, rose petals, and juniper berries. The taste reminds me of Las Vegas: the desert in bloom outside the city. I finish the drink and order a beer, which doesn't remind me of anything.

I sit at a table on the sidewalk and drink alone, camera in the empty seat across from me. The shadows of palm trees stretch. The air cools in a way that feels deliberate, like air-conditioning turning on.

No news on Jack.

No responses from my sources.

I look at recent photos I took of a director having lunch with a producer. They're practically worthless. The director and producer have names people recognize, but no one knows or cares about their faces. They are ugly men. They look ugly in the photos, their faces mottled with the redness of drinking too much for too many years.

My phone vibrates on the table, and I reach for it, hoping for news of Jack from one of my sources. Instead, it's a text from a paparazzo turned awards-show photographer. A selfie from a red carpet event, eyes bugged out and mouth open, press pass around his neck. **It's so nice to actually be INVITED to things!!!!** Winky face.

I finish my drink. I'm not going to order another one. I'm going to go home and wait for news. I'm going to meditate. I'm going to fucking pray.

It's so nice to actually be INVITED, he said, like that was an honor, like that was the goal, like years of chasing people in the street had led to a press pass and an hour of standing beside a red carpet taking pictures of people who spent five hours getting groomed and manicured and styled, seven months dieting and exercising. Those photos. Those red carpet photographers. All of them getting the same boring shots. They will never do what I do. They have given up. I delete the text.

It's so nice to actually be INVITED, he said. Like it was something to be proud of.

The delivery guy can't find my apartment.

"I'm trying to get you your goddamn salad," he huffs into the phone. His voice is familiar, and when he finds my door, his face is too. Another ex-paparazzo, I realize.

He hands me the cardboard box. "Ben? Is that you?"

"Yeah, that's me."

"It's me, man. What's up?"

The bottom of the box is warm, the oil from the salmon greasy against my fingertips. "Uh, I don't know. You know."

"You still doing the pap thing?"

"Yeah, yeah. You?"

He laughs. "Does it look like it?"

"I don't know. I guess not."

He cranes his neck and looks into my apartment. "This is a nice place. Must be going pretty good."

"Yeah. It's okay."

He nods, keeps looking, as if adding something up.

"Do you need me to sign something?" I ask.

"Nope," he says, not looking at me. "It's all on the app. Leave me a good tip, hey?"

"Sure." I ease back into my apartment. Something about the way he's looking at it makes me uncomfortable.

He smiles. "Yep. Pretty nice place there, Ben."

"Thanks."

"Yeah, must be going real well."

"Yes." I hit the word hard. Definitive. Not like a celebrity in an interview, pausing, forming a lie.

"You know, this delivery gig is better money than being a pap was." His smile fades. "Guess it's different for you."

"Maybe."

"You know," he says, "I remember when you first showed up. A lot of shit has gone down since then."

I don't ask him what he means by that. I don't want to know what he's referring to.

"Thanks for the food," I say. "I'm going to eat now."

"Yeah, you do that." He looks at me for a few more seconds, unblinking, and then turns and goes.

I throw the takeout container in the trash. And then because that doesn't feel like enough, I take the entire bag to the garbage chute across the hall and drop it in. I stare at the black hole after it falls, listening to it land. I go back into my apartment and lock the door, slide down and sit with my back against it, palms on the floor, trying to ground myself. I close my eyes and see his face, the same as it was in crowds of paparazzi, shouting, shoving, jeering, laughing. Back when we used to be in crowds, before.

chapter three

I knot and re-knot my tie in the bathroom mirror, watching Jack on the TV. He is on two channels: On one, there's a movie he made three years ago called *Spanish for Mercy* in which he played the patriarch of a family of homesteaders. On the other, two entertainment reporters discuss the scandal, trying to come up with a hashtag for it.

An *L.A. Facelift* producer tweets and then deletes: *if everyone could leave our beloved Jessica alone right now that would be great . . . she needs privacy not vultures swarming around*

I run a comb through my hair and then wash my face.

Tonight, there's a private party for a philanthropist / tech overlord. A millionaire wunderkind who donated money to Jack's environmental nonprofit last year. These are the connections you have to look for. If you are open to them, they are everywhere. The millionaire's girlfriend's makeup artist tipped me off, got me on the list. Some celebrities disappear when there's a scandal; others hide in plain sight. If Jack is the latter, he'll be at this party. Or at least someone who knows something will be there. Of course, I can't bring my camera, just my phone. I need to look like a guest, blending in.

The event isn't for another hour. I drink mineral water and flip back and forth between the two channels, still standing in my bathroom. I like to watch TV standing up just like I like to eat standing up. Shoes on. It just makes more sense to me. A text could come in, telling me where to go. I could be out the door in a minute.

In *Spanish for Mercy*, it is winter. It is 1864. The crops are not growing. Jack strikes at the frozen ground with a shovel, at first plaintively and then violently, cursing the gray sky above him, the fruitless earth below him, the circling ravens. He falls to his knees and presses his head to the dirt, punching at the soil with his fists and then running his fingers through it, lovingly, pleadingly. *Forgive me*, he says again and again. *Forgive me*.

On the other channel, there is a slideshow of girlfriends as the two entertainment reporters narrate his dating history. The costar he dated when they were both teenagers on their first movie set. The models in quick succession in his early twenties. The rumored fling with the much older actress. The Olympic skier. A few more models, and then just one model for two years. And then Jessica, introduced through mutual friends at a dinner party, the way normal people meet.

"Just a stunning couple," a lithe, mean-looking entertainment reporter says. Her coanchor is an overly botoxed man who makes his assistants take his dick pics, supposedly. If the story ever comes out, a shot of him leaving the studio in disgrace will be a decent paycheck.

"A Montana native, Jessica met Jack shortly after relocating to Los Angeles to work on *L.A. Facelift*," he says. "The pair has been together for a decade. I gotta tell you, Cheryl. You just don't see that kind of longevity in celebrity marriages nowadays."

"Well, let's not forget that he used to be a bit of a playboy."

He winks at the camera. "Who hasn't been a playboy at some point? Jack, if you're watching, you have an open invitation to appear on the show. And also, Cheryl here is single."

"I think every woman in America is single if Jack Whitlock is."

I go back to the other channel and watch Jack watch the sunrise. A close-up of his face. A quiet folk song. That's better.

I'm at USC, a paparazzo texts me. **I'm going to hang out at the dorm and see if that chick Sasha turns up.**

I don't know why he texts me. I don't know why any of them do. In the early days, I got a sense of validation whenever a paparazzo asked for my number, added me to a group text thread, but that feeling is gone.

Twenty minutes later, he texts again: **i got kicked out they thought i was some pervert**

When it's time, I take Santa Monica to Beverly Hills, park on a darkened, palm-lined street, and walk down the hill.

I give the doorman my name, and he says, "You look familiar."

He scrutinizes me. We scrutinize each other. Has he kicked me out of somewhere before? Does he work for Mia Luna? I put my hand in my pocket and touch the sharp edge of the quartz.

"I get that a lot," I say.

The doorman taps his clipboard. "I can't place what I've seen you in."

Relief. I let go of the crystal. "I do a lot of background work."

"Huh," he says. "Well, have a good night."

The interior ballroom is lit with violet strobe lights. Girls in silk lingerie descend from ropes and climb back up. In the far corner, a golden staircase leads to nowhere, each step filled with presents. A very famous DJ who has never been photographed with his sunglasses off plays a remix of a remix. Waiters on hoverboards serve champagne. The ceiling is outfitted with planets and stars. Neon letters on the wall: *THE FUTURE.* My heart sinks. This place looks like a child's party in a nightclub. It isn't Jack's scene.

I kill time at the bar, hoping to overhear someone say something or to gain a new source or to learn about the kind of VIP room he'd be in.

"You work these kinds of events often?" I ask the bartender.

She doesn't even look at me. "I'm not interested."

"I'm not hitting on you."

"Sure you're not."

The guest of honor sits on a platform surrounded by velvet rope. He watches the room, not smiling. I order a sparkling water and tip a different bartender twenty, but when I try to press her for details about the guest list, her smile tightens and her eyes dart to the millionaire on his throne. "I've got an NDA."

"Those aren't always enforceable."

"And ninety thousand dollars in student loans. I need this job."

She turns her back to pour more champagne. A projector on the wall opposite the DJ shows photos of the birthday boy. Each one includes a celebrity. Each one taken by an event photographer. Some by the same paparazzo turned event photographer who taunts me on occasion. There are no event photographers here tonight. Why is that?

I filter through the crowd, watching the slideshow, looking for someone I know. Politicians. Other people from tech. A few socialites and would-be socialites. A trapeze artist descends from the ceiling, scatters a fistful of glitter down on us all as she flies overhead. She catches my eye and winks, her face the same shape as Ellory's in the violet light.

An elbow in my side. Terrence Tower, who runs the eponymous *Tower Blog*, lowest form of celebrity news. An almost unreadable website both in design and in content. He steals paparazzi photos without licensing them, puts his own watermark on them when he's feeling especially bold. He traffics in conspiracy theories he calls Tower Tales.

"How'd you get in here?" I ask him. He is wearing black frames with no lenses. His trademark red suit.

"I was about to ask you the same thing," he says.

"I was invited."

"Bullshit."

He motions to a girl dressed as an alien, handing out cupcakes. "How old do you think she is?"

"I don't know. Twenty-three?"

"That's an awfully specific number."

The slideshow changes to an image of the millionaire in Hawaii with a pop star, on a golf course with the governor, at a winery with a professional football player. I keep looking for Jack. I at least want to see him in the slideshow. His face would be centering, would reassure me that the photo will come and the money will follow. I think about my car payment, my rent, my gym membership, my last grocery run. Why is it so expensive just to exist here? The Mia Luna money was supposed to last longer.

Terrence waves his hands around like he's conducting a symphony. "All of this is a front for something evil."

"Sure it is."

"Don't be so sarcastic. We could work together on this."

He leans in, speaks loudly into my ear: "Child sex-trafficking ring."

"I haven't heard anything about that."

"Of course you haven't. No one has. No one except me."

"From where? From who?"

"I can't reveal that."

"Then I'm not interested."

"You paps are never interested in this kind of stuff. Makes me wonder if you're in on it."

I finish my water. "I have to go talk to someone else now."

"Who?"

"Whoever."

I circle the room, looking for a door, a dark hallway, anything. Finally, a photo of Jack on the slideshow. The millionaire beside him presenting a check. Both of them smiling in tuxedos. A banner behind them reading *Salton Sea Preservation*. An audible murmur pulsates in the crowd. The sight of him has given everyone permission to speculate, to share theories and rumors. The Salton Sea is one of Jack's main environmental causes. He lent his voice to a half-hour documentary about it. Tonight, I tell myself, I will go home and watch it again. The images of the shrinking shoreline, the beaches blanketed with dead fish, the pelicans lifting up at sunset, one by one. *This was once a paradise*, his voice says. *To me, it still is.*

A woman nearby says, "Jessica must be devastated. She's such a sweetheart."

Another woman responds, "She's the fakest person I've ever met, I swear to god. That's what you get when you marry the most famous actor on the planet. I mean, come on."

I turn to her. "You know Jessica?"

She blinks at me, her pupils big in the semidarkness. "We met once at a dinner."

"You're not still in touch?"

"No. Like I said, we met *once* at a *dinner*."

I move through the crowd, listening to others talking about Jack, not talking about Jack. A talk show host approaches the millionaire. Regular people would be surprised to see her here—she's built her brand on being relatable and funny. Even though she is beautiful—Pilates arms and glossy hair—she projects a bumbling, awkward, *I'm just a regular gal* persona when she interviews famous people. She tweets about skipping the gym to get tacos (*I'd rather have extra guac than a six-pack*), posts pictures of a blistering sunburn on Instagram (*TFW you fall asleep at the beach*), and acts starstruck by other celebrities on the red carpet. Her former assistant once told me that a *New York Times* columnist comes up with all those witty captions, that there is in fact an entire team of people ghostwriting her personality.

Tonight, she is wearing a silver dress and looking sleek and poised and lethal as she approaches the millionaire. There are no cameras to pretend to trip in front of. No interviewers asking her to talk about the struggles of postpartum weight loss. The millionaire comes down from his seat and hugs her from across the velvet rope. She puts her hands to her chest, smiling as she speaks graciously to him. She would not want to be photographed here. I take a surreptitious shot with my cell phone, trying to guess how much it'll be worth.

What a fool I was to even think there might be a chance I'd see Jack. His name is in whispers around me, but he is somewhere else.

At the bar, a Hollywood trade reporter who exchanges good reviews for sex asks me who I am. He waves his glass of red wine around, sloshing it onto his white button-down shirt, his eyes focusing and unfocusing.

"Who the hell are you?" he keeps saying.

When I start to answer, he puts his hand on my chest and makes eye contact with the floor. "You're nobody."

"That's right."

Terrence Towers appears over his shoulders and mouths the words *he's a drunk* at me. The trade reporter whirls around to look at him. "You little rat. Go back to that basement where you blog from."

Terrence says to me, "I hear he's in on it."

"Say it to my face," the trade reporter says. "Say what you're gonna say. I'm not going to read it on your blog, because no one reads blogs anymore."

"Oh, I'll say it. I know what's really going on here. The underaged girls. The yachts. The private beach clubs. The code words they use. Every time someone orders an ice cream sundae with extra strawberries and no pecans. You know exactly what I'm talking about. Don't think I don't know what's going on here. I'll say what I just said to Ben. I think you're a part of it."

The trade reporter finally makes eye contact with me. "Oh. Oh, I do know who you are. You're the one, aren't you? You're the one who took that picture. There's people who want to kill you, but you know that, you know that." He whirls around, spilling what's left in his wineglass. He drops the glass and it shatters, but he doesn't notice. His eyes are nearly closed as he cups his hands to his mouth. "Security. Security, there's paparazzi here tonight."

A few sets of eyes flick in our direction.

"I'm out of here," I say to no one.

"Sure, Ben," Terrence calls after me. "Run. Run away from the truth."

As I leave, the image of Jack and the millionaire appears on the wall again. He's looking directly at me, telling me I'm right to go. Telling me to keep looking.

Out on Robertson Boulevard, a trio of thirty-something C-list reality stars tumble out of an Italian restaurant. It's the kind of place that has appeared on so many of those *Where to Dine in LA if You Want to See Celebs* lists that it's become the culinary version of an overcrowded national park that got famous on Instagram. Gone are the days when *real* celebrities—celebrities like Jack—would grace its patio. The portion sizes are smaller, the prices are higher, and the reservation list is six months deep with tourists hoping to see a Hollywood legend. They crane their necks toward the host stand each time someone new enters, completely unaware that the reality stars and influencers they're dining alongside are as good as it's going to get.

The thirty-something reality stars notice me, even without my camera, even though I'm barely looking at them. They know paparazzi the way bodyguards and personal assistants know me, but for a different reason.

The one in the trucker hat careens toward me with his arms spread wide. "Ben! Hey, man, how you been?"

"Good. Just heading home."

The two women he's with, an ice blonde with a severe bob and a brunette with tattoos—I can't remember which is his girlfriend—hang back, posing as if I'm photographing them. Trucker Hat takes me by the arm and pulls me away from them. "Listen, man. Listen. Take a look at this."

He takes out his cell phone and glances back at the women before showing me the screen. "Pretty hot, huh?"

The photo is of the blonde, draped over a velvet couch and wearing black panties. Her hands are on her breasts. Her nails are chipped. Trucker Hat raises his eyebrows, like we're in on this together. I can't tell what I'm looking at, other than the obvious. I haven't been following this narrative, because it isn't worth enough money to me. Is the photo relevant because it's of his girlfriend or because it's not of his girlfriend?

"Why are you showing me this?" I ask.

"Aw, come on. You know why."

The photo looks like it was taken by one of those boudoir photographers. Someone with a grubby little studio in the Valley who advertises on Facebook. Elegantly Undressed Boudoir, or something like that.

I look back at the girls, who are still posing.

"I don't have my camera on me," I tell them.

"Well, that's not very professional," the tattooed brunette teases.

"Use your phone. The other guys do that."

I oblige them, maybe because I feel sad thinking about that boudoir studio, maybe because I want this interaction to be over. They ask to see the photos I've taken of them, and when I show them, they're displeased.

"Fuck, I look fat."

"It's the angle. It's a bad angle."

I delete, take the photos again, delete, take the photos again.

Trucker Hat folds his arms across his skinny frame, shakes his head, smirks.

At home, I call the photo agency, but they don't want the shot of the talk show host in her silver dress approaching the millionaire. It's not worth the legal trouble. I don't even bother mentioning the reality stars.

"Call when you find Jack Whitlock," they say.

I feel keyed up. I pace the balcony. A text message full of indecipherable but threatening emojis. I want so badly to turn off my phone, or to drop it over the railing and listen for the sound of it smacking the pavement, but what if someone calls or texts about Jack? I imagine the phone hurtling toward the ground, ringing. Instead, I go inside and drink filtered lukewarm tap water, standing in the bathroom, ending the night exactly as it began. And I wait.

It isn't long before my phone lights up.

chapter four

It's a grainy, thirty-two-second video, shot in a kitchen at a horizontal angle by a phone that must have been propped up on a shelf—probably against a stack of plates or cookbooks. Sasha is perched on the marble island in a lace bra, long neck and arched back. Jack stands in front of her in a tuxedo, holding an Oscar statue. *What are you doing?* she says, giggling. He parts her legs. Pushes the statue between them. *Oh*, she moans, a sound of amusement, and then unexpected pleasure.

I replay the video over and over, each time focusing on a different detail: the potted orchids on the counter, his left hand on her knee, his open mouth. I watch with fascination, arousal.

Everybody on Twitter is saying some variation of the same thing:

do NOT watch the Jack Whitlock video at work

haha I watched the Jack Whitlock video at work and now I'm fired lmao fml

You can search "Jack Whitlock video" on here but just be warned that what you see is going to change your opinion of Jack Whitlock forever.

An actress who once starred in a movie with Jack tweets: *I just think it's really disrespectful to the Academy.*

* * *

Strangers convene on Jessica's Instagram, in the comments of an anniversary photo of her and Jack, as if they'd planned to meet there. They speak to each other like they're not using her account for their conversation, like she isn't there at all:

yoooo do you think she knew?????

Jessica might wanna delete this one

Yikes guess her man wasn't faithful

who would have expected this from JACK WHITLOCK literally crying right now

Ummm if hes hooking up with randoms . . . im available!!!!

There's an *L.A. Facelift* marathon on HGTV—not a coincidence.

Although Jack has never appeared on his wife's show, he is there.

He is there when she tours a mid-century home in Glendale, points at the view of the golf course and says, *My husband would love that.* He is there when she asks a divorcée what she envisions for her new home in Sherman Oaks and the woman says, *A handsome man like yours.* He is there when she says, *We like that restaurant* and *We wanted a saltwater pool too* and *We love having a fireplace.* The guests on the show are normal people renovating their homes with her help, and they are incapable of hiding how eager they are for these whispers of him. They are desperate for more. *And does your hubby like to grill?* they ask, and Jessica smiles brightly, saying *Yes, he loves it*, before pivoting to a discussion of whether the original banisters should stay. When the guests hug her, it's as if they're touching him too. It's the closest they'll ever get.

Despite my efforts, and despite how badly I want to find him, there are no tips coming in. Not yet. The leaks aren't coming from anyone I know or anyone who knows anyone I know. There are no sightings of Jessica. Sasha seems to have been erased from the internet entirely.

So I take it on intuition. Sunset all the way from Beverly Hills to Malibu. Even though it is less efficient, there is something about this drive—my favorite in Los Angeles—that contains all the undulating possibility of the city. Los Angeles is not a city that presents itself to you; it is coy, withholding, vulgar and brown and then sweet and soft and green when you least expect it. I love the way the road curves through the shadowy corridors of Brentwood and Pacific Palisades, offering flashes of gold through the trees before finally opening up to the mist of the Pacific, the coastal eternity of Highway 1. Each gated entryway holds something more valuable than luxury: the truth.

And of course I think of Jack when I pass through Bel Air. I think of the possibility of him in his great big house, alone, or with Sasha, or with someone else entirely. Last night I watched one of his early career movies, in which he was a poet in the South of France. His suits were seafoam green and gray, as if he was the only cool thing in each room. His hair was slicked back, and he smoked long cigarettes, and after he punched a man outside of a party, he looked past him, at the water, the man's pain and blood suddenly so separate from him, just another image he was observing. And that's how I feel when I see the ocean, when I pass the families and first dates and roommates. They are right beside my car; I could roll down the window and talk to them, touch them even. But I wouldn't know them, and they wouldn't know me.

I park and walk to Nobu, hoping to catch him slipping into a private dining room. No luck. I head to a ribbon of shoreline beneath a row of mansions. The sand is wet and choked with seaweed in the exact shade of dark green a politician's daughter recently colored her hair. I know this because I was in the process of selling photos of her—the first photos of her new hair color—when she scooped me by sharing a selfie to Instagram (caption: *new hair, who dis*) which caused the photo agency to lose interest. *This is happening more and more*, the agency said. The photo set would have been worth gas money at best, but still, I needed it.

June Gloom in August. Clouds stretch across the cool Pacific. Fog hangs over the sand. The ocean roils. The sun hasn't pierced the marine layer yet. It is damp and quiet and ugly. The mist creates an invisibility cloak for everything, everyone. I close my eyes and try to manifest Jack materializing from the vapor. He stands in front of me, positions himself, finds his light, his angles. Spreads out his hands like Jesus.

I open my eyes. Empty beach, empty ocean, empty sky.

I watch the waves, as if the water will reveal an answer, but the ocean is patternless, random. So I leave the beach. I pace around Malibu Village past warm, inviting shops selling vegan yoga mats, healing crystals, hand-poured candles, lavender-sage facial oil. Could he be inside the Enchanted Coast Reiki Center? The doors are closed, the shades drawn. Businesses close all the time so that celebrities can browse without the prying eyes of the public. *Sorry to have missed you*, the sign says. *Be well and follow us on social media to learn more about our new dog reiki offerings.* Finding nothing, I give up and drive to the Beverly Hills Hotel. It's sunnier there, at least. When I arrive there's a line of cars stacked front to back on the hill. Other paparazzi. My heart thumps. Could he be here? Lunch with Jessica at the Polo Lounge to assure the public that all is fine? No; I would have heard about it from the loose-lipped room service attendant. I might have even heard about it from one of Jack's people. They never communicate with the paparazzi, but these are unusual circumstances. They have a narrative to control.

I grab the last available spot—farther uphill than I'd like—and jog toward the rosy palace. The paparazzi are huddled by the blooming pink azaleas, their cameras hoisted. An obsidian black Maybach rolls out, the windows down. A red ponytail, fresh lip filler. Relief. It's not Jack. It's a comedian with a controversial new Netflix special. She is worth taking a picture of, but I wish I didn't have to.

The car pauses. The cameras flash. She's gone before I get a shot.

One of the other guys pats me on the back. "You just missed her."

"No shit," I say.

He shows me his photo. "Not bad, eh?"

"It's out of focus."

"Who cares," he says before sauntering off to his ugly sports car. The rest of us stay, hoping someone else of note will emerge from the valet. We are desperate, edgy, bouncing on the balls of our feet. No one has gotten their shot yet today. Net income for the day will be zero for me; I can sense it. Less than zero, actually, if you factor in gas.

The sun sets peach, softening the energy of the group.

There is talk of the comedian in the Maybach. Talk of Jack, of course. No one has any leads, which soothes me. Discussion of a recent blind item on a celebrity gossip site: *Guess which A-list golden boy is heading to rehab.* Is it Jack, the group wonders.

"Of course," someone says. "It's textbook. Say it's sex addiction, go to a rehab center, come back and get back to business, blah blah blah. Meanwhile, there are real people with real addiction problems."

"I gotta admit, I'm surprised by this. And nothing surprises me."

"He'll bounce back. You know he's going to be in that movie that's in development over at—"

"Nah, they want someone younger."

"I heard there's nude pictures of Sasha, if that's even her name."

A few of them take out phones, looking for the photos, looking for any trace of her. But she's a ghost.

As the periwinkle sky turns indigo, everyone prepares to pack it in, talking about plans for the night: a sushi date, a friend's backyard barbecue, a stepchild's school play, an improv show.

Not me.

I know I will go home and comb the blinds for something more than *golden boy heading to rehab.* I know I will flip through the stack of glossy tabloids on my counter, alone.

"Any plans, Ben?" someone asks.

"I might meet up with someone," I say.

"Like a date?"

"Maybe."

"You still doing that thing?"

"What thing?"

"Using dating apps to find sources."

"Who told you that?"

He nudges me. "A little unsolicited advice? Clock out every once in a while. I've been doing this a while and I've seen what it can do to you if you're not careful. There was this one guy who disappeared—"

"I'm fine," I tell him.

I download a new dating app when I get home, upload a recent photo to my profile, which was taken with a tripod in my apartment, against my sterile gray living room wall. *Ben, 30, photographer*. I don't know what else to say about myself.

I swipe through profiles. An introverted graduate student who likes going out for drinks, a behavioral therapist who spends weekends at Disney, a project manager in an open marriage. An actress.

Her face isn't familiar. If it was, she'd be on the celebrity dating app. Still, I never rule out anyone who might be spending time on set. We match and she messages me right away, starts telling me about the shitty audition she just had. *I want to get drunk*, she says.

At the wine bar, we order a bottle of garnacha, and she drinks three glasses in quick succession. She says it feels like four on an empty stomach.

Her teeth are stained red, and she says, "The only way to get anywhere in Hollywood is to fuck someone. You're a whore if you do or a bitch if you don't."

"What movie is that from?" the bartender asks.

"It's not *from* anything."

The bar is dark, almost too dark to read the menu, and she puts her hand on my leg, moving her fingers upward, kneading my inner thigh.

"What do you think about Jack Whitlock?" I ask her.

"Why do you care about *him*?" she says, putting her head in her hands. "He doesn't have the kind of problems I have."

When she goes to the bathroom, I put money on the bar and leave.

I round the block and duck into a different bar, order a soda. When I hand over my credit card, the bartender looks at the name for ten seconds too long. Then she looks at me. Something in her eyes feels like a trap. She takes her phone out of her back pocket and starts texting someone.

"Just close it out," I say, my voice shaking.

I go outside and call an Uber, pace the small parking lot of a Japanese restaurant, refreshing my email.

On Twitter, from a Mia Luna fan account: *he's at Manzanita Bar in Frogtown*

My legs and arms are numb. I force myself to breathe. The little car on the Uber app is stuck in traffic. It pauses, moves, gets off at the wrong exit. Ten minutes away changes to thirteen. The electric sky above blocks out the stars. The neon *Open* sign at the restaurant goes dark. The car is fourteen minutes away now. Time is moving backward. Time is frozen. The driver is going the wrong way. Sixteen minutes away.

My phone rings.

"Hello? Is this the Uber driver?"

My stomach curdles. The line is bloated with silence.

"Can you hear me?" I say into the phone. "Can you see me?"

On the app, the Uber driver is now five minutes away.

"Leave me alone," I say into the phone, and when there is no response, I say it to the street, to a man exiting a restaurant with a phone to his ear.

He tilts his head. "I wasn't even looking at you."

"Are you calling me?" I say.

"Uh, no, I'm talking to my girlfriend, asshole."

The call disconnects. A pair of headlights flashes behind me, and I nearly collapse. But it's just my Uber. I check the license plate three times, ask him four times if he's really Rashad.

"Yes, I'm really Rashad."

"Can you prove it somehow?"

"Either get in or don't."

I get in.

"There are people who want to hurt me," I tell him as we drift down the highway, surrounded by other Ubers, faceless drivers, faceless passengers.

"That sucks," he says. "You want music or no?"

I thought it would go away, I text Eddie.

I'm scared Eddie

I'm scared of the people who hate me

it's been more than two years and it's not getting better. sometimes i think it's getting worse

As usual, he says nothing.

Alone on my balcony at 1 a.m., I think about calling Ellory. She would tell me to relax, to breathe, to get a glass of water, to sleep on it. Or she would say, *Ben, I told you something like this would happen*. Her number is no longer in my phone, but it doesn't matter; I have it memorized.

Ellory.

Ellory with her cornfield hair. What would she think of this apartment? There's a man who has been showing up on her Instagram lately, but I can't tell if they're dating. He has a beard and a tattoo of a sparrow on his forearm. I've come to know his forearm from the photos where it appears resting on a table beside a latte or a beer at a bar I recognize. Trivia night. She's probably introduced him to her friends, her family. I wonder what it will feel like when she finally posts an image that makes it clear that they're together. Arms around each other at a party. A selfie like the one of Jack and Sasha. I wonder what she has told him about Los Angeles, about me. She deleted every photo of us a long time ago, but left the one of her hand holding the keys to the apartment we used to share. Caption: *new beginnings . . .*

Did she leave it on purpose? I can't ask, because we don't talk anymore.

Beyond my balcony, the lights shimmer, the night ephemeral, the city endless. Between the sirens, I hear the howling and barking of coyotes, all their vocalizations making a tuneless song.

las vegas, three years and three months earlier

chapter five

Jack Whitlock is everywhere.

At the restaurant where I work, he appears in multiple places. The TV above the bar, the free postcards at the host stand, the signed photo in the manager's office. And the booth. Everyone wants to sit in the booth where the famous scene from *Double or Nothing* was filmed. On a neighboring wall, there's a photo of it: Jack in a tuxedo, as Frank, a Las Vegas mobster with a vulnerable side, clinking champagne glasses with a woman in a chartreuse gown. She's his fiancée, and he doesn't know she will soon sell him out to his rival. The scene is romantic on first viewing, sad and ironic on repeat viewings. Tourists like to sit in the booth, order champagne, and re-create the exact image. The Bluebird is a diner, not the nice restaurant it appears to be in *Double or Nothing*, but we keep champagne stocked so guests can drink it and pretend to be Jack Whitlock. And it's him they want to be, not the woman playing his fiancée. She's good enough but does not have what he has, that thing people call *star quality*. A concept I didn't understand until I saw his movies.

Tonight is *Double or Nothing* night, the anniversary of the film's release. When I arrive for my shift, a long line of couples dressed in tuxedos and chartreuse gowns streams from the door.

I have worked here for five years, first as a dishwasher, then a busser on the less desirable morning shift, and now a busser on the evening shift, which is as far as I plan on going—anything more would be too much interaction. I have seen this night play out before. Occasionally, some of the women look like the actress from the movie, but no one looks a thing like Jack Whitlock. Not even close.

The restaurant is showing *Double or Nothing*. They've been showing it all day, will be showing it all night. Since its existence, Jack Whitlock has been a presence in my life, like the mountains, the desert, the sky. Not a choice, but a part of the infrastructure. As a teenager, I went to a drive-in theater on nights when I felt lonely, and more often than not he would be there on the screen. His face above me, the glass of the windshield between us, but still he would be there. I could count on that. Even when the radio in my car stopped working, I could see him, I could read his lips.

They're playing the *Double or Nothing* soundtrack on the tinny restaurant speakers, the movie on mute. Jazz with an undertone of menace. I pause to watch a few minutes of a scene. It's an early one, shot on location outside the Flamingo. Most Las Vegas movies are shot in Los Angeles. It's easy to tell; the landscape is too green, the homes are too nice. But *Double or Nothing* was actually filmed here. Every second of it. In an interview, Jack Whitlock said that was important to him. *I had to get to know Vegas*, he said. *And I found I really, genuinely love it*. Las Vegas locals are used to hearing people from out of town talk shit about the city—it's gross, it's depressing, it's soulless. Jack's praise meant something. When he said, *I love Las Vegas*, I knew that included me.

I watch him make his way into the casino, the twinkle of slot machines haloing his frame. His posture is confident, but his eyes are searching, anxious. His character is new to Las Vegas, newly engaged, new to a vast fortune. He has everything, and yet he is plagued with dread. In his suit, he stands in front of a floor-to-ceiling window, looking out over the city. He touches the glass. At the end of the movie, he will die in this room. It's as if he already knows. He was thirty when he made *Double or Nothing*, just three years older than I am now, but his melancholy makes him older.

I keep watching him.

Julie, the bartender, flags me down. "Ben. I need more champagne."

"I'm early. I can't clock in yet."

"It's fine. We're swamped. You're in here tonight with me." The high-tops are crowded with empty glasses, overflowing ashtrays. A bachelorette party, all dressed in chartreuse gowns, orders Double Tequila or Nothing shots. Above us all, on the TV, Jack drives through the desert in a blue convertible.

I trade my sneakers for slip-resistant black dress shoes and clock in. The schedule says I'm here until close, but in a twenty-four-hour restaurant, close could be midnight, morning, twenty years from now. I am aware of the undefined endpoint of this job, this city.

Thirty minutes from the border of California. My whole life a fixed object in the current of tourists from Los Angeles, watching them arrive on Friday, watching them leave on Sunday. I should be going back there too, I keep thinking, but I'm from here.

My internet search history: *apartments in Los Angeles*, *what*

Los Angeles neighborhood should I live in, should I move to Los Angeles, moving to Los Angeles what should I know.

I tie the black apron around my waist, grab a beverage tray, and start clearing champagne flutes. They're plastic tonight. We go through so many on *Double or Nothing* night it's easier that way. Julie keeps the champagne flowing as the costumed guests filter in and out. A local news station stops by for a quick segment. *Stay tuned for an exclusive look at the house Jack Whitlock rented right here in Las Vegas during filming*, the reporter says. The movie finishes and starts again. Sweat collects on my back as I pass from the bar into the kitchen, into the humidity of the dish pit, where Ramon keeps his head down and feeds water glasses into the steam. The swearing of the cooks, as they sear steaks and slide chilled shrimp cocktails over the line.

"I need hands here," Chef bellows, making eye contact with me. "Ben, I said hands."

"Sorry, Chef."

"Don't be sorry. Be running food."

I heave a tray onto my shoulder and hustle out into the dining room, past the bar, where Julie shouts at me for abandoning her section, and land at the *Double or Nothing* booth. I read from the ticket, "Wedge salad, mushroom omelet, side of fries."

A couple dressed as Frank and his fiancée, the gender roles switched. The guy in a dress, the girl in a tuxedo.

"I was afraid you'd say no," he says to her, quoting the movie incorrectly. I drop the food where I feel like it. Let them switch the plates around.

"I was *sure* you'd say no," the girl corrects him. And then she looks up at me. "Right?"

"Yeah," I say. "Yeah, that's right."

"Can you take our picture?" she asks me.

I put down the tray stand and take her phone from her. I wait while they arrange themselves in the frame. She has smooth hair and an easy smile. She's very photogenic. Most people tense up in front of a camera, but not her.

"Ready?" I ask. They nod and I take it.

She meets my eyes for a few seconds longer than she needs to. "Thank you."

I hand her phone back to her, noticing the freckles on her cheekbones, which didn't show up in the photo. She gives me a twenty.

"Oh," I say. "Thanks."

On the TV above the bar, Jack counts his own money. He runs his hands over it, mouthing the numbers.

I take out the trash for Julie. The movie ends and starts, ends and starts. Jack arrives in Las Vegas, falls in love, gets rich, drowns his brother in Lake Mead, weeps at the shore. Marriage. Betrayal. Death. Credits. Rebirth. The bar fills and empties. A giveaway of a signed poster. Some free DVDs. An extra from the movie gives an interview: *Everybody at work thought it was so neat they let us be a part of it.*

On my ten-minute break, I eat cold fries over a trash can. When I return, the bar is peppered with tuxedos and chartreuse gowns but also locals in jeans and promotional T-shirts from neighborhood casinos: *Our customers are winners!* Everyone is hammered and talking about the movie.

"The guy," a man in a hotel polo shirt says. "The guy, Jack. They gave him a key to the city."

"Uh-huh," I say, emptying an ashtray into the trash. Jack smiles down at us benevolently.

"I was working here when they filmed it," a passing server chimes in. "I was an extra. I met him."

"What was he like?"

"It was a . . . It was like a beam of light. Like getting blasted in the face by headlights, meeting him. Some famous people, you're like, yeah, okay, that's that guy. Jack Whitlock, it's headlights. Pow."

I carry the bus tub to the kitchen, bring it back, fill it again. The speaker plays the sad song from the credits. That enigmatic, unsettling final scene: Jack running down Las Vegas Boulevard at night, perhaps toward something, perhaps from someone. No cars, no people. The sky is black, the neon lights out of focus. Critics and film students and professors and audiences have asked for years: Is it the afterlife?

The bar is nearly empty.

Julie polishes glasses. A few industry people, fresh from shifts at nicer restaurants, arrive for our reverse happy hour and order two-dollar beers.

And there she is. Alone at a high-top, the girl in the tuxedo. I don't usually want to talk to other people, but I want to talk to her. I pass by with a pitcher and refill her water. When she doesn't look up, I ask, "How'd the photo come out?"

"The photo?"

"The photo I took of you and your boyfriend."

"He's not my boyfriend."

I rest the pitcher on her table. "Hmm."

"I'm not telling you that because I want you to know I'm single, if that's what you're thinking."

"I'm not thinking anything."

"You look like you're thinking something."

The song swells and continues. She has removed the tuxedo jacket and the bow tie, unbuttoned the top button of her white dress shirt. I can see the outline of her bra beneath. There are other guests entering the bar. Other people who need water, glasses cleaned, tables wiped.

"Can I get you something besides water?"

"No, thanks. I'm going to find a ride soon."

"I can give you one. Back to your hotel. Or apartment."

"Apartment."

"I figured."

She finishes the water. I refill her glass again. "What does that mean?"

"You tipped me twenty dollars just for taking a picture. You're a local. Either that, or you were flirting with me."

"I'm a local," she says. But she smiles. The movie soundtrack ends, and a pop song from the radio comes on. Something different for the first time that night. And I can feel it, the shift.

"I'm Ben," I say.

Her eyelashes are light blond, like prairie grass. We shake hands.

"When is your shift over, Ben?" she asks.

My car is filled with the detritus of restaurant life—empty cans of Red Bull, unwashed aprons—and she is clean, so clean sitting in the passenger seat. She rolls down the window. The smell of rain, even though it's not raining. The sound of bars and restaurants as we fly down Sahara, hitting green lights all the way to the Maryland Parkway.

"I haven't had a lot of people in my car," I say. "Sorry about the mess."

"I'm not judging."

"I just realized you didn't tell me your name."

"It's Ellory Fox."

"Is that a stage name or a real name?"

"It's a stage name and a real name."

Finally a red light. I look over at her. "You're a performer of some kind?"

"Trying to be."

"What do you perform?"

"Burlesque. At dive bars and shitty downtown venues you've probably never heard of."

"Try me."

"But I want to work in one of the shows on the Strip. I have a Jack Whitlock character, hence the whole, you know." She gestures to her tuxedo. "Turns out you can't really do burlesque as a career unless you're on the Strip, and even then . . ."

The light changes and I turn right.

"Sometimes my friend Steven and I, the guy that was there tonight, sometimes we busk on the Strip. Dressing up, taking photos with tourists. Some people tip. Some people don't. You can't legally ask them to."

"I figured you were a college girl."

"I am—I was—I just graduated."

"So I was right."

"Did you go to college?" she asks.

"No," I say. "I just bus tables at the Bluebird. Sometimes I work catering gigs. And I'm a photographer, but not really."

"Not really?"

"I'm a wildlife photographer. Or at least, I want to be. No one has ever paid me for it."

"Does it only count if you're getting paid?"

"I don't know. Maybe." I catch her eye again. "Would you perform for free?"

She shifts in her seat, her change in posture indicating I've said the wrong thing. "The turn is here. On the left."

I put my blinker on. "Thanks," I say. I can barely hear my own voice.

Her neighborhood is cool and dark and quiet. Big old oak trees, 1970s town houses.

"I'm sorry," I say.

"For what?" she asks, then points at the entrance to an apartment complex. "I'm right there."

I stop the car at the curb. "Any plans?"

"For what?"

"Your life," I say. "Or just tonight." It's the kind of thing that would sound so cool in a movie, coming from Jack Whitlock.

She laughs charitably, which is the worst sound in the world. "Thanks for the ride."

After she's gone, I drive west in silence. When I get back to my apartment, I put on *Double or Nothing*. The company is nice.

On my day off, I take the Great Basin Highway north to Lincoln County. The open desert, where some people believe there are UFOs among the stars, alien creatures looking down. But that's not what I'm here for. I park my car on the side of the road, where the other cars are already waiting. The desert is windswept and gold. Magic hour. The silhouettes of men waiting with cameras.

The sun dips below the mountains, turning the air cold. And it's then that he appears. Ghost. White hair, pale blue eyes. A cremello. Cowboys used to say these horses were blind. Thinking them useless, they set them free. Ghost is old and strong and famous. He has his own Wikipedia page, five social media fan pages, a short documentary, and us, all of us.

I hold my camera like the other men hold their cameras, pretending that I am just as good as them, even though we all know that's not true. No college, no real photography training. I'm just a person who saw the Ghost documentary on TV as a teenager and knew, instinctually somehow, that I wanted to take a picture of him.

He moves fast, his hooves kicking up dust. I raise my camera. I watch Ghost, just a blip of white in the blue evening. And then I run after him. *What are you doing? What are you doing?* the other men say, laughter and anger in their voices. *You moron*, they say, and they're right, but still I try, my feet carrying me through the dust, my camera in my hand, my heart believing in the impossible. Ghost is just a phantom now, but I can still see him. I've been doing this for years—coming out to the high desert with a camera. First a shitty one, then a better one. This is the closest I've ever been to him. I want it so bad, even as he runs away from me, and I think to myself that it would be so much easier with a telephoto lens like other men have, to take Ghost's picture from far away, but I don't really want it like that. I want it like *this*. This way. Sprinting across the desert as the dirt turns to gold and the sky to fire, the entire landscape a warning saying no, no, no but my pumping legs and arms and hot blood say yes, and I do get a few pictures. Pictures where he is just a white spot, a patch of snow. But I know. I know he is there.

chapter six

I get drunk and find Ellory on Instagram. Photos of her on small stages, sometimes dressed in that tuxedo. I message her and ask if she would ever go on a date with me. She writes back: *maybe*

Sober the next day, I type: *I'm sorry if that was weird.*

She says, *I don't mind weird*

I take her to a movie theater in a casino, because that is what locals do. How is it possible we've never met before, I keep thinking as we drive up Charleston, the crown of red mountains in the desert hovering on the horizon past clay-roofed apartment complexes and billboards for personal injury attorneys. How many times did we pass each other in air-conditioned malls as kids, in the darkness of windowless bars as adults?

We quiz each other on this as we enter the parking garage, as we pass through the sliding glass doors into the casino, which smells the way casinos always smell—cigarette smoke and the coconut fragrance they pump in—which is to say it smells like home. And we are both comfortable here, passing through the maze of slot machines, because we know these places well. This is where we grew up.

"My family moved here from Texas when I was six, so I guess I'm not really from here," she says.

"That counts," I say.

"What about you? Are you really from here?"

"Third generation."

"Are you serious? No one has multiple generations of family here."

A cocktail server maneuvers in front of us, and we give her space to pass with her tray of beers.

"Well, my grandparents are dead and everyone else is gone," I say. "Except my parents, who aren't going anywhere."

"Your family has seen so much of this city's history," she says. "Really, it's amazing."

"I've never thought of it like that before."

We ask each other more questions. Where did you go to high school, did you go to the water park on the Strip as a kid? Where was your first job? Your graduation?

We encounter a series of near misses: a coffee shop I started going to after she'd already quit her job there, a party she went to at my apartment complex. I imagine myself standing on my balcony, listening to voices and music. And Ellory just below, in the hot darkness of someone else's living room.

The movie theater is in the back of the casino, near the bowling alley. An idea for a second date blooms in my mind, but I stop myself.

"It's this thing they do here called Western Wednesdays," I say.

"I know about Western Wednesdays."

We buy our tickets and go in. The theater is surprisingly full for a weekday. The movie begins: Jack Whitlock is a cowboy, riding a black horse in the white snow. Ellory leans closer to me, smelling like amber. "You think that would be better than my *Double or Nothing* character?"

After, at the lobby bar, we drink tequila sodas and look at the tiger shark encased in formaldehyde.

"I heard he's real," she says. "And he's slowly decaying. It's really sad."

I move closer to look at the shark, his face frozen, mouth open, body suspended in blue. He does look real.

"I prefer to photograph animals when they're alive," I say.

"Tell me about that. The wildlife photography."

"I shouldn't have said anything. I'm not really a wildlife photographer."

Ellory's lipstick is red. I imagine her selecting it. I imagine her painting her eyelids gold. "So what are you?" she asks.

"I'm a busser at the Bluebird."

"There are worse things."

"There are."

"No, really," she says. "I love the Bluebird. It's cool that you work there."

I crunch on a piece of ice. "Come on."

"I mean it. It's a Las Vegas landmark. You're a part of that. You should be proud."

"You don't think it's pathetic that I'm not even a server or a bartender?"

"No, I don't." She sits back on her stool and regards me for a moment. "You like to be in the background."

I shift my focus to the shark, meeting the dead animal's eyes instead of hers.

"Am I wrong?" I hear her ask.

"No."

"That's not an insult."

"Really?"

"Yeah, really."

Ellory smiles and I feel myself smiling back. "You're kind of, I don't know, disarming me."

"Good," she says. She raises her glass. "To the Bluebird."

"Sure, I guess. To the Bluebird."

We drink and stare ahead at the shark, as if it might move. I look at Ellory. "Can I ask you something? Why'd you say yes to going on a date?"

"I don't know. I just felt like it."

"It's that simple for you?"

"Yeah." She laughs. "How do you make decisions?"

We order another round. I feel very comfortable around her, a feeling I'm not used to. We talk about casino pools. The one she swam in when she was growing up, it turns out, was across the street from the one I swam in. I look at the dead shark and think about that distance, those two lanes of traffic that separated us.

Two weeks after the movie date, she texts me a string of question marks. I look at them, count them, as if there's a hidden answer there.

My internet search history: *jobs in Los Angeles*

I type *photography jobs Los Angeles* and then delete it and type *Ellory Fox*. There she is, and there's the venue where she's performing. A supper club near the Strip but not on it.

She calls me. Her voice sounds confident, because she actually is confident. "What are you doing tomorrow at dawn?"

"Nothing."

"Meet me on the Strip, where it intersects with Russell," she says. "There's something I think you should see."

* * *

On south Las Vegas Boulevard, there is a motel with a big pink fiberglass elephant in the grass. There is a wedding chapel built of redwood. There are strip malls with taco shops and psychics and discount T-shirts. *Someone in Las Vegas loves me very much*. There is a view of the freeway, thick with Los Angeles traffic.

"The other night I was at this club at Mandalay Bay with some Cirque du Soleil people," Ellory says. "We ended up staying until close, which was, like, five a.m., and I wasn't tired so I went outside for a walk. And there was something that made me think of you. I don't know. Maybe it'll happen again."

"You thought of me?"

She laughs, bumps up against me—by accident, or on purpose maybe. "Don't read into it too much. You brought your camera, right?"

"I did."

We keep walking. The diamond-white *Welcome to Fabulous Las Vegas* sign comes into view.

"I hate to break it to you," I say, "but that thing is always there."

She holds her index finger to her lips. And then she smiles. "Do you hear it?" she asks.

I stop and listen. The rare almost silence of the city. The hum that prevents total silence: electricity, traffic, occupied hotel rooms, graveyard shifts. And then I hear it. The coyote howls once, a single unwavering note held for one, two, three, four, five, six, seven seconds. A response.

"There," Ellory whispers.

They appear on opposite sides of the street. They find each other in the center.

"How did you know?" I ask.

"That they'd be here again? I didn't. I just hoped."

How could she possibly know I have photographed them beneath the canopy of lights on Fremont Street, in the parking garage of the Stratosphere, at the front entrance of a casino, in the gardens of luxury high-rises, in the dirt yards of trailer parks. That I have watched them pick through trash cans at bus stops, hunt for rabbits in flood channels, move in packs on golf courses. That I have heard the rumors of slain family pets—a limp tabby cat in a mouth, a bloody chihuahua in a backyard—and felt the stucco neighborhoods tense with fear, anger, but it has never changed the way I feel about them.

"I love coyotes," I tell her.

"So do I."

Wildlife advocates like to say coyotes were here first, but I know that isn't true. They are here because they are opportunistic. They have made themselves a part of our ecosystem.

I raise my camera and watch the two coyotes through the viewfinder. They wag their tails like dogs, touching noses. The city is gold and green and blue glass behind them. The photo has to be perfect. Wildlife allows for no do-overs. It doesn't matter if the light is shitty or the lens is out of focus or there's a slightly better angle.

I take it.

Afterward, they spot us and scatter, trotting south across rocks and dirt and trash toward the airport.

"Can I see?" she asks.

I show her.

"You know, sometimes when I photograph an animal I don't even look at the picture I take," I say.

"Why?"

"I don't know. I guess it's enough to have it."

She looks so pretty in this light, her eyes wet in the direct sun.

"I've been seeing coyotes everywhere lately," she says.

I feel jumpy on the way to Utah, a trip I'd planned on taking by myself. We're driving to the Tushar Mountains so I can photograph a herd of mountain goats. When I invited Ellory, she didn't say no like I thought she would. She doesn't overthink things like I do. She is impulsive, self-assured.

"Why are there mountain goats in Utah anyway?" she asks.

"They were reintroduced in the 1960s. Some biologists brought a few over from Washington and they reproduced. They're doing well."

"Still, must have been disorienting for those first mountain goats."

"I hadn't thought of that."

She is wearing aviator sunglasses, and I can't tell what she's thinking, what we're doing. Usually, I hike alone, do most things alone, but I don't say that, would never tell her how scared I was when she said she'd come along. After the hike, we'll camp. There are separate tents in the trunk of the car. *Quite an elaborate date you have planned*, she said, and I felt like I'd done something wrong.

She unscrews her water bottle and takes a long drink. "How do you know about these kinds of things?"

"I guess I watched a lot of nature stuff on TV growing up. There wasn't much else to do."

"There wasn't much to do in . . . Las Vegas?"

I think of my parents' house, the blinds down, the TV always on in the living room, where we ate together, not talking. Even when I was a child, we treated each other like roommates.

"I'm going to stop at this gas station," I say.

I fill up the tank and she buys us breakfast burritos. We make it to the trailhead before anyone else. It's still morning. The point is to avoid the afternoon rain that's been forecast. We move through the pines in silence. Ellory hikes in front of me, her bare shoulders shiny from the sunscreen she's just applied. A faint white streak not quite rubbed in. I want to touch it, want to touch her. This sudden desire for closeness is making me stupid. I am so used to the barrier of restaurant behavior: the smile, the *Can I take that plate out of your way?* Even with coworkers, I've rehearsed and perfected the rituals: coffee in the break room, the after-work drinks, cigarettes in the parking lot, the **hey man can you cover my shift** texts.

"How many girlfriends have you had?" she asks.

"None."

"None. Really?"

I think of a few drunken encounters: a sloppy make-out session in the darkness of a tiki bar, sex with a tourist whose bachelorette scavenger hunt included a one-night stand with a local.

"I guess I've dated, but not seriously." And then because I don't want to elaborate, I point to a pale purple flower with a yellow center. "Utah columbine."

Ellory takes a picture of it with her phone. I wonder if she'll post it to social media later, if I'll appear in the image at all. My arm, my shoes, my shadow.

"I haven't dated seriously either, not recently anyway," she says. "Every time I meet someone interesting, they leave."

"Transient city," I say.

"Are you going to leave?"

"Are you asking me that because you think I'm interesting?"

"That depends," she says.

"On what?"

"If you're sticking around."

I study the back of her head. Her hair, soft and blond.

"I haven't left yet," I say, which is not a lie. "You love Las Vegas, don't you? You're one of the five locals who actually love it."

"Oh, come on, there are at least twelve of us."

"And you're this Las Vegas archetype. You're a showgirl."

"Burlesque isn't the same thing, but point taken. And yeah, you're right. I do love it. I always have. I think it's the most interesting city in the world."

There's a mountain bluebird, Technicolor blue. We stop to look at it.

"The Nevada state bird," Ellory says.

I almost tell her about the hypothetical plans I sometimes make for a life in Los Angeles, about the California tourists whose plates I clear, about how I've only been there once, as a child, to see the ocean on a class trip. Never with my parents, who are scared of crowded highways, long drives. But instead I say, "There are things I like about Las Vegas."

"What things?"

"The animals. The money."

"What about your family?"

I think of my parents, the way we communicate in happy birthday texts, like former coworkers. But I don't want to say that. I can sense she's close with her family, that she has a lot of friends. So I say, "Of course, yeah, my family is something I like about Las Vegas."

We continue on. The trail rises. My calf muscles burn, tighten, release.

"Can I come see you perform?" I ask.

"Eventually."

"You've seen where I work."

"Everyone has seen where you work."

We break the tree line in time to see the cloudless sky. The altitude isn't bothering me today. A miracle. Strips of snow in green grass. A near-vertical trail.

"Just another mile to the summit," I say.

I imagine the goats waiting, grazing in an alpine meadow. Black eyes and white fur. My camera is in my backpack; I can feel the weight of it. And then a shift in the wind, thunderheads bruising black. A rumble and a flash. Downpour. I don't want to turn back, but for the first time, there is someone else here. It isn't just me. Her skin is slick with water and her eyes are wide. "This is crazy," she shouts over the pouring rain. We're soaked before we even get our jackets on. If I were alone, I would keep going; I would will it to blow through.

"Let's turn back," I say.

We hurry back into the forest, moving faster with each crack of thunder. The trail is muddy. The rocks are slick. Finally, the glint of metal through the trees. My car. Thank god. Once we're inside it starts hailing. Hard pieces of ice like hammers on the roof. My heart pounds against my rib cage. I reach for Ellory without thinking, her face suddenly between my hands, and I kiss her hard.

The smell of her, like jasmine. The heat of her, like lightning.

"Fuck camping," she says. "Let's go to a hotel."

In Parowan, we run across a cracked parking lot through the downpour to a neon vacancy sign. They give us the only room they have left—one queen bed—and when we get inside, she touches her fingers to my jawline and we just stand there at the threshold of the room, the door still open. A pause in the rain. There is a cereal factory in a neighboring town, and the air is suddenly sweet.

"What should we do?" I ask.

She leans into me, mouth close to my ear. "I think," she says, "we should take our clothes off."

I close the door.

She lifts up her arms, as if to cue me to pull off her shirt, so I take the wet material in my hands and slide it up her body. She kicks off her hiking boots, her legs still muddy from the trail. She steps out of her shorts. And then she's standing there in her underwear, waiting for me to make the next move. Her bra is thin and lavender. I take it off, and then she's lying on the blue comforter, which is patterned with illustrations of cowboys. I kiss her freckled shoulders, and then her lips, and she moans softly and says, "I can feel how hard you are through your clothes." And it's true, but hearing her say it emboldens me. I slip off her panties, drop to my forearms, move between her legs.

She is wet and tastes like the desert. Sage and mesquite. And she tells me exactly what she wants as I move my tongue inside her, her breath hoarse, her voice getting higher. I hold on to her hips and keep going, until she's pushing against me, and she is so warm now.

I hear her voice from above me. "I need you naked now."

"Yes, ma'am," I say, which is not a thing that I would ever say. Maybe it's the kind of thing a real man would say, a man like Jack Whitlock, and maybe, just maybe, in my wildest fantasy, this is how Ellory sees me on this queen-size bed in Utah. I get undressed quickly, my hands shaking as I pull off my clothes, but I am not shaking from fear but from whatever magic has turned this ordinary motel room into a place I've never been before. Her eyes are closed when I push myself inside her, still closed when I'm moving slowly and then open when she tells me to keep going. I let myself move faster, her hands on my shoulders, and then her hands on my ass, pulling me deeper, and then her hands on my face, both of us looking at each other.

She is loud when she comes, which makes me come, and I know in that moment that I will never recover from that sound, not for the rest of my life, that I will never stop hearing it, that no matter what happens, I will always be chasing it, desperate to hear it again.

We stay naked for a while afterward, listening to each other breathe, listening to the rain. We stay naked until we fall asleep.

In the morning, it is bright and cool. She is lying on her side, white sheets pooled around her waist.

I touch the tiny dragonfly tattoo on her rib cage. "What's the story with this?"

She laughs. "I got it at the ten-dollar tattoo place downtown."

"What does it mean?"

"It doesn't mean anything. It was cheap and pretty and I liked it."

"I want to learn all the things you like," I say. Another sentence I'm surprised to hear from myself. But her face remains open and accepting. She doesn't mock me for only pretending to be someone who knows the right words; she treats me like I actually know them, and maybe with her I do.

"Okay," she says. "Sit up."

I maneuver so I'm leaning against the headboard. "This way?"

"Yes," she says. She slides on top of me, takes my chin in her hand, and kisses me. Her tongue in my mouth, the soft skin of her inner thighs against my legs. There's nothing separating us. And then I'm inside her again, which feels so easy, easier than anything has ever been.

"I like it like this," she says.

I close my eyes and rest my forehead against her chest, listening as she tells me what else she likes: my hands on her hips, my tongue on her nipples when she is close. She likes to say my name, likes to hear me say hers, likes to bite and be bitten—but not yet, not until we really know each other. There are other things we'll do then too. *Then*. It sounds so good, the future, an invitation to go there passing from her body to mine. It's a gift, to know what her sweat tastes like, to feel her shudder against me. I memorize all of it, as if there will be a test, as if I might never get it again. Her palms are pressed against the mountains on the wallpaper. I want to tear a piece off and take it with me, to prove to myself that this actually happened.

* * *

The next time I see Ellory, I show her photos of Ghost. She is at my apartment for the first time, which means something. She brings takeout from a Greek restaurant, and she tells me she's a vegetarian, which is a new thing I learn about her, and there is so much more to learn, and I'm not afraid anymore, not really. And that night is the third time we have sex, her on the kitchen counter, legs and arms around me. "I've never done this in here," I say.

And fuck, that sound she makes. I'd give my life for that sound.

We have one of those nights I've heard about but have never actually had before. One of those nights where you stay up talking and fucking until it's all part of the same conversation. And when she says, *You feel so good*, she isn't just talking about my body but about me as an actual person, and I don't know that I've ever felt good to anyone in that way. She wants to see the photos of Ghost again, and I show her and she asks what it was like seeing him in real life, says she's seen the documentary, and I do not tell her that once I was so angry I didn't get the shot I wanted, I punched the window of my car on the drive back to Las Vegas. I do not tell her the wind whistled through the cracked glass, that I had to work an extra few shifts at the Bluebird to pay for the damage. No. Instead, I kiss the crown of her head and I hold her and I tell her it was exhilarating, really, it was incredible, it was beautiful.

chapter seven

My apartment is in one of those stucco-and-red-clay complexes everyone in Las Vegas lives in at some point. A corporate property management company has given it a made-up, vaguely European name, Artezza, because god forbid anyone reference the actual desert. It is nice in the way a midrange hotel is nice. A pool, a gym, a leasing office with complimentary coffee. *Resort-style living*, the website says.

Before I signed the lease, the property manager gave me a tour of the model unit, a first-floor apartment full of gray IKEA furniture and inoffensive wall art. A place no one will ever actually live.

"Your unit," the property manager told me, "will be just like this one."

When I asked to see the actual unit, she said it wasn't possible; the current tenant hadn't vacated yet. "But don't worry," she said. "When he does, the maintenance crew will shampoo the carpet, deep clean the refrigerator, and dispose of anything that's been left behind. It'll feel brand-new."

I had already seen four other identical apartment complexes and received four other identical tours that day, so I agreed to move in, not because this apartment complex was the best but because I was tired of looking. I signed the documents, paid the security deposit. A hundred dollars. It was so easy. The property manager handed me the keys and said, "Enjoy your stay."

Las Vegas can be an impersonal place, even when you live here. It's the feeling of drinking a gin and tonic at a hotel bar on the Strip, looking out at a pool full of tourists. It's an apartment complex, anonymously turning over tenants.

But the more time Ellory spends at my apartment, the more it feels like home. She makes observations about the color of my couch, the blackberry sparkling water in the fridge, my shampoo, my clothes, my sheets. All of my decisions, which previously seemed like reflexes, are suddenly purposeful in her eyes. It's as if I've fallen into a previously unknown galaxy, a universe where I could have a girlfriend. That's where this is headed, or maybe that's where this somehow already is, despite how impossible a romantic relationship has always seemed to me. We hike to the top of a mountain in Red Rock Canyon, high above the layers of Aztec sandstone, the hazy mirage of Las Vegas below. She takes me to a party and doesn't seem to mind how bad I am at talking to the people there. She pulls me into the bathroom at a concert, lifts up her silk slip dress, and puts my hand between her legs. I can't believe I'm wanted this badly. At a crowded bar in the Arts District, she looks up at me through the blue light as if seeing me for the first time. There's glitter on her collarbones, and she puts her arms around my neck and says, *Take me home.* And I'm so elated to be on the receiving end of those words. This feels good but also dangerous; I don't need a reason to stay. And it's fucked up that I haven't told her I want to leave. But still, I was eating off paper plates before I met her, and when she offers to shop for real ones with me I experience a specific type of kindness I didn't know existed. We spend a Sunday under the fluorescent lights of various thrift stores, choosing from the ones other people have discarded. Alone this would be a chore, but with another person it's enjoyable somehow. I can feel my heart expanding to hold something new. Ellory buys a mug from a casino that doesn't exist anymore. Just like me, she stood on the Las Vegas Strip as a teenager and watched them implode it. The crack of the explosives, the structure curtsying into a cloud of dust, the sudden empty lot.

That night, I wash the new dishes by hand. After, I call her at her apartment, where she is getting ready to perform in a variety show at a downtown speakeasy called Giggle Water. She puts me on speakerphone and talks while she does her makeup. I can hear her roommates in the background. Their music, their boyfriends.

"You sure you don't want me to come tonight?" I ask.

Laughter from one of the roommate's boyfriends. A commercial for a used-car dealership in Summerlin.

"Fridays are better. I'd really rather have you there tomorrow. But maybe"—she pauses to drink water—"I could come over after?"

"Yes," I say immediately, past the point of pretending I'm not desperate for that.

"It'll be late. After midnight, probably."

"It doesn't matter. Just come over."

After I hang up, I finish the dishes. I dry them carefully, these first objects I bought with another person.

Her body is cool and dusted with shimmer that night when she slips into bed wearing only the Jack Whitlock tuxedo jacket.

"I'm still in character," she teases and starts to slide it off her shoulders.

"Leave it on," I say.

The sex is gentle at first, and then harder, from behind, her hair in my hands, her voice in the dark breathing *yes* like a secret. And in this anonymous apartment, we could be anywhere. She climbs on top of me, and I put my hands on her lower back, feeling the material of the tuxedo jacket as she moves back and forth.

When I come, there is a twinge, a shudder, a sharp sudden sadness I can't locate.

After she is asleep, I get dressed and walk around the apartment complex. I find myself outside the model unit. The lights are on. I look inside at the blue walls, the fake fruit in the wooden bowl on the coffee table, the empty bookshelf, the vacuum lines on the rug, the framed photos with no people inside.

The next day, on the drive home from a catering gig for human resources professionals, I miss my exit on the 15 and keep going. And then I pass the exit after that, and the one after that, until I'm outside the city, in the cracked heat of the open desert. And I want, what I desperately want is to cross the state line and feel the difference of being in California, so I do it. And then I'm in Baker. I'm in Yermo. And it doesn't feel different enough so I keep going, and then I am halfway to Los Angeles when I realize what I'm doing. I pull over near Barstow, on the soft shoulder of a frontage road. It is just as hot here as in Las Vegas, the sun molten as it sets. A cluster of auburn burros stands on the other side of the highway, watching me, their expressions blank.

* * *

After a shift at the Bluebird, I drive to Ellory's smelling like fried food. She is in her swimsuit, looking for a towel.

Her roommates are huddled on the couch, still hungover from the night before, watching the Jack Whitlock movie where he plays a wealthy widower. He is alone in a living room, painting a white wall blue.

"You want to go to the pool?" Ellory asks me.

"Sure. I've got to get this smell off of me somehow."

Her apartment complex's pool is just like my apartment complex's pool. In fact, her apartment complex is just like my complex. Sometimes when I'm there, climbing the stairs to her second-story unit, I go up one flight more as if I'm going to my apartment.

The pool sits directly behind the leasing office, visible through wide glass doors so prospective tenants will see it and imagine themselves sunning beside it, diving in, drinking beers with neighbors who will become friends.

I don't want to know my neighbors, but Ellory knows hers. As we walk past the fenced-in dog run, she lifts her hand to wave, to greet them by name. She is warm with strangers, knows when to begin and end interactions. I am comfortable with the one-word blips of communication in a busy restaurant, the passing greetings people exchange on hiking trails, the silence of the men who are also waiting for Ghost. There's an understanding we're doing this alongside one another, not with one another.

Ellory unlocks the gate to the pool. The water is lit from underneath, turquoise, orb-like. Overhead, palm trees rustle and grackles call back and forth. It is too early in our relationship to ask if she'd leave Las Vegas with me, if she'd leave at all.

We swim in silence, touching, not touching. We sit at the edge with our legs in the water. Beside me in the dark, she looks up at the sky, her eyes on the beam of the Luxor.

"The other day I drove halfway to Los Angeles," I say.

"Why?"

"I don't know."

"You don't know?"

"I guess I was photographing something."

"What were you photographing?"

"I don't know. I don't know what I was thinking."

A week earlier, after she realized the pool was open twenty-four hours, we took mushrooms and dove in naked after dark. My first time skinny-dipping, my first time doing psychedelics. Both seemed ordinary to her. The water was warm and I floated on my back, dissolving one limb at a time. I was certain that I was coming apart and being put back together as Jack Whitlock, but I kept it to myself. At dawn, we had sex in the shallow end, just like in *Double or Nothing*.

Ellory slides back into the pool, backstrokes from end to end. She rests her arms on the edge. "I think the Giggle Water thing might become more permanent."

"Oh yeah?"

"I mean, I *hate* that name. But it's a cool venue."

"It is."

"And the owner has got some connection to a show on the Strip. So that could lead to something."

"What does more permanent mean?"

"They want to do regular burlesque nights," she says. "A few nights a week. Dinner-show thing."

I push my index finger against my thumb, feeling my waterlogged skin. I look at my fingernails. "That sounds good."

"I like the people there. It's a good group. I think some of the waiters do a trivia night together. And there's another performer who is super into hiking."

"That's great."

I slip into the water and put my arms around her, willing myself to also want a life here.

chapter eight

I am waiting in the mud. Yesterday, it rained in the high desert. There's a temporary lake, silver beneath the white sky. Pronghorn antelope ran beside my car on the drive here, their hindquarters white, their posture so straight, somehow formal, even in their panic to get away from me. If I don't leave in forty minutes, I will be late for my shift at the Bluebird.

A tawny mare appears at the shoreline, fuzzy colt behind her. She lowers her head and drinks. I have seen her before, but the baby is new. The baby is white. White like Ghost.

I have a better camera now. I hold it to my eye and watch them. The colt is hiding behind its mother, just an idea of an animal. I wait for it to get the courage to approach the lake. The surface is still, reflecting the empty sky above. Down the road there's a bar with photos of UFOs on the wall and alien-themed burgers, and I think I would rather go there and get drunk with conspiracy theorists than clear another table at the restaurant, collect empty glasses at a wedding. Twenty minutes later, the colt is still behind its mother. I should really go. It's a ten-minute walk to the car. But I decide to push it just a little more. I can walk fast, drive fast. I have started running in the mornings. Jogging west on Tropicana at sunrise, I often imagine a mountain lion a mile away. It's not an impossibility.

Last month, on the news, there was footage of one in a Las Vegas neighborhood. A 130-pound adult male tumbled over a wall into a backyard. The family took photos with their phones through the sliding glass doors of their living room. Shitty photos. I could have done better. I should have been there. It should have been me.

The light is really beautiful right now. The mountains are still. Ten minutes pass, and finally, the little white horse steps out from behind its mother. I know this horse is part Ghost; I can see it in his blue eyes, his pink skin beneath his white hair. I start taking pictures.

When I am holding my camera, when there is a subject in view, when I am pressing the shutter-release button, there is nothing else that exists. Oblivion.

The mare turns her head, spotting me. Her baby turns too. I move closer and they let me, they actually fucking let me. They are frozen beside the water, watching me approach them from the sagebrush, watching me watch them. I stay longer than I should.

I am an hour late for work. The assistant manager asks me again and again what my fucking problem is, and I show him the photos and say, *This, this is why I'm late*, expecting some sort of capitulation from him, but he just shakes his head and says, *Unfuckingbelievable.*

I look at the autographed photo of Jack Whitlock in the office, willing the assistant manager to fire me, to give me a reason to say, *Maybe this is a sign I should leave Las Vegas.* Like it's a new idea.

I try to sell the photos, but no one wants to buy them. It's my fault, maybe. I just don't know enough about that part of it.

Of course, I could put them on one of those fan sites for Ghost, could send them to someone who runs one of the Instagram or Facebook pages, but I'm not just going to give this shit away. For the first time I realize it. This is worth something.

The mountain lion shows up again. This time, they tranquilize him and bring him to a wildlife expert.

This is bad, the wildlife expert tells the local paper. *He shouldn't be prowling neighborhoods for food. This behavior is troubling.*

A different wildlife expert says, *Euthanasia is the humane solution.*

And then they all agree: It's the only thing that can be done at this point.

In the pictures, the animal appears to be sleeping.

I search the internet for other photos of other mountain lions and find an article about one that lives in the Hollywood Hills. His range is small, the article says. Too small for a mountain lion. Nonetheless, he is thriving there. Residents of the surrounding neighborhoods give starstruck quotes about rare encounters with the animal, describing him like one would describe a god, a work of art, a celebrity.

This is the problem with people in Las Vegas. A mountain lion showed up in someone's backyard and no one had any reverence for it.

The restaurant is busy and the catering gigs are plentiful. The money is good. This is Las Vegas, land of hospitality. I am able to remain in my apartment, even when the rent goes up. I buy a king-size bed. A real one, brand-new. Ellory does burlesque three nights a week at Giggle Water. Then four. There is talk of the Strip, finally. A routine inside a giant martini glass. Very glamorous stuff. Onstage, she looks happy. Actually happy. She arrives from her dressing room blanketed in perfume, warm from applause. Her friends hug me when I meet them and look at us, saying, *The showgirl and her boyfriend who works at the Bluebird, it's so Las Vegas I want to die*. They're nice to her. They remember she's a vegetarian when they invite her to dinner. I go with her to trivia night with a few of them, because this is important. These are the things you do in a relationship that are important. We spend time with her family, and they're nice. Nice to her, nice to me. It's more than I deserve. I introduce her to my parents—a lunch at a smoky neighborhood restaurant with video poker and well-done burgers. Afterward, she doesn't say that the lunch is awkward, even though it was. She doesn't say that meeting my parents revealed something about me, even though it might have.

My internet searches are questions now: *how do I tell someone I want to move*.

I try to sell photos and can't. I go to the desert, the mountains, the lake, with my camera.

"You should be a wildlife photographer," one of Ellory's roommates says, stoned on the floor of the apartment. "Ellory showed me a photo you took of that famous horse. It's good."

"Thanks," I say.

"He is a wildlife photographer," Ellory calls from the kitchen. The blender whirs; she's making frozen margaritas. She appears holding three glasses in two hands.

We sit on the floor and drink. The balcony door is open, letting in the night air. I can smell cigarette smoke from the man who lives below, a blackjack dealer. Ellory shows her roommate some of my other photos on her phone. Mule deer, mountain goats, bobcats, kit foxes.

"But they're mostly of the white horse," the roommate says. "You must like taking his picture."

"Well, yeah, he's famous."

"Ben only likes animals that are famous," Ellory teases.

Another roommate enters and turns on the TV. *Double or Nothing* is on. She leaves it. Jack Whitlock in the living room. All of us in Las Vegas.

"God, he is just beautiful," the roommate says. The rest of the girls nod. So do I. We all watch in silence. Ellory looks at me in the dark, the light from the screen on her skin. She reaches for my hand. Her fingers are soft and cool. And in that moment, I love her so much, the graciousness in her eyes. The trace of a sunburn on her shoulders, hair parted down the center, toenails painted red.

Later, in bed, I ask her, "Do you want to live here forever?"

"Forever is a long time," she says. "Why?"

"Just thinking."

She is falling asleep on my chest, too tired to process what I'm saying. Maybe that's why I brought it up. I listen to her breathe. Outside, a car alarm. An open window with music.

The next day, I work a catering gig for a wedding at the Flamingo. The ceremony is outside even though it's too hot, behind the casino, where the eponymous flamingos live. I enter through the same entrance Jack Whitlock used in *Double or Nothing*, even though it takes longer. It's nice to get an approximation of that feeling.

The flamingos dip their heads in the water. They alternate between standing on one leg and standing on two. At the nearby day-club pool, a DJ is encouraging partygoers to *make some noise*. He screams something about *titties*, and the crowd cheers. During the ceremony, the bass from the day-club overpowers the recording of the wedding march. The bride wears a coral-colored dress in the same shade as the flamingos' feathers. Her three daughters from her first marriage are her bridal party. They do not smile when they walk down the aisle. I pick up discarded wineglasses and restock napkins. At the reception, held in a ballroom where I once worked a barbecue luncheon for a painfully boring self-storage convention, the daughters sneak alcohol and loudly talk shit about their new stepfather. Overhearing this, their mother takes them outside. I trail them and watch. Their red faces, their tears, their eventual apologies.

I feel a sudden impulse to take a picture.

The bride sees me. She points a finger. "Why are you staring at us?"

"Super creepy," her daughter says.

After their first dance, the groom asks me if I'm some kind of pervert or something.

"Of course not," I say.

The couple leaves a negative review for the catering company, mentioning me specifically, but not by name, because they didn't ask, so no one really knows.

* * *

In early September, I work an evening wedding at a golf course on the far west side of town. This neighborhood was desert when I was a kid. Before all the master-planned communities, the outdoor mall. I imagine a future in which golf course sprinklers run dry and the grass dries up. Coyotes hunting quail in the sand.

In the present-day version of this golf course, I am parking my car in a far part of the lot designated for staff. I am wearing black dress pants and a long-sleeve black dress shirt per the couple's request. It is muggy, uncharacteristically muggy. Grasshoppers swarm on the pavement. Some of them have been crushed, run over by cars and stepped on by people, and the smell is distinctly chemical. The clouds expand, darken, turn into thunderheads. The final storm of monsoon season.

The venue is outdoors. A group of men attempt to erect a tent that clearly none have ever set up before. The wind lifts the canvas. The rain is coming soon.

"Where should I go?" I ask the catering manager.

She puts up her hands. "I don't even know. We're behind. A bunch of the cater waiters are stuck in traffic. Just . . . go placate the bridal party. Offer fruit or something."

Nobody plans for rain in Las Vegas. It's why our tires are so bald, our wiper blades perpetually in need of replacement.

The catering manager, who is both sweating in the uncharacteristic humidity and close to crying, motions to the stucco bungalow by the bar. "They're in there."

"Okay. I'll go in there."

"Good luck."

In the bridal suite, the maid of honor argues with the hair stylist. The bride's curls aren't holding. Her hair is wilted, her eyes wet.

"You should have used more hair spray," the maid of honor says. "Where did you go to cosmetology school? Supercuts?"

"Does anyone . . . need anything?" I ask.

The bride turns and offers me a small smile, her lip quivering.

"Don't you fucking cry," the maid of honor tells her. "It'll ruin the glue on your lashes." The rest of the bridal party sits on the floor, drinking champagne in tense silence.

The maid of honor turns to me. "More champagne." I go and get a bottle from the bartender, and when I hand it to her, she says, "This is hardly chilled."

"Do you want me to get a different one?"

"Will *a different one* be cold?"

"I don't know."

She rolls her eyes and passes the bottle off to a bridesmaid, who opens it. The cork pops in celebration. No one cheers.

A wedding photographer navigates the room. "Everyone just pretend I'm not here. I'm going to take some candids."

The maid of honor turns to her. "And her dress and her bouquet? And some posed shots of the group? You'll take those too?"

"Yes," the photographer says. "I'll take those too."

The bride seems tired and hungry, the end result of starvation and spin classes and five-figure contracts from wedding vendors. During the ceremony, her curls completely fall out. After the vows, one of her fake eyelashes detaches itself and needs to be reglued. The glue is black and it gets in her eye, making her eye black. She rubs it with her fist, creating a mess. The groom and his groomsmen drink whiskey from a flask that reads *TEAM GROOM* and chant, *One vagina forever one vagina forever one vagina forever.*

The wedding is terrible, but I know the couple will look through the photos and try to find happiness in their frozen smiles. On each anniversary, the bride will share the photo where she looks thinnest and say it was the most magical day of her life.

It pours. It pours and the tent is leaky. I burn my hand re-lighting a Sterno. People complain that the chicken is dry, the fish underseasoned. The couple's golden retriever bolts when he hears the first thunderclap. The bride's mother misses the first dance looking for him. The flower girl vomits. The best man gropes a bridesmaid at the reception.

"Staff use the porta potty," the father of the bride says when I try to use the restroom inside. He motions to the flooded golf course, deliberately not making eye contact with me.

I splash through waterlogged grass, soaking the dress shoes I bought just for this. The water around me is mixed with sewage, I realize, when I get to the porta potty. Inside the rancid plastic structure, I dab the rain off my face with toilet paper. It dissolves and sticks to my skin. The scent of human shit rises from the pit below the toilet. A trapped grasshopper buzzes against the door, trying to get out. A hundred yards away, the band plays love songs, but I can't hear a word.

During the couple's last dance, the groom is so drunk the bride is holding him up. The bride smiles at the watching crowd, laughs at the suggestive comment the best man makes when it is time for the newlyweds to retreat to their hotel room.

When it is finally over, I stand beneath the awning outside the hotel, waiting for the rain to let up. I'm thinking about the leftovers I have at my apartment—a plastic container of chicken and potatoes from a different wedding. I am thinking about driving out into the desert to look for Ghost, driving to the Strip to look for coyotes, driving to Red Rock Canyon to look for burros. Anything but this.

Beside me, someone lights a cigarette. "Wait—Ben? Ben from the Bluebird?"

I turn. "Eddie?"

"Shit, man. I haven't seen you since I quit." He shakes his head. "Ha. The fucking Bluebird. I don't miss that place." His cigarette goes out and he relights it. "Want one?"

"I only smoke when I'm on break at the restaurant."

"You're still there, then?"

"Busing tables."

"What the fuck—they haven't made you a server yet?"

"I don't want that."

"Suit yourself," he says.

"How have you been?" I ask.

The rain quiets. "I'm just in town for a wedding," he says.

"The Osworth wedding? I was working it."

He takes a drag. "Nah. Different one. Inside, thank god. Leave it to Las Vegas to hit you with the unexpected flash flood, right?"

A boom of thunder rolling around the bowl of the valley.

"Maybe I will have a cigarette," I say.

Eddie grins. "There you go."

We smoke in silence. The cigarette hits me, and I feel dizzy on an empty stomach.

"So guess what," he says. "I moved to LA a year ago."

"That's great."

"That's not all of it." He pinches his cigarette between his thumb and pointer finger. "Guess what I do."

"I don't know."

Eddie can't stop grinning. "Get this. I'm doing paparazzi photography."

I take a too-deep drag and cough. He laughs. "Easy there, bud."

A car passes and we step back to avoid being sprayed by water. The puddles have turned to tiny rivulets. They'll flow downhill from here, filling the flood channels on Alta Drive, the place where so many homeless people sleep beneath the city. Every monsoon season, someone drowns.

"I didn't even know you were into photography," I say.

"Here's the thing. I'm not. This shit is, like, so easy, Ben. A trained monkey could do it, though, for real. You don't need to know shit about photography to do what I do."

I consider this for a moment. "Really?"

"Really. I bought a camera, watched a few videos on the internet, and *bam*." He snaps his fingers. "Money is unreal. Un-fucking-real. Actually, I just sold a photo of that hot singer chick who came into the restaurant that one shift. Remember?"

"Maybe."

"Fifteen fucking thousand dollars."

"Thousand?"

"Yeah, thousand. Easy money. Well, not always *easy* easy. Sometimes they don't want their pictures taken. But all things considered." He laughs. "All things considered, it's pretty goddamn easy."

I roll back and forth on the balls of my feet. My shoes are still soaking wet. I'm going to throw them out when I get home.

"Huh," I say.

He nudges me. "I see that face. I see those wheels turning. Everyone thinks you're this inscrutable fuck, but I see you."

I toss the cigarette butt onto the wet street. "Maybe I need to get in on that."

"Better than doing this shit. No offense."

My phone buzzes with a text from Ellory. I put it on silent. Eddie gives me another cigarette. I light it.

"You're a paparazzi," I say. "Really? You run around chasing celebrities, that whole deal."

"Paparazzo, dude. With an *o*." He elbows me. "I'm just fucking with you. But, yeah, it's crazy, right? I moved out to LA and started doing the same thing I was doing in Las Vegas. Restaurants. And eventually, I get this valet job at a really nice spot in Beverly Hills. And I keep seeing all of these guys, these paparazzi, posting up, taking pictures of the celebrities who would eat at the restaurant. And these paparazzi are approaching me, giving me their numbers, wanting me to hit them up whenever someone famous comes in. So I'm doing that for a bit, getting a little cut of their profits in exchange for the info, and then I'm like, duh." He hits himself on the forehead. "Why don't I just do what they do? So, yeah. I bought a camera, learned how to use it, and now I'm the one juicing people for info, getting the shots, selling them."

"Just like that, huh?"

"Easy." He holds up a pretend camera. "Point, shoot, sell."

"And you like it?" I ask.

"I like it okay. And I love, love, love, the money. Last month, I flew to Cabo and got some nice photos of that actress from *Headhunter* on vacation with that basketball player. Making out on the balcony. I'm not even going to tell you how much I got paid. I don't want you to, like, kill yourself."

"I think I saw those photos on a magazine at the grocery store."

"Fucking right you did. You should consider it, Ben. I'm serious. Anyone can do it. I know LA isn't for everyone, and people in Las Vegas aren't always down with California, but who cares when the money is good. And it's kind of exciting. Running around like a spy. Better than, I don't know, busing fucking tables, man." He looks at me. "Or catering a wedding."

I don't know why I lie but I do. "My girlfriend and I have talked about moving to Los Angeles."

"You have a girlfriend? Sorry, I didn't mean that like it sounded."

"Her name is Ellory."

"Well, there you go. Move to LA with Ellory. Hit me up if you actually do it."

"Maybe later this year."

I think about the high desert, sprinting toward the mountains, a gash of red on Ghost's neck after a fight.

The rain stops. "I should probably get going," I say.

"Sure." He puts up his hands. "Don't let me hold you up. You still got my number?"

I check my phone. I do.

And as I'm walking away, he adds, "It's just like wildlife photography."

I turn back. "What?"

"I know it's a weird analogy, but it's true. Paparazzi photography is basically the same thing as wildlife photography. You've got these skittish subjects who are running away from you and—"

"Are you saying that because you know that I do wildlife photography?"

He laughs and sort of cocks his head at me. "I didn't know

that about you. Honestly, no one at the restaurant really knows what your whole deal is. But that's good, man. Look at you. You're already halfway there."

I wipe the rainwater off my face. "Yeah."

"And it helps to have someone in mind," he says. "A celebrity you really, really want to take a picture of. Do you have someone like that?"

Jack Whitlock, I think, but don't say it. Instead I just nod.

At the apartment, I shower and put my clothes in the washing machine.

Do you have someone like that?

I eat the leftover wedding food at the kitchen counter. I can't sleep. I text Eddie: **Good seeing you. I kind of want in on the whole thing haha**

I can't bring myself to tap out the word *paparazzi*, which sounds made-up.

Eddie doesn't respond.

The next day, I text him again: **I'm serious.**

He sends a thumbs-up emoji.

chapter nine

For a week, I keep it to myself, until I can't stand it anymore. Then, on a Saturday in the mountains above Las Vegas, I finally tell her: I want to move to Los Angeles. Not abstractly, but actually. I don't tell her how long I've been thinking of this, that if she'd known this about me on our first date there wouldn't have been a second. But I'm still not lying. Not really.

"There's a job," I say.

"What kind of job?"

"A photography job. I don't have it yet, but I could."

She rests her hand on an aspen tree, turns back, and looks at me. "Are you asking me to come with you or telling me you're leaving?"

"I don't know. I didn't think about that part."

"Wow," she says. She turns ahead and keeps going. The trail is steep. We're at eight thousand feet and I'm feeling the elevation, amplified with the pressure of her back turned to me, the hurt in her voice.

"I shouldn't have said that. It's not that I didn't think about it. I did. It's just, we've only been dating for, like, five months. It would be crazy to ask you to move with me."

"So you're not going to."

"I'm going to."

"Really? It doesn't sound like it."

"Ellory. You know you're my first real relationship."

Her voice softens. "I know."

I stand beside her. I put my hand on her arm. "Would you move to Los Angeles? Or, would you do long distance with me if I did?"

"For how long?"

"I guess . . . indefinitely."

"Indefinitely," she repeats, turning it over.

We hike in silence to the saddle in the mountains, a bridge in the land thick with bristlecone pines, the oldest living things on earth. Their trunks are pale and twisted, clay molded by the wind. She asks me where I want to eat after this, a conversation we often have at this point in a hike. Maybe she isn't going to address my question now or ever again, I think. Maybe I have to keep asking. I consider the possibility of going to Los Angeles without her. Consider the possibility that perhaps that's what she wants.

"I'll eat anywhere," I say. "Pizza would be good."

"I've heard LA pizza is terrible," she says. "It's something about the water, apparently."

"Can't be worse than Las Vegas water. Drinking Lake Mead. Drinking water from the place where the mob dumped all those bodies."

"They treat that water. It's not literally the body water."

We look at each other, neither one of us giving in.

Back in the car, on the drive down, I say, "You're not going to make this easy on me, are you?"

It's the wrong thing. She tilts her head as if hearing my voice for the first time and not liking the way it sounds. "Excuse me?"

"I'm sorry, I shouldn't have—"

"You can't even decide if you're asking me to move with you to another state, asking for a long-distance relationship, or breaking up with me."

"I'm not breaking up with you."

"Well, maybe you should be. Maybe that's what you want."

"Jesus," I say.

The ponderosa pines turn to sagebrush, the thick forest opening to desert. The car in front of us drives ten miles under the speed limit, red brake lights flicking on and off. "Look at this asshole," Ellory says.

I pull over, put the car in park. I look at her. "Listen. I fucking love you."

"What?"

"I love you."

"Why are you pulled over?"

"I love you. Come to Los Angeles. We haven't been together long enough for me to say that, but I'm saying it."

"Which part?" she asks.

"All of it."

"You're asking me to move to another city. To leave my job, my friends, my family—everything, everyone."

I cut the engine, unbuckle, and turn to her. "Then say no. If it's too much, say no."

"And then what? Then you go without me?"

I put my hands up. "I don't know. Maybe."

"I told you when we first met that this is why I wasn't dating," she says. "Because everyone leaves. You knew that about me. And you probably also knew you wanted to move, didn't you?"

"I don't know."

"Ben. Don't lie."

"In a way I knew," I say.

"That's very selfish," she says. "You're a very selfish person."

I reach for her hand. "Ellory, didn't you hear me? I said I love you."

She pulls away. "Saying that now for the first time is incredibly manipulative."

"You're right," I say. "But I did mean it."

"I don't want to be this person, this, like, wet-blanket girlfriend who says, *No, you can't do that.* I really don't like that you're making me this person."

"I'm not," I say. "I saw Eddie the other night, this guy who used to work at the Bluebird, and he's out there and he's a photographer and it's going really well. And he's doing these cool gigs that pay really well." And then the first outright lie: "And he's offered to mentor me."

"What kind of photography gigs?" she asks.

"Celebrity stuff."

She snort-laughs. "Like . . . a paparazzi? Those still exist?"

"Apparently the money is great. And the work is easy."

"That's crazy," Ellory says. But it isn't judgment I hear in her voice. She puts her hand to her cheek, taps her fingers against her skin. She opens her door. "I need some air."

"Ellory."

I get out too. We stand in the dirt by the road. There's a long silence. A car passes. Suddenly, I really want a cigarette.

"I could finally do something with photography," I say.

"And this is what you want to do?"

Out in the foothills, something moves. An animal. A burro,

maybe, or a horse. But neither one of us acknowledges it. The animal moves closer. It is a horse, it turns out, but not the one I care about. We both watch it. It's dark brown, head to the soil, grazing on what little vegetation there is.

I put my arms around her.

"I can't do long distance," she says.

Sometimes it's a conversation. Sometimes it's a debate. We talk for hours after midnight in her bed, in my bed. We argue in a casino parking garage. We text about it while I'm breaking down boxes behind the restaurant, while she's out at a bar with her roommates. Sometimes it feels like we're making plans, dreaming. Other times, it feels like we're fighting. Sometimes we don't talk about it at all. We talk about other things—movies we want to see, hikes we want to do—but then I realize that even when we're not talking about it, we're still talking about it.

She does one of her Jack Whitlock performances at a bar. A divey place that serves oysters—a menu item that should seem out of place but doesn't. I sit alone in a booth, watching her remove her tie, her jacket. Her hair is gold in the light. Her false eyelashes throw shadows on her skin. She falls to her knees, her back, looks at the audience from upside down. It's the music from *Double or Nothing*, I realize. Why did I never realize she performed to the score? Has it always imbued this routine with such a sense of sadness or is there something about this night, something about this bar, something that's changed between us?

When it's over, she orders a negroni and joins me in the booth.

"This paparazzi shit came out of nowhere, Ben," she says. "I don't get it." I can feel another fight starting, but the tone in her voice remains neutral. "I think . . . I think you need to explain it better."

I realize then that in spite of all our arguments and circular conversations about Los Angeles, the job is the one thing we haven't really talked about. I don't even know how she feels about it.

"Do you have a problem with it?" I don't mean for it to sound as antagonistic as it does, but mercifully, she doesn't take it that way. She sips her drink and considers.

"I don't want to be judgmental," she finally says. "I want to be open."

"So what don't you understand?"

"I just . . . Since when is this your dream? It's fine if it is, but there's a stigma about what you're talking about doing. You have to know that."

I try to remember things I've seen and heard about paparazzi in real life, but every image I picture looks like it's from a movie. "I could see there being a stigma," I say.

"But have you really thought about it?"

I haven't. "I think I can do it in a way that's ethical." A bartender passes by and clears my empty glass. I ask him for water, trying to be clearheaded about this.

"Next up," the announcer says, "we have Miss Flamingo herself. Put your hands together, ladies and gents, for Virginia Hill."

The woman appears, cloaked in pink feathers, dancing to Sinatra, balancing on one leg and then the other.

"Think of it like journalism," I say to Ellory. "Or art. Or think about how good the money will be."

"Ben," she says over the music, "I asked you if this is your dream. If this is really what you want."

"This is a way for me to actually be a photographer, even as someone who didn't go to school for it and doesn't have those technical skills and that business savvy."

"Couldn't you get those things? You make decent money. Take a class."

"And then what? Become, like . . . some Las Vegas wedding photographer?"

"There must be other options," she says.

"Not here."

"I doubt that's true," she says. "And what about the wildlife photography? You could really do that, you know. As a career."

I look down at my hands, the red light from the bar on my knuckles. "I don't think so."

"Ben."

"Maybe I don't do the paparazzi thing forever. Who knows if I'll even like it. I just want to be in Los Angeles."

She takes a long drink. "Why LA?"

"It's a big city, and people are doing interesting things."

"You're describing the city we already live in."

"It's different. I don't know; it represents something different."

"But you don't even know what that is," she says.

"Exactly," I say. "I want to be around, I don't know, some possibility. There could be other jobs too. Better ones. Maybe there *could* be a chance to do something real with wildlife photography. I could decide on an end point for the celebrity stuff. *We* could decide on that. If you came with me. Even if you didn't. Like . . . a contract, almost. A specific commitment that will expire."

"That's a bit much."

Virginia Hill stands on her tiptoes, raises her arms to the ceiling, and then extends them like wings.

"I'm serious," I tell Ellory. I reach for a bar napkin, a nearby pen with the name of an upscale casino on it. Casino pens migrate, moving miles away from the properties they belong to. At the Bluebird, my apron is filled with them. So is my apartment. If I move to Los Angeles, I'll try to leave them behind, but I know, somehow I know, they'll end up there with me.

I start writing.

"You don't actually have to write it down," Ellory says. "We can just talk about it. Honestly, Ben, I just want you to be able to live with yourself."

"Do you think paparazzi are bad people?"

"I'm sure they're not all bad people, but it seems like sometimes they do bad things."

I tap the pen to the napkin. "We can decide on all of it together. What I will and won't do."

"I haven't told you I'm coming with you. And besides, this is something you should decide on your own. Really. I think it should be up to you."

Virginia Hill finishes her performance. The sparse audience applauds. A guy at a neighboring booth lights a cigarette, and the smoke drifts over. The lights dim again, indicating another interlude, and for another second, Ellory looks like Jack Whitlock. It's something in her eyes. It has to mean something. I reach for her forearm and touch the fabric of the tuxedo jacket. And then I return to the napkin. "I won't ever go on anyone's private property."

She looks at me. The light changes from red to yellow. A flicker of her eyebrows that says, *Okay, keep going.*

"I won't do anything illegal. And I won't take a photo of someone who is in danger."

"What kind of danger?"

"In danger of hurting themselves or someone else. And nothing that would ruin someone's life. Unless they deserve it. Do you think that's too much of a gray area?"

Ellory is silent again.

"I feel like you have an opinion," I say. "Come on."

"No. I'm not going to do that."

I scratch out *unless they deserve it*. And then I repeat it out loud. "I won't do anything illegal. I won't take a photo of someone who is in danger. And I won't ruin anyone's life." I fold the napkin and put it in my pocket. "What do you think?"

She's still silent. I look at the far wall, where there's a mural of a lagoon. Pink flowers and palm trees, white clouds and mountains. A place that might not even exist.

I put my hands on Ellory's. "I'll do it for six months, tops."

"Let me think about it," she says.

I don't hear from her for five days.

I compose and delete text messages:

am i ever going to hear from you again haha

If you need to take some time I get it

is everything okay

On the sixth day, I call out of work. I chain-smoke cigarettes on the small stucco balcony, watching *Double or Nothing* through the sliding glass door. I pretend it's real, that Jack

Whitlock isn't just arriving in Las Vegas at the beginning of the movie but is stepping into my apartment, standing there beside me. He doesn't say anything, just looks at me with affection.

I walk to the gas station for another pack of cigarettes. I've never smoked this much in my life. I sit at the row of slot machines in between two men who are often there, drinking thirty-two-ounce fountain sodas and sliding money into the machines. People from other places think it's so unique that there are slot machines in gas stations and grocery stores, but to me it is ordinary; it means nothing.

"You can't sit there if you're not gambling," the cashier says.

I put my hands up. "Fine. I'm going."

I stand outside in the sun, long enough that I can feel it burning me. I let it.

My phone buzzes in my pocket.

Ellory: **come over**

I light cigarettes off of each other on the way, and when I get there she says, "Jesus, did you walk here?"

"Yeah, I guess so."

"You look awful." She reaches for me and we stand there, holding each other in her living room for a long time.

"I think I need a shower," I say. "Are your roommates home?"

"No, they're not." She leads me to the bathroom, closes the door, and turns on the water. She undresses first, her eyes on me as she unzips her dress and lets it fall to her feet. Then her underwear. New tan lines underneath. A pool day I wasn't there for, or maybe the Colorado River. A warning of how quickly her life could contract to no longer include me.

The room is hot with steam, and she lifts up my shirt. "I

smell like cigarettes," I say. "I'm sorry. I've been smoking too much."

She unbuttons my pants, sliding them down with my boxer briefs. "You always apologize for that, but I don't care if you smoke. I've never told you not to."

In the shower, she washes my body with rose soap. "Now you smell like me."

I touch her dragonfly tattoo, circle her nipple with my index finger, put my hands in her wet hair. She is so perfect; I'm terrified.

She reaches up and cups my chin, her thumb against my lip, pulling my mouth open. She pushes me against the wall of the shower and kisses me. And when she touches me I make this involuntary sound like a throat clearing or a laugh and she says, "Let's go to my room."

In her bed, everything is clean and white and warm, sheets perpetually fresh from the dryer somehow. I don't have to be told to lie flat on my back, I just do it because I know what she wants, I'll know that forever. Wet skin, water from her hair dripping onto my face as she climbs on top of me. I could drown in it, I could die. She doesn't hesitate to pull me inside her. I make another involuntary sound only this time it's words. "Fuck, I love you so much."

And it occurs to me in a moment of panic that this sex might not be about love; maybe she was bored and it's just sex or maybe she's doing this to say goodbye to me. I close my eyes and try to be okay with that; no, I open my eyes and memorize her collarbones, her pale breasts, her belly button. Her fingertips are on my chest, and I can feel her pulse in each one as she moves against me. And I'm so deep inside her, trying not to come because if this is it, I want it to last. I think of frat boys hungover at the Bluebird bragging, *Yeah, I fucked her for hours*, and I want to be those men not because I want to brag too but because I don't want this to end. I want it to last until it's dark outside, until it's morning again, until it's winter, until this apartment building is demolished, until the city is unrecognizable, until there's nothing left.

She rocks back and then falls forward against me, her chest pressed against mine, both of our hearts beating. Her face against the pillow. She doesn't move.

"Is it okay?" I ask. "Do you want to keep going?"

Ellory lifts her head. She looks at me seriously. "Ben," she says.

"What?"

"Ben, I love you."

"You do?"

"Yeah, I do." She laughs. "Fuck it, let's do it. I'll go with you."

I text Eddie: **Believe it or not I'm taking your advice and moving to Los Angeles. Could we meet up when I get there? Maybe you could help me figure out the paparazzi thing.**

The night before we leave, Ellory and I go to a buffet on the Strip for a last dinner with her family and friends.

The line to get in is long and full of tourists. One of Ellory's roommates keeps rubbing her back and asking in a low voice if she's sure, if she's really, actually sure.

Ellory smiles at me. "I'm sure."

"What are you even going to do in LA?" her cousin asks.

"Ben's going to do some photography," Ellory says, and I

feel both relieved and hurt that she's not more specific. "And the manager from Giggle Water is trying to connect me to gigs out there."

"We're going to hike a lot too," I add.

"Where's your family?" the cousin asks me. "Didn't they want to say goodbye?"

"They don't like the Strip."

Inside the buffet, in line at the stir-fry station, Ellory's mother says brightly, "You'll go to the beach all the time."

"Ellory doesn't like the beach," her cousin interjects.

"Everyone likes the beach," her father insists.

We sit at a big table, eating prime rib and scalloped potatoes and pizza and spaghetti and sushi and pad Thai. Las Vegas food, which is just every food in excess.

"Well, Ben, you must be pretty special," one of the roommates says, "to get the most Vegas girl I know to leave Vegas."

A friend from Giggle Water puts her arms around Ellory and looks at me. "I can't believe you're taking her away from us."

Ellory's mother smiles, shrugs. "Ellory has always been adventurous."

"And a bit impulsive," the roommate says.

"Mmm, that's true," the cousin says, covering her mouth as she finishes chewing her food. "I remember how she learned to swim by just jumping into the pool."

"Last year she woke up one day and just randomly decided to hike to the bottom of the Grand Canyon," the roommate adds.

They all share stories like these until they finally end up on me. "And this relationship. It happened so suddenly."

"And now you guys are, like, super serious."

They all look at me, as if waiting for an explanation. I put my hand on Ellory's leg and squeeze.

"We are," she says, pausing to drink soda through a straw. "We are super serious." I hope for a moment she'll share the story of how we met, or elaborate in some way, but she doesn't.

"It feels right," she says, and then returns to her salad.

I lean into her and ask, "Are you okay?"

"Yeah," she says. "Just really hungry."

I text Eddie again: **Leaving for Los Angeles tomorrow. Really psyched. Let's grab drinks.**

yeah for sure, he says, and it's a relief to get a response, even if it's one exclamation point short of an enthusiastic one.

Ellory eats plate after plate of food.

After a few hours at a bar for tourists who like finding hidden gems on vacation, even if those hidden gems are heavily advertised, I'm at Ellory's apartment, in her bed. She's in the hallway bathroom, brushing her teeth with her roommates.

"I'm sorry, but I don't get it," one of the roommates says in a drunk whisper.

"Don't get what?" I hear Ellory ask.

"Ben. I'm serious. What's the appeal?"

"Come on, let's not do this again. I love you, and I'm going to let this go because you're drunk."

"He's just kind of . . . I don't know. He's sketchy. Not, like, dangerous, but there's something off."

Ellory sighs. "Seriously, stop."

"He doesn't say much. He just sort of hangs back and watches. He's, like, the opposite of you."

"Yeah, I know. I like that about him."

The faucet runs and then stops.

"I'm following my instincts here," Ellory says. "And honestly, I don't have to defend my boyfriend or justify my choices."

In the morning, in the parking lot, we stand by our separate cars filled with our separate belongings. All of these items that will soon be combined. She's wearing a white T-shirt and black sunglasses, the easy glamour of a slight hangover.

"I've never done this before, you know," she says.

"What?"

"Moved in with the guy who brought me a wedge salad at the Bluebird."

"I hope not."

She hooks her fingers through the belt loops of my jeans. "I'm serious, though. I've never lived with a boyfriend."

"I know," I say. "I wish we could drive together. I know you hate the 15."

"It's okay. It's all an adventure."

On my way out of Las Vegas, I stop at the Bluebird. I park in the back lot and enter through the loading dock. In the break room, a server clocks in. Seeing me, he asks, "What are you doing here? I thought you quit."

I gesture in the direction of the office. "Just picking up my last paycheck."

The office is open and empty. Jack Whitlock looks back at me from the autographed photo above the desk. I lift it from the nail on the wall, slip it inside my jacket, and take it with me.

los angeles, amid scandal

chapter ten

Go-Go's owner isn't happy.

"His name is spelled *g-o* hyphen *g-o*. Go-Go with a hyphen, as in go-go dancer. Not Gogo all one word, which isn't anything."

Go-Go is tiny and fairy white, except for the soft fur on his tail, which is royal purple, like it's been dragged through a third grader's art project. He walks cautiously in tidy little circles around the members-only indoor dog park before dropping down onto his belly. He cradles his head, which seems too big for his delicate body, in his paws. His pink tongue hangs out, which is kind of his whole thing, or at least the thing that got him 4.1 million followers on Instagram and an exclusive sponsorship deal with the world's largest online pet toy retailer. Go-Go yawns, closes his eyes, and promptly falls asleep.

A collection of admirers hover with cell phones, going *aww* whenever Go-Go does anything. He curls his body into a fox-like ball, burying his nose in the fur of his stomach.

"What a perfect baby," a woman says solemnly.

The dog's owner moved here to be a comedian, and when that didn't pan out, she adopted Go-Go—then named Scamper—and figured out quickly that he had more screen presence than she did. But she isn't jealous of his career. No, no, of course not. I know this because she talked about it when she appeared on a special episode of *L.A. Facelift Celebrity Edition*. The celebrity in the episode was Go-Go, not Go-Go's owner. But a human had to be there to talk to Jessica Hartley about Go-Go's future mini dog mansion in Pasadena. Walking through the construction site—carrying Go-Go in his little pink hard hat—the owner explained, "He wants an entertainment room, a snack room, and a guest room for friends." A different host might have acknowledged the absurdity of the moment, but Jessica smiled serenely, nodding, taking it seriously, which seemed to me a kindness. "I've got to tell you," Jessica said, extending her hand for the dog to lick. "Our daughter is a big fan of Go-Go."

"And is your husband . . . a . . . fan of Go-Go?"

Jessica laughed. "Our dog is also a big fan of Go-Go."

"Let's set up a playdate."

Jessica put her hand on the scaffolding of the mini mansion, turned to the camera, and smiled. "Once Go-Go's dream house is complete, we'll throw him a housewarming party."

A lesser paparazzo would dismiss this as meaningless TV banter, but my inkling is that the dog housewarming playdate happened, or at least something happened, because Jessica and Go-Go's owner follow each other on Instagram. They engage with each other's posts. On Go-Go's owner's account, there's a shot of an outdoor dinner party at Jack and Jessica's Bel Air mansion. Jack is not pictured, but I recognize the infinity pool. Go-Go's owner appears at the table eating lamb and drinking wine. *I thought u and Go-Go were both vegetarians*, someone says in the comments.

I have been combing through Jessica's social media for days. She hasn't posted since the scandal broke, but there is still much to be discerned from the existing content. The potential friendship with Go-Go's owner is *something* because unlike the couple's more famous friends, Go-Go's owner is easy to find. A quick glance at the dog's website tells you exactly where to find him and his owner almost every day. And today, they are at Paradise Paws Canine Club, giving out plant-based dog biscuits.

"It's just that so many journalists forget the hyphen in his name," Go-Go's owner is saying. "Can someone get me a sparkling water?"

When the small crowd temporarily dissipates, drawn to another famous dog—Otto the three-legged schnauzer—I approach Go-Go's owner. "Hey. I'm Ben."

She is swiping at her phone with her index finger. "Hi."

"Dating app?" I ask.

She looks up at me and, seeing me for the first time, draws her phone to her chest. "What?"

"It's hard, isn't it? Dating in Los Angeles."

Go-Go wakes up and trots over to her. He plants himself at her feet and sits down, his back to her, his big eyes on me. "Huh," she says, looking down at him. "Go-Go doesn't like you."

"What makes you say that?"

Go-Go continues his unblinking stare.

"Look at his posture. He's protecting his mama." She crouches down and coos in the *speaking to a dog* voice, "Are you protecting your mama?" She combs his fur with her long purple nails and says to me, "We ran out of the dog treats. You should have come earlier."

"Oh, no, that's okay."

She stands. "Where's your dog anyway?"

"My dog?"

"People usually bring dogs to these things." She gestures at the animals running in circles nearby. "It's a dog park."

"I don't have one."

"So, what, are you just a fan of Go-Go? You want a picture with him? It's fine, just don't touch him."

Go-Go remains pressed against her, eyes on me. He parts his lips and shows me his tiny bottom row of teeth.

"I came to see you, actually."

She pockets her phone. "Who are you, again?"

"Ben."

"What is this—another one of those fetish things?"

"What? No."

"Because I gotta tell you, I've had it with these dog-fetish people."

"*Dog*-fetish people?"

"Yes, they're clogging up my DMs. I have a filter on my email that's supposed to keep them out of my inbox, but they get through. They don't ever come to events, so I've got to say, you're a first."

"Okay, but I'm not a *dog fetishist.*"

"Don't say it like that. Like you've never heard of it. Like you don't believe it exists." She scoops up Go-Go and cradles him against her, rocking him like a baby. "Poor Go-Go is terrified of these freaks in our DMs."

I shake my head. "Yeah. You're right. I have heard of them. I think I read about it on Terrence Tower's website?"

She nods. This is good.

"Yeah. The *Tower Blog*. Those people make me sick. Just the thought of them . . . well, you know. Those people make me sick," I repeat.

"Me too."

"And I think, I just think, uh, that what you do is so important, right?"

She kisses Go-Go's wet black nose. "How do you mean?"

"It's just . . . important." I gesture to Go-Go. "To celebrate how cool and special dogs are."

"In a nonsexual context."

"Of course. In a nonsexual context. One hundred percent nonsexual." I stall, thinking of something else to say. But she is looking at me now, giving me her attention. Behind her, two huskies start howling, trying to match each other's pitch.

"Fucking huskies." Go-Go's owner shakes her head. "I'd never adopt—"

"Adoption. That's another thing I admire. You're bringing so much awareness to that. You know, the whole adopt-don't-shop thing."

"I've dedicated a lot of time to speaking out against puppy mills."

"I know. And I so value that."

She takes out her phone again. I'm losing her. "Go-Go has an event in Long Beach, so I've really gotta be wrapping up here. Traffic. But did you want a selfie with Go-Go or something?"

"No. I just wanted to talk to you about . . . Well, I'm a photographer—"

"Oh," she says. "I know what you are."

"And you're friends with—"

"No." She puts a finger up. "Absolutely not."

"If you'll just—"

She begins backing away. Her eyes are wide and angry. "I know what you're trying to do, Ben." She says my name like it's a bad word, or maybe so that she'll remember it, so she can warn someone else about me. "You know, shame on you. Shame. On. You. Jessica is a mess right now. And she's in Montana with her family, so you can just give the fuck up." She holds Go-Go tighter.

"I can offer money."

She continues to back away. "Stay where you are."

I put up my hands. The huskies howl. More dogs join in.

"You are so much worse than those disgusting, awful people who harass me online, who message me all the unspeakable things they want to do to my baby. You are lower than low. You are the devil. You and everyone like you, you're the worst people in this city. Don't come any closer. You are goddamn dangerous."

"I'm not going to hurt you. I'm not going to hurt anyone."

She laughs. "Yes, you are." She points her finger. "That's all you do."

At a nightclub in Hollywood, I pass my card to the bartender and he takes it. No one comes here anymore, but they used to. Jack used to, when he was in his twenties. When he was young and single and his hair was a little bit longer, a little bit messier. There's a photo of him I revisit often: He's exiting the club in sunglasses, holding hands with a lanky Romanian model. A cigarette in her hand like an accessory. Everyone around them parting, letting them out onto the sidewalk. Their easy elegance. Their half smiles. A car waiting for them. No photos exist of him inside the club, so it's impossible to imagine what booth he sat in, what drink he ordered, if he ever danced.

"Nobody famous comes here," the bartender tells me. "But, sure, I'll let you know."

He is desperate for the cash. Desperate in general. I can see it in his eyes.

There are people worse than us, I text Eddie. **That has to be true.**

The bartender is talking about how cool it would be to see Jack Whitlock, but I can barely hear him over the music. The following week, he texts often. A talent agent's brother came through, he thinks. A bus driver for an indie rock band. Useless shit like that. Eventually, he is just texting to check in, to stay on my radar, as if I am supposed to do something for him and not the other way around. I block the number. I should have known it would be hopeless.

On a Wednesday, the sky is ash and the air smells like a campground. There's a fire burning in the Santa Monica Mountains. The winds will shift in a favorable direction soon, city officials say, but for now it's best to stay inside if you can, cover your mouth and nose if you have to leave the house. From my balcony, I see people with silk scarves across their faces carrying takeout from the vegan sushi restaurant on the corner.

A downtown bar offers wildfire shots—Fireball whiskey and Malibu rum—until the internet calls it offensive, forcing them to apologize.

I sit on the couch and look at my phone. Celebrities, bored in their houses and needing attention, make social media content without the guidance of PR teams and managers. A comedian jokes about hot firefighters. An heiress throws a pool party and posts videos of her friends dancing in bikinis beneath the orange sky. *Pretending it's snow lol*, an influencer tells his followers, sharing a video of ash falling on a beach set to the song "It's Beginning to Look a Lot Like Christmas."

I watch the video of Jack and Sasha again and again, as if his posture might contain a secret message.

E! News officially confirms what Go-Go's owner told me: Jessica is in Montana. She was spotted at the airport in Kalispell two days ago with her daughter—someone took a picture with their phone and posted it online—presumably on her way to her parents' ranch, where she grew up. The photo was taken near baggage claim, a taxidermy elk on a nearby wall. She has her head down and is holding her daughter's hand. A fashion blogger notes that Jessica is wearing a vintage Pendleton coat and carrying Hermès luggage from the fall 2013 collection.

Other paparazzi, also bored in their homes, text me, text one another, considering flying there, speculating about the security at the ranch, the restaurants and stores they might find her at in the small towns that dot the region.

Would it really be worth the flight?

I don't want to find her. I want to find him.

E! News says that while Jessica has not released a statement, coworkers and guests from *L.A. Facelift* have expressed their support, noting a petition that's circulating, calling on paparazzi to pledge to stop taking pictures of celebrities' children. A local news station interviews the creator of the petition, who says, "The situation with Jessica Hartley and her daughter is a perfect example of why this issue matters. Here is a woman dealing with a serious personal crisis, flying home to be with her family, as she should, and not only is her privacy violated, but the privacy of her very young daughter, who will grow up and see those pictures, is being violated too."

The reporter nods. "Imagine her growing up and seeing that video of her father."

"I wasn't talking about that."

I text Eddie: **that video wasn't even taken by paparazzi**

Music from the apartment next door. The people who live there are in the habit of celebrating hyper-specific events—a second interview at a production office, a cat's birthday—and a day stuck inside seems like no exception. I listen to their voices, the sound of the door opening and closing as more people from the building find their way to the party.

I go out to the hallway, standing there barefoot.

A woman in a white tank top opens the door. The heat from the apartment hits me. People are dancing in the living room. There's a sheen of sweat on her forehead. She smiles. "Who are you?"

"Ben. I live next door."

She pulls a pack of Camels from her back pocket and smacks the bottom with the palm of her hand. "It's too hot in there. I'm going out for a smoke. There's a wildfire, but"—she pulls out a cigarette and puts it in her mouth—"what's the difference."

I laugh. "Right."

"You want to join?"

"Thanks, but I'll stay inside."

She shrugs. "All right. You going into this party?"

"I don't know any of those people."

"Neither do I," she says. "I'll see you."

I watch her move down the hallway until she's gone. I think about following her, or going into the party, meeting my neighbors. I picture myself standing there with a beer when she comes back inside, asking her name, talking to her. But instead I just listen to the people on the other side of the door. They're talking about the wildfire. The containment percentage is low. Some of them have friends in the area where it's spreading. They're worried. But eventually their conversation turns to other things—mutual acquaintances, favorite coffee shops, vacations—and soon they're just talking, just being together. And I get it, how a party like this might feel good.

"My name is Kendra," she says in the video. "And my roommate is hooking up with the biggest movie star on the planet."

She has two hundred followers when she posts it, which quickly balloons to thousands. In the video, she is sitting on the floor of her small bedroom. There's a California state flag and string lights on the wall, a collage of Polaroid pictures. She has a demeanor I recognize from the service industry, friendly but not genuinely nice. The video is long enough to be monetized. She spends the first few minutes talking about herself and her apartment, what she likes and dislikes about her neighborhood. Eventually, she arrives at her point. "So my roommate—well, my now ex-roommate—is this girl, Sasha, who some of you may have heard of. And the other night she came home at, like, two a.m. I could hear her in the kitchen talking to some guy whose voice sounded really familiar, but I couldn't think of where I knew him from. I was in my room, with the door closed, studying for the GRE because I want to go to grad school so I don't have to work in retail for the rest of my life . . . whatever . . . and so"—she pauses to drink from a pink water bottle—"so she thinks I'm asleep, clearly. And she goes to her room with this man. And, guys, they have the *loudest* sex. Like, I put on headphones and I could still hear them. So annoying." She pauses to drink water again. She taps her manicure on the exterior of the bottle. "The next night, we have a party at the apartment and she gets drunk, and she keeps going *I shouldn't tell you guys this* until finally we're like, *Okay, you have to tell us*. And then she tells us. She has been hooking up with Jack Whitlock"—she pounds the floor beside her for emphasis—"in this very apartment. Of course, no one believes her. He's the most famous person ever? Like, why would he be in our apartment? So we're like, prove it. And she passes me her phone, and, well"—she takes another big sip; she smiles—"legally I don't know if I can say the rest. But, like . . . let's just say I realized where I knew that voice in the kitchen from."

I do the obvious thing. I find Kendra's email address and send her a message. It is easier to start from a place of belief than skepticism—a celebrity guru told me that once. Or maybe he said it to a crowd of people, to the internet, to the whole world.

I don't ask her if she's telling the truth. I ask her where Sasha is. What did she mean by *well, my now ex-roommate*? Are

Sasha and Jack still sleeping together? Are they in a relationship? Is that why they've both vanished?

I give Kendra proof of who I am, what I'm capable of, promise her I'm good for the money if she wants to talk.

She doesn't respond.

I refresh my inbox again and again. A new wave of threatening emails:

you are TRASH

You have no idea how many of us there are. We're everywhere and we're never going to stop.

going to make u regret what u did

But nothing from Kendra.

The next day, she takes down her video, which is how I know she wasn't lying.

The fire spreads. An actor's house burns to the ground. Next door, there is another party. People want to be together during times like these, I hear one neighbor saying to another in the hallway on the other side of my door. They introduce themselves to each other, start talking about their jobs, where they're from originally. These are the kinds of easy friendships Ellory would form.

I look at her Instagram. She is in a sequined bodysuit at a club on the sixty-third floor of a hotel, the lights of the Las Vegas Strip behind her. Her hand is on her hip and she is smiling with red lipstick, a showgirl smile. *This is truly a dream job . . .* the caption begins. Finally, she got what she wanted. I type and then delete *congratulations*. In another tiny square on my screen, she removes a tuxedo jacket and then begins unbuttoning the white shirt. She slides her hands down her body. Her eyes close. I touch myself, remembering a dirt road in the desert, the back seat of my car, her underwear pushed aside, the way she held my head in her hands and told me she'd never been this close to another person. And for a moment I'm there, but after I come I'm back on my couch looking at her face on my phone. This is the only version I know of her now, what she gives of herself to the internet.

chapter eleven

The smoke clears and I leave my apartment. I walk to Jack's dermatologist's office. Waiting outside offices has worked out for me in the past; there's a chance it could work with Jack. Oftentimes, there are procedures that can only be performed in a dermatologist's office, things that would make a house call impossible, forcing the celebrity out.

It was easy to figure out who his dermatologist is—about six hours of work total, which is nothing to me. In the end, it took a trip to the library, reading back issues of celebrity magazines until finally a half-page spread: *Top Skincare Tips from Dr. Ruby, Derm to the Stars!* After two hundred words about the difference between retinols and retinoids, I arrived at the pivotal sentence: *Dr. Ruby's A-list client list includes Sondra Neal, Lil Monstah, and most notably, Jack Whitlock.*

On the internet, rumors swirl about where Jack is, where Sasha is, whether Kendra was really her roommate. The speculation intensifies, reaching the crescendo of frenzied fan fiction: He's at a Buddhist retreat. She's hiding in a penthouse he's paying for. He's driving to Mexico; she's heartbroken in a Toyota Tercel, trailing him as he crosses the border. They're together, playing house in his mansion. They're in separate rehab facilities.

Five blocks away from the dermatologist's office, the lead actor of a long-running sitcom throws a glass of wine at me.

"We don't want you here," he says. He sounds like his character, a bumbling Brooklyn literature professor, not himself. He stands on a restaurant patio, holding a now-empty wineglass. His assistant sits at a nearby table, intently looking at her cell phone. The wine is red and my shirt is white—light colors when it's warm and sunny, an obvious desert survival tip.

"I'm not here for you," I say.

"Doesn't matter. None of us want you here. Get a real job."

"Congrats on the show getting renewed," I say.

"Hey, fuck you."

I keep walking. I'm a few blocks from the dermatologist's office when I realize I'm being followed. A man is behind me, and then he's beside me, facing me and doing this weird, wide-legged sideways jog like he's in an exercise class. I think of the emails, the text messages, the DMs saying, *you're going to regret what you did we're going to make you regret it just wait until we get you alone.*

I keep my head down and move faster, but he keeps pace with me, looks directly at me, very intentionally, so I can't convince myself it's all in my head. My heart palpitates.

"Hey," he says. "Hey. Can I talk to you for a sec?"

I turn a corner and he stumbles but keeps up with me. "Hey," he says again. "I know you can see and hear me." His voice is desperate, not threatening.

"I'm not going to engage with you," I say.

He continues to jog in place. "I saw you back there. I saw him throw that wine on you."

"It happens."

My shirt sticks to my chest, the skin clammy and cool.

"He really got you, huh?"

"It's fine." I can see the tall arch of the building where the dermatologist's office is. The top floor. "I need to be somewhere, okay?"

"Can I have that shirt?"

"What?"

We both stop.

"I know it's weird," he says. "But I'm a really, really big fan of his and I'd just love to have your shirt that he threw wine on."

I look at him. "A hundred bucks."

"Done." He grins.

"And I need something to wear. Give me your shirt."

We both remove our shirts and pass them to each other. His black button-down is too big for me. It smells like sweat. He doesn't put mine on; he stands shirtless on the sidewalk holding it, his hands trembling. "Wow," he says. He holds it above his head. Opening his mouth, he takes the material and twists it, attempting to wring the liquid out and drink it.

"Can I have the money?" I ask.

He fishes around in the back pocket of his jeans and withdraws a twenty. "I can write you a check."

I point to an ATM. "Cash."

"There's a fee."

"Take the money out," I say, and walk with him to the ATM. We don't look at each other when he hands the rest of it over. We can sense each other's desperation, the way animals can. Lately, I have been depleting my savings, charging bills to credit cards.

The smell of his shirt is a distraction as I walk the rest of the way to the dermatologist's office, but when I get there I'm the only one, which is a good thing. The office closes at five. I have three hours. I stand there for every second of the time.

The workday ends. There is no sign of Jack Whitlock. I give it another half hour.

Dr. Ruby himself walks out of the glass door of the building, looking like a photoshopped version of a person. His movements are purposeful. A clear sign that I should follow him.

Dr. Ruby enters an unmarked black door beside a sandwich chain. I wait five minutes and go inside. Immediately, there is a small, windowless waiting room outfitted with baroque red wallpaper and framed paintings of cats. An antique princess phone rests on the only piece of furniture in the room: an armoire below a mirror. From somewhere undetected, jazz music plays. I lift up the receiver, listen to the dial tone, and then press O for operator. I can hear a phone ringing in a room I can't see.

"Feline Club," the voice says, both on the line and through the wall.

The name sounds familiar, like something I read about in a magazine years ago.

"Yeah, hi," I say. "I'm here for the thing with Dr. Ruby."

"Are you a patron or an assistant?"

I can't tell which lie will be more convincing. "An assistant," I say, wondering if it's fate that the sweaty man's shirt is more professional than the one I was wearing before.

A buzz, and the black door on the wall clicks open. I turn

the glass knob and enter. The next room is a lot like the previous one, just bigger. It's windowless again, with the same wallpaper, the same cat paintings, but there is a small bar and some tables. This is someone's idea of a Prohibition-era speakeasy, not an actual Prohibition-era speakeasy. There is something derivative about it, something try-hard. A distinct sense of almost-but-not-quite. A Santee Alley version of a designer handbag. A woman in glasses stands behind the bar. She smiles when she sees me. "You're here to assist Dr. Ruby?"

"Yes," I say, more like an affirmation than the truth.

She opens the door to a narrow hallway. "They're just getting started in the Ragdoll Room. Last door on the left." There is a menu on the wall beside her: *tonics and elixirs to aid with the process*.

In the hallway, which is lit entirely by a single candle, I look up *Feline Club* on my phone. There's a website and a smattering of articles. It's an expensive club for *distinguished women*. The website links to an Instagram account and I go to it and scroll. There are photos from this space, various rooms with various vaguely recognizable people in them. The kind of people who are famous-adjacent. The daughter of an actor, a celebrity hairstylist with her own line of deep-conditioning masks. In one photo, a collection of well-dressed women with very good skin and teeth crowd together, holding blue cocktails. The caption reads: *Last night, our Feline Club members enjoyed an exclusive screening of a documentary about California's shrinking Salton Sea, narrated by Jack Whitlock. Plus, themed cocktails!*

Okay. His place in all this still feels tenuous, but at least there's something.

I follow the hallway to the door marked Ragdoll Room, passing rooms named after other kinds of cats. Sphinx, Bengal, Siamese, Manx, Snowshoe. I don't know what I'm going to do, what I'm going to say, what I'm going to see when I enter the room. I breathe in, breathe out, trying to channel the energy of Dr. Ruby's assistant, whoever that assistant might be, whatever that assistant might be doing.

I figure I can at least start with the nonchalance of a person who has done a job before. No knocking. I open the door and step inside.

The room is nothing like the rest of the Feline Club. It is spa-like in nature, glowing in hues of soft pink and white. Two of the walls are mirrors, as if one might host a yoga class here. In one corner, there is the largest Himalayan salt lamp I've ever seen in my life. In another, a healthy fiddle-leaf fig, stretching up toward the ceiling. On the far wall, a light installation from a well-known artist. Five women recline on chaise lounges. They are dressed in long silk bathrobes and they have the kind of smooth skin and lean muscles that are directly correlated with a lot of money and a lot of time devoted to the business of self-care. Two of the women are from a reality show. On the show, they are bitter rivals. The show's best-known scene is one in which they are standing outside a wine bar, trading insults. *You're just a crab with hair extensions*, the younger one famously says to the older one. The phrase resulted in a T-shirt line, branded wineglasses, and a partnership with a sustainable seafood brand.

They seem to be getting along now, sitting beside each other drinking amber beverages garnished with herbs. The room has the tenor of a very subdued bachelorette party. Dr. Ruby turns from the table he's setting out equipment on and faces me. "They told me you weren't coming."

"Pardon?"

"They said you were sick. You're here to assist, no?"

"Yes. I'm the assistant."

Jack Whitlock in my mind, his cool gaze passing over the casino floor. I am following him, I tell myself. This must be the way through. Dr. Ruby shakes my hand, and I think, these hands have touched him, anointed him with oils and burned him with lasers.

"Have you done this before?" Dr. Ruby asks.

"No, I'm new."

He waves me over to the table. "Okay, well, come take a look. I'll show you what you need to know. It's not that hard."

I stand beside him, listening to the women in their robes speak in their yoga voices. They're looking forward to the process, they keep saying. The process is very effective. The process is very exclusive.

Dr. Ruby hands me a mallet. He points to a crate. "They're in here," he says.

I can't say, *Who is in there*, so I just nod. But I feel sick all of a sudden. The mallet looks like a movie prop but it is heavy like real life.

"First," Dr. Ruby says, "we're going to show one to the ladies. They like to see them. It's important to them that they know this is the real deal. Have you ever seen one before?"

"I don't think so."

"They're very endangered. And I have to make sure you're aware that this is not FDA approved. You signed an agreement so you should already know that, but I'm required to say it verbally. You are not to speak about this. Not even to your girlfriend."

"I don't have a girlfriend."

"Good," he says.

He rests his palms on the crate. There is something moving inside. I can't see it, but I can feel it.

"Some people find this upsetting," Dr. Ruby says. "It's our responsibility to ensure that there is no discomfort experienced by the women here. That includes the treatment itself and the preparation leading up to it. Do you understand?"

"Yes." I concentrate on his hands, trying to discern if he has touched Jack since the scandal broke, if he had to alter his treatment to counteract the effect of the stress.

"We'll begin soon," Dr. Ruby says to the women. And then to me: "Just waiting for the temperature to adjust."

"Dr. Ruby," I say. "Can I ask how Jack Whitlock is doing?"

"I can't speak to that."

"I was told that you treat him."

He drums his fingers on the crate. "By who?"

"A friend, I think."

"It's a delicate situation."

"Of course, I just—"

He clears his throat. "Now. After I open the crate, I'll take one out. I'll show it to the ladies. I'll explain the treatment to them. Then you and I will use the mallets to swiftly immobilize the contents of the crate. Aim for the skulls and it will be fast and humane. You will replenish drinks and ensure client comfort while I extract the material from the glands."

A shudder from within the crate.

"You can set down your backpack, by the way," Dr. Ruby says.

The acknowledgment of the backpack and the camera within makes me flinch. I'd rather leave it on. I'd rather have the ability to leave. There's an anxious energy emanating from the crate. The movement inside is intensifying. I imagine myself at home, standing up at my kitchen counter, fully dressed, shoes and clothes, ready to be on the move.

"I just want to say, about Jack—"

"What did you say your name was, again?" he asks. And I can tell I've pushed it too far. I am being sloppy, I know it.

"Scott," I say.

"Scott, don't they usually send a woman to help with this?"

"I don't know."

He holds up one finger and turns away. "I'll be back shortly," he says to the room.

"We'll take another round of tonics," one of the women says, tapping her empty glass. "A little more of the drops in these ones."

"Of course. And thanks for your patience," Dr. Ruby says. But he doesn't ask me to get the drinks or to do anything. I see him remove his cell phone from his white coat as he exits the room. The crate trembles. Something cries. Something hisses. Whatever they are, there are two of them. They are angry. They are afraid.

I think suddenly of Ghost. His wide blue eyes. All the horses in the high desert running away from me.

I know that when Dr. Ruby returns I will be asked to leave. The women have finished their drinks and they are placid, resting in their seats, delicate arms folded. The crate trembles more violently now. Something scratches. Whatever is inside can sense that something horrible is about to happen, that once the key is in the lock and the lid is lifted, there will not be much time left.

The door opens, and Dr. Ruby is back, this time with a security guard. I know he is a security guard because I've seen him somewhere else before, have probably been kicked out of somewhere else by him at some point before, maybe I have even been hurt by him at some point before. But it's hard to remember, and it doesn't matter. It's all an endless scroll now, a dream, a nightmare, a blur.

He discreetly signals that I need to follow him. Dr. Ruby doesn't look at me. He smiles at the women, who don't even notice him. Their eyes are closed, their expressions serene and blissful. This building could be demolished with them inside and they'd yawn and shrug and drift off to sleep. In direct contrast, the creatures in the crate are whimpering now, a shrill pleading that is so much worse than any other noise they've made.

"Come on, Ben," the security guard says, and the fact that he knows my name is enough to signal it's over. But I can't stop looking at Dr. Ruby's hands on that crate, his power to still the animals inside, those fingertips that have felt the pulse moving below Jack's skin. I go with the security guard, knowing the offer to do this the nice way is valid for only so long. We leave the room and shut the door, and in that dark, narrow hallway, he tells me I'm not a very good liar, and I know that isn't true. I'm a great liar, and getting better at it every day. Sometimes I hate that about myself, but not that often. Not anymore.

Before the security guard throws me out into the hot sunlight, I hear Dr. Ruby talking to the women, promising that after this treatment they will be younger, more beautiful than their peers, or at least it will appear that way. Their soft applause and other noises of approval. The sound of the crate opening.

chapter twelve

A stylist texts me: **Need photos of Laura in new Versace. Alfred Coffee, Melrose. 9 a.m.**

It's purely a money gig, the kind of job I hate. But I have no choice but to take it as I look for him. Soon the Mia Luna money will be completely gone.

A text message from an unknown number: **was it worth it?**

I am both groggy and panicked, which shouldn't be possible. I get dressed. An alert on my phone. Another. Another. A surge of joy. His name. There is a screenshot of a text message exchange, verified by TMZ.

Sasha: **are you back in town yet**

Jack: **Not until the 20th.**

Sasha: **i want ur cock in my ass**

Jack: **Baby, all I've been thinking about is fucking you. Just FYI we need to find a new place to meet. Jess wants me to be more discreet.**

It's thrilling, this glimpse of him. His punctuation, the fact that he calls his wife Jess and not Jessica, the fact that she knows—has probably always known. I read the word *baby* again and again, hearing his voice.

LOVE IS DEAD, a clickbait website moans, doing a retrospective of Jack and Jessica's relationship.

Strike and a spare: Their first official date was at a bowling alley!

J&J were #babymoon goals in sun-drenched Portofino

The pair was known for their backyard 4th of July fêtes

Photos of their wedding, their house, their daughter.

Somebody tweets: *damn everyone in Hollywood is so fucked up*

Can't believe she knew and was cool with him sleeping around!!!

I'd never let my man do that

This kind of thing is the result of our messed up society if you really stop and think about it.

The conservative news pundits and Christian influencers are running with it, screaming about infidelity and anal sex. *Hollywood's liberal agenda.*

I make some calls, reminding the city's eyes and ears that I am here, I am still looking, I will be the first to get to him.

I wait for responses, and when there are none, I drive to Alfred Coffee. I hit every red light on the surface streets, tapping my finger on the steering wheel as I wait at intersection after intersection beneath the kind of smog that looks like rain clouds. Parking is as bad as I knew it would be.

A stream of texts from the stylist:

where are you

Versace gave us these clothes under the condition Laura be photographed in them that's like the whole point of looping you in on this

you take photos, we all get paid, press, etc, remember??????

I'm getting out of my car when she calls. "You're usually good for these, Ben, what the fuck. I'm about to text a different guy."

"I'm here."

"This is supposed to be easy."

"Tell her to wait."

"She's on a very tight schedule."

"I'm on my way. I'm literally walking there."

"We're supposed to all work together."

"I know, I know. We are. We are working together."

At least it's consensual, Ellory said once, toward the end. *When they call you and you do it that way.* I had just returned from photographing an actress pretending to inspect a bottle of coconut water at a Walgreens. Label out.

Jesus, I said. *You make it sound like sexual assault.*

She said nothing, just stood at the kitchen counter, slicing a papaya. I knew better than to tell her that I preferred it the other way, when the celebrities weren't in on it, when they weren't posing, when it was as exhilarating as chasing an animal in the wilderness. When they weren't giving it to me. When I had to take it.

After photographing the model at Alfred Coffee, I go home and message a background artist from the dating app: *how's it going*. Her face is familiar to me. A shiver of realization when I place her: pouring coffee for Jack Whitlock in a noirish detective movie.

On the TV in my bathroom, *E! News* is showing Jack and Jessica at last year's Oscars, arms around each other and laughing like newlyweds. *In happier times*, the chyron reads. I reread the leaked text messages, rewatch the grainy video, study the photo of him on that girl's bed. I am restless and Los Angeles is pulsing with rumors, the coastal air sweeping through the city.

The girl from the app says she's bored and lonely. *Let's hang out*, I reply. She comes over and says, "Is this real leather?" when we fuck on the couch. I can smell her self-tanner and feel the hard beads of her hair extensions, and I can recognize another person who is trying to construct an identity. She asks me to look at her and when I do I see a sadness that is exactly like my own, but that's not what we're doing here so I focus on something—anything—else. When I come I say *Fuck* to the gray walls of the apartment.

After, she fixes her lipstick in my bathroom, leaving the door open as she talks to me. Looking at her combing her hair with her fingers, I feel a surge of tenderness.

She puts her jeans back on and faces me. She's wearing a sheer turquoise bra—a knock-off of the more expensive version all the influencers got for free last month. "Who's the most famous person you've taken pictures of?" she asks.

I start listing off names. She interjects: "What about Jack Whitlock? He's so hot."

It's satisfying to hear her say his name.

"I'd really like to photograph him," I say. "Now more than ever."

"I always thought he was the monogamous type. I know that's naive, but I don't know . . . he always seemed so . . . perfect."

I find her shirt on the floor and hand it to her. "Have you ever heard anything about him?"

"No. But I met him once."

"Really?" I try to sound surprised.

"Yeah, during one of my many prestigious gigs as a *background artist*," she says, rolling her eyes. "I hate when people call it that. I mean, we're just extras. I don't need to be patronized."

"I like calling things what they are too."

"Do you? Because your profile says photographer."

"And yours says background artist."

"I've been meaning to change that," she says.

"Yeah, me too."

She sits down on the couch, begins lacing up the straps on her open-toed wedge shoes.

"So you met him on set?" I ask.

"Yeah, about a million years ago. On the set of *Catalina Phantoms*. I was the waitress at the restaurant. Remember? When they're having dinner after the guy gets murdered?"

"I do remember."

"No, you don't."

"Yes, I do. You had black hair in that."

She finishes with her shoes and stands. "I did. Good memory."

"I've seen it a few times. I thought you looked familiar."

"People are always saying that."

"It's good."

"It's because I look like every other girl."

She isn't wrong. There's a homogenization in the women I meet, the women I photograph. Everyone is a copy of a copy of a copy of a beautiful girl from a music video. Their distinct features cut and contoured and pulverized until they are replicas of someone original. "Your hair looked good in that," I say.

"You're just being nice."

"I'm not nice."

We smile at each other. In a different context, this interaction might almost be romantic.

"So did you talk to him?" I ask.

"Once. And only because he made a point of saying hello to everyone on set. He introduced himself to all of us. It was very classy. I know he was just doing it because he's professional, but when he shook my hand and looked at me it felt like . . . It sounds stupid, but it felt like we knew each other. Like we had always known each other. And then I talked to the other extras and they all felt that way too."

"Is that the only contact you've ever had with him?"

"Yes," she says. "What do you think about the rumors that he and his wife were swingers?"

"I never rule anything out."

"Me either," she says, walking over to the kitchen island, where my camera shines beneath the anonymous track lighting that every apartment in this building has. She runs her fingers over it. "Maybe you'll be chasing me around someday when I'm famous."

"Maybe."

"I should go. I have to get to hot yoga."

"Would you text me?" I ask.

She smiles. "Yeah, okay."

"If you're on a set and you hear anything about Jack, or anything interesting that might help me get a shot of a celebrity, text me. I'll give you a cut of whatever I sell it for. That's what I do for everyone else."

Her smile fades.

"I don't have any extras in my contact list," I say. "You could be a big help."

"Oh," she says. "Oh, I get it now."

After she's gone, it starts to rain. A rare, late-summer shower. Outside, there's a courtyard where people from my apartment building are gathered beneath umbrellas, taking videos of the gray sky with their phones. I recognize their faces; they are often there, drinking wine. The courtyard, like so many courtyards belonging to apartment buildings in Los Angeles, is a gathering place for transplants who have found themselves far from home. The clouds darken, threatening thunder, and then it begins to pour, soaking the eucalyptus trees, the palms, the bougainvillea. Rain is a gift in Southern California. I stand at the edge of the courtyard, letting it soak my clothing, watching the water droplets hit the fountain, smelling the wet soil of the garden, listening for the sluicing of tires in puddles on some distant highway.

I exhale the air from my lungs, inhale for four seconds, hold my breath for four seconds, release. Box breathing. I learned it at a transformational breathwork workshop in Burbank after Ellory left. I told myself I was there looking for someone from a TV show, but I was doing it for myself. What would she think, I wonder, about this Jack mess? Would she be disgusted with him? Would she be surprised? Or would she feel sorry for him?

Puddles gather on the brick walkway. Inhale. Exhale.

I feel deeply alone, just for a second.

It passes.

los angeles, two years and eleven months earlier

chapter thirteen

Our apartment is at the base of a hill. On our first night there we walk the narrow, winding road to the top. It is impossible not to make comparisons. For me, they're all positive: The hills in Los Angeles seem to undulate, containing mystery. How different from Las Vegas, which is a valley, open and obvious. Here, yards are full of succulents and trees are heavy with lemons—so heavy the fruit falls from branches and rolls downhill. In Las Vegas, the plants are sunburnt.

Ellory appears stunned, like she's been deposited in an unknown country after a red-eye flight. I can't tell if that means she's unhappy or just unsure.

We pass a house draped with Tibetan peace flags, another with a Pride flag, another with a white sheet billowing from a window, a pro-choice slogan written in black marker.

"That's nice," I say. "People standing for things." I can hear in my own voice the transparency of what I am trying to do: convince her. But she is here, I keep reminding myself. She is here.

"They seem to," Ellory says.

I take her hand as we enter Elysian Park. I say, "I'm so happy to be here with you."

"I'm happy to be with you too," she says.

We follow the dirt path that rises up, up, still up. Up into the pinky-blue haze of skyscrapers. Las Vegas is a city-themed city; there is a version of skyscrapers at the New York–New York casino, but it isn't real.

The sun sets. Ravens croak in eucalyptus trees. On Valentine Street, we pass a massive silver-green century plant, an agave that will bloom once and then die.

Still, she is mostly silent.

At a market, I spend forty-six dollars on hunks of fancy cheese. "I got it," I say to Ellory at the register, as if the Cambozola, Esrom, and Mahón will convince her.

We eat on the hardwood floor of our new apartment. The nice cheese paired with a gas station bottle of merlot. I watch her watching the shifting tree branches outside, people passing on the sidewalk.

We have no furniture yet, so we spread out a sleeping bag in the bedroom. In the dark, I kiss her like it's a question. I go down on her, filling the room with sighs. She sounds different, softer. I stop and ask, "Do you want this?"

"I wouldn't be doing it if I didn't want it."

We slide around on the slippery nylon of the sleeping bag, fumbling until it feels good.

She whispers into my neck, "I don't know if I can be loud here."

"You should," I say. "I want you to."

Afterward, we open up the windows and listen to the intermittent hooting of a horned owl. The air smells like figs.

I text Eddie. **I'm here. Drinks soon?**

He responds the next morning: **busy this week but maybe next**

Mentally, I insert something like *Welcome to LA, dude!*

Ellory and I walk to a bakery for coffee and scones. "I got it," I say again.

And he's offered to mentor me, I told Ellory in the mountains that day, and even though it wasn't true I find myself irritated with Eddie, as if he had made that promise.

We sit on the front steps of our apartment because neither of us has anywhere to be. She is still waiting to see if the manager from Giggle Water has any leads on gigs in Los Angeles. And I should start work soon, but I don't know what starting means. There is no actual start date. This is not a job anyone has asked me to do. But I think maybe that's the point of Los Angeles; it is a place where everyone is opting in.

Ellory's phone rings. One of her old roommates. She goes inside to take it.

"It's good," I hear her say. "I like it so far."

She returns to the steps with a glass of iced tea.

"Did you mean that?" I ask. "That you like it?"

She leans in and kisses me. "Don't do that."

We spend the rest of the day responding to Craigslist ads for cheap furniture. In between emails I text Eddie: **I'm in Echo Park by the way. Can't remember what part of town you're in.**

"Someone in Koreatown has a queen-size mattress for free," Ellory says. "Where is that?"

We drive there, circling the building where the mattress is located again and again, unable to find parking.

"Is there seriously no parking here?" Ellory asks.

"I know," I say, but it doesn't bother me. I like this crowded city, which is somehow both enormous and claustrophobic. I feel absorbed, swallowed whole.

We pay for a spot in a cramped lot behind a restaurant.

Twenty dollars for the hour, which is more than either of us has ever paid for parking. A lifetime of casino garages with thousands of spaces like a perpetual welcome sign. In Los Angeles, there is no invitation.

By the end of the first week, she's already talking about driving to Las Vegas to perform at Giggle Water.

"They said they'd have me back whenever," she says. The boxes on the floor beside her are still sealed with packing tape.

"What about the gigs here?"

"I don't know what's going to happen with that."

"I thought you said there was a good burlesque scene here."

She opens a box marked *miscellaneous* and considers the contents. "It's different."

"Not really the big fish / small pond Las Vegas thing."

"What does that mean?"

"Nothing. You'll figure it out here."

"I know that," she says. She pulls a spatula from the box and holds it, not making any move toward the kitchen. "And I'll work on it. I am working on it. But for now, would it be the worst thing to occasionally drive home for a gig here and there? I can crash on someone's couch or stay with my parents. A lot of people do that—go back and forth."

"Yeah," I say. "Of course. That makes sense."

She stands and picks up a pale pink weekend bag, the same one she carried to and from dressing rooms in Las Vegas. I think of her car, which is still full of her things. The hardwood floor creaks beneath her bare feet as she gathers what she needs.

"Are you leaving, like, right now?" I ask.

"It's Thursday. I could beat the weekend traffic."

She stops in the center of the apartment, in the sun, where dust particles gather in the light. "You're looking at me like I'm leaving you for good," she says.

After she's packed, I walk her to her car and kiss her through the open driver's-side window.

"I moved here because I love you," she says. "But I'll always love Vegas too. And this gig will be good."

"I'm going to find a couch while you're gone," I say. "I'm going to do some other things with the apartment. Things you'll like."

"Okay. Good."

Standing there in the street, I feel very sad.

That night, I scroll her Instagram feed. This version of her is happy, neatly contained in asymmetrical squares. I look at the one photo she's posted from Los Angeles, a photo of her hand holding the keys to the apartment. Caption: *new beginnings . . .*

And then I go back. Back to photos of her onstage, in dressing rooms, at parties with friends, hiking in the desert, camping in the mountains. I am so far back that I've encountered a version of her long before me, one who can't hurt me, can't be hurt by me.

I don't even realize that I've double-tapped each one until a text message from her interrupts my hypnosis: **all these notifications must mean you're missing me**

I am, I say, and then I shut off my phone and go to sleep.

The next day, I buy a purple couch at a yard sale, get some plants from a shop that specializes in rare cacti. All these things to make the apartment into a home. I send her photos. **Great,** she says. **Thanks for doing that.**

I text Eddie again: **hey so I'm pretty settled in and I don't have any plans this weekend. Are you around? Can we meet up?**

The dots appear, indicating a response, but then they're gone.

I go to the movies and watch Jack Whitlock. It makes me feel less alone. I think about what it would feel like to be in the same room as him. I think about him like he is my only friend in Los Angeles. I fold the autographed photo from the Bluebird into a sweater and put it on a shelf in the closet.

Ellory returns at 10 p.m. the following Monday, after staying an extra day in Las Vegas to avoid the Sunday traffic. Her face is bare and she is wearing a yellow dress.

"Is this new?" I ask.

"We went thrifting."

"It looks nice on you. How was the show?"

"Really good. They said I can come back and perform pretty much whenever."

"That's good."

"But?"

"I didn't say but."

"You were about to."

We sit on the couch together. She touches my face. "You have to relax. I'm here."

We go to a comedy show at a natural wine bar. The comedian makes hyper-specific jokes about Los Angeles, and Ellory laughs politely because we're in the front row and he's making eye contact with her. We drink too much and then go to our apartment and cook eggs on the stovetop, both of us waiting for the smoke alarm to go off like it always did at her place, but it doesn't.

We fuck desperately, in a way we've never fucked before, sitting up and facing each other, legs intertwined, her hands around my neck, my arms around her waist, our bodies communicating urgently, just in different languages.

"Harder," she says. I feel like we're going to break each other.

"I want this to work," I say, like a prayer.

The next day, we hike the Mount Hollywood trail in Griffith Park. A row of skinny palm trees, the white letters on the hillside, the dome of the Griffith Observatory perched neatly on a hill overlooking the city. The sun turns the sky blue. I reach for her hand.

"We could hike here every day," I say.

"We should," Ellory says.

I take a photo of her smiling at the top.

"We should take one together," she says, and then waves at a nearby group of women. "Excuse me, could one of you take a picture of us?"

I put my arm around her. She reaches up and touches her fingers to mine.

"Cute," says the woman taking the picture. "Now do one kissing."

I laugh, a little embarrassed, but Ellory pulls my face to hers. The women cheer. In the photos, we're happy. I look at them for a long time, standing there saying nothing. We don't have many photos together. I don't have many photos of myself.

Ellory continues talking to the group of women and then turns to me, beaming after they wave their goodbyes to us. "We exchanged numbers and we're going to go hiking."

"How do you do that?" I say. "Make friends so fast."

She smiles and shrugs. "Most people are friendly."

At a bookstore in our neighborhood, we buy Los Angeles hiking guides and wildlife guides. As we walk back to our apartment, green birds fill the sky above us.

"Parrots," Ellory says. "How is that possible?"

They sing and move in a chorus, parting and regrouping in random patterns.

She touches my arm. "You should take a picture."

I point my camera at the flock of green and shoot. The images are unremarkable, but she says they're good.

Later, I learn that there are parrots in Bel Air too, the descendants of pets released during a fire. They bred, became feral, adapted. Bel Air, the same wealthy neighborhood where Jack Whitlock lives. And even though the fire was in 1961, before Jack moved there or was even born, I can still see him standing on the terrace of a doomed mansion with an open cage in his arms, watching a green bird fly away.

"Maybe Eddie retired," I say to Ellory at a coffee shop with no tables. "Maybe he made so much money he retired."

"I thought he was supposed to train you on everything."

We order cold brews and walk out onto the sidewalk. The weather is perfect, again.

I could tell her that he's not responding. It would be the truth and she would be sympathetic. *People can be so flaky*, I imagine her saying.

I put my arm around her shoulders. "I'll figure it out."

We go to a burlesque show that night. The cover is forty dollars and every performer is dressed as Marilyn Monroe. The people at the table next to us ignore the performances and talk loudly about a movie that is in development, about what it is like to work in development, about how everyone who has ever done well in development has started on the desk of someone named Patrick. Ellory's phone is on the table, and I can see that her friends are sending her pictures; they're all out at a bar together, missing her.

Ellory motions to the stage. "They all look like they want to be actresses."

She responds to a text message and then places her phone face down. "Sorry. I'm distracted. I've been looking for gigs, and it seems like you have to know the right person and I barely know anyone."

I rub my thumb across the top of her hand. "Maybe we shouldn't have come here."

She looks at me with surprise, and then relief.

"I meant to this show."

"Oh, yeah," she says. "Maybe we shouldn't have."

Three days later, I call Eddie and he doesn't answer.

"I'm sorry to keep bugging you," I say in my voicemail, "but I could really use your help."

I wait for a response, and when it doesn't come, I tell Ellory that Eddie is busy—maybe family stuff or travel, I'm not sure.

"He gave me some good advice, though," I say. "I feel pretty good about getting started on my own."

I feel sick, thirsty. Can't swallow. I type *places to see celebrities in Los Angeles* into my phone. At the top of the list is an outdoor shopping mall in Hollywood.

Ellory is on a hike with the women we met on the Mount Hollywood trail. I wonder if she's told them what I'm doing, if they judge or accept it.

I drive to the outdoor shopping mall and park in the garage. I walk past a makeup store, a yoga apparel store, a group of girls in pink hot pants doing a choreographed dance in front of a fountain. What am I looking for?

Come on, come on, I keep thinking, looking for cameras, listening for familiar voices. I watch a college-aged man in a denim jacket exit a juice bar, sunglasses on, phone pressed to his ear. I imagine he is Jack Whitlock's assistant, that he's as close as I'll get. It's possible.

I buy a seventeen-dollar sandwich I can't afford and eat it while walking around. Maybe this isn't going to work, I think, stepping into the way-too-nice lobby of the restroom area. There's a man sitting in a chair by the ladies' room. He has a camera in his lap. I draw in a breath. A poreless woman with beautiful posture appears from the restroom. The man rises from his seat with his camera and begins taking her picture.

"Security," she calls out, and the man scrambles for the elevators, smiling. He's gotten his photo.

"Wait," I say, following him. "What happens now? Who do you sell it to? Where are you going next?"

"Fuck off," he says. The elevator opens and he gets in. After the doors close, I realize I've been holding my breath without meaning to. I let it out. I start laughing, caught off guard by an emotion I don't recognize. I feel drunk, exhilarated.

* * *

I type *where to find other paparazzi* and nothing helpful comes up. I look at the *places to see celebrities in Los Angeles* list, and it reads like a different language to me. I don't know these neighborhoods, these restaurants, the difference between West Hollywood and Hollywood, what's in West Los Angeles and what's in East Los Angeles, what's going on in the Valley.

I settle on a cocktail bar that the internet says is popular and upscale and *classic Hollywood* in hopes that that means something to someone famous. It's humid and loud inside and the lights are red and the bar is full of tourists talking about studio tours, the Hollywood sign, how overrated Los Angeles is, and how much they don't want to come back. They're drinking vodka cranberries and craning their necks, looking for celebrities just like I am. The crowd is thick, and then it thins out.

The bartender makes eye contact with me. "You. You've been here for a while. You've got to buy a drink or leave."

I order an old-fashioned, because that feels like what I should order, and then another, and then I'm drunk on an empty stomach, surrounded by tourists as desperate as me.

I bum a cigarette off a couple from Michigan outside the bar and think about calling Ellory for a ride, but to do so would be to admit I don't know what I'm doing.

My vision blurs. I hop from one foot to the other. "Can I get a ride from you?" I ask the Michigan couple.

"To our hotel?" they ask, suddenly flirtatious. "We can just walk."

"Never mind," I say, and stumble into a waiting cab.

The next day, I take my laptop to a coffee shop and study recent paparazzi photos until closing time, making lists of where they were taken. Sometimes the captions just say *grocery store* but other times they say *grocery store in Beverly Hills* and from there, as long as the celebrity isn't using their own reusable bags, which they're usually not, it's just a matter of identifying labels. This brings me to Gelson's, where I wait in the parking lot, at first in my car and then on my feet.

"My girlfriend is just inside grabbing something for dinner," I say to the guy corralling grocery carts, and he shrugs like he doesn't care.

Every man who passes in and out of the grocery store has a Dodgers cap and a beard and sunglasses, and every woman has a matching yoga set and defined abs. They all look like they could be famous, making it impossible to tell who is actually famous. I realize, suddenly, I only know to look for Jack Whitlock, and he isn't here, probably would never be here, probably has people to do his shopping for him. I raise my camera every time someone exceptionally attractive or interesting or surreptitious passes by, but what then? Who am I supposed to show the photos to and ask, *Is this anyone?*

I go to a steak house in Sherman Oaks and finally, for the first time, I see a crowd of them. The guys with cameras. It's strange to see an idea from pop culture come to life, to become a part of that idea. I count them: nine men, dressed in hoodies and blue jeans. It's a uniform of sorts, too casual for the steak house's dress code, but still serious, utilitarian. Their posture is relaxed and they're talking to one another, standing close together like friends, which surprises me. I think of Ghost. Me and the other men, waiting. I can expect the same, I tell myself. Not a brotherhood, necessarily, but tacit acceptance. I can expect that.

The men look up from their conversation as an SUV approaches. It's a nice car—but regular-person nice, not rich-person nice—and they greet it with familiarity, fake jeering and flipping it off, saying things like *Well, well, look who it is.* The driver stops to talk to the valet, who, like the photographers, laughs and smiles, clearly joking around with someone he knows until an actually nice car appears and then it's back to service industry how-are-you-doing-this-evening mode. The SUV heads to a lot marked for self-parking. I follow it with my eyes, watching the door open. Another man in the unofficial sweatshirt and denim uniform. Eddie. He joins the others but doesn't see me. How is it possible that he doesn't see me? I'm here too.

"Hey," I say. "Hey, Eddie."

He is tanner than the last time I saw him, and even though it wasn't that long ago, there is something different about his posture, his shoulders squared and his chin angled slightly up, causing him to look down at me. The version of him I know from Las Vegas—hunched over a bus tub, grinning and lighting cigarettes on the loading dock—is a completely different person. "Oh, hi," he says in the voice of a guy at a party pretending to recognize someone.

"Eddie," I say, like I'm reminding him of his own name.

He looks around. "What are you doing here?"

"Are you serious? Come on, you know why I'm here."

The other men go silent, communicating to one another with their eyes, a conversation I'm not a part of.

"I've been texting you," I say.

A low *ooooh* from the other men. *Eddie, your boyfriend is maaaaad.*

My face goes hot. "I . . . yeah . . . I, uh, moved here. From Las Vegas. Like you said I . . ."

Eddie coughs into his hand. "I didn't expect you to actually . . ."

"I thought we could get drinks. Now that I'm here."

"Yeah, I don't really have a lot of free time."

"Or just one drink. Coffee, whatever."

"Definitely," he says, looking past me.

"I'm confused. You knew I was moving here to do this. Like, you've seen my texts. Don't you remember our conversation when you were in Las Vegas? For that wedding? Remember?"

"Look, I was pretty fucked up that night. I don't know what to tell you."

"What?"

Eddie is still looking at the restaurant. The others are too. His voice shifts to signal the end of a polite conversation. "Anyway, so cool that you moved here. Good for you."

He smiles and turns away. *Who is that?* one of the other guys asks him, and he waves the question away with his hand. And then someone says something I can't hear and they all laugh.

"What the fuck," I say, to myself, mostly, since he isn't listening anymore. I don't know what else to do, so I take out my camera.

I stand behind them, wishing I could understand their conversation, wishing I was above average height, wishing Eddie would turn around and say, *Ha ha, just fucking with you, man, come over here, I'll show you how this all works.*

I watch them watch the restaurant. Eventually, they go still and silent. A woman in sunglasses appears from inside, pauses on the steps in black heels with red soles. The men come to life. They start nudging one another—again, there's a sense that they're in it together, but not with me. Eddie is at the front, moving so confidently that the others appear to defer to him. He is liked here. He is respected. He is good at this. *A trained monkey could do it*, he said that night in Las Vegas, smoking cigarettes in the rain. Maybe he lied.

I don't recognize the woman, but she's tall and beautiful and I trust the reaction from the men. They raise their cameras and move toward her, soldiers pushing forward, and I'm so in awe of this I freeze for a moment, but then I do as they do. I raise my camera, aim it at the woman, every light in California reflected on her sunglasses. And me. I'm a part of that. I take her picture again and again.

And then a thud against my shoulder like I'm being tackled by a linebacker, if I had ever played football.

I'm down on the ground, my face pressed into the dry dirt of a cactus garden.

I wait for a *let me help you up* and it doesn't come, because the shove was intentional. I turn onto my back and inspect the broken lens. The men smile down at me.

One says, "Sorry, bro."

The others laugh.

"Gracie," Eddie says to the woman. "You look beautiful, beautiful. Give us a smile."

I stand and spit out the dirt.

"What the fuck," I say again, this time so he can hear it. But he doesn't look at me. Maybe he doesn't want to be reminded where he came from.

At home I tell Ellory it was an accident.

"It seems intentional," she says.

"Maybe just hazing. It'll pass."

She gets a bag of frozen peas and holds it against my face. She is an angel in this moment, so nonjudgmental. "Lie down," she says. I go to the couch, and she sits beside me on the floor, icing my face, her free hand finding my fingers. I start to tell her about Eddie but then don't.

Lying in bed with her that night, smelling her perfume and feeling the warmth of her palm on my chest, I say, "It'll get better."

But the next time is worse. Outside a bar on the coast, they take my camera and throw it into the ocean. The waves carry it away.

"You threw it *far*," they say to the one who hurled it across the beach, into the water.

"Y'all keep forgetting that I played professional baseball before this," he says.

"I don't get why you're not helping me," I say to Eddie. "Or, like, at least acknowledging me."

The men laugh. "Did you hear that, Eddie? He wants to be *acknowledged*."

"Yeah, Eddie, the least you can do is *acknowledge* him."

"Fine, whatever," I say to Eddie's back as he walks away from me. "Be a dick."

The others smirk and sneer, scuttling off to their cars.

Mine has been towed. I type *retrieving vehicle Pacific Coast Highway* into my phone, but there is no service.

"Can anyone help me?" I ask the retreating figures of paparazzi, the empty beach, the setting sun, the disappearing tide. It takes three hours and four bus transfers to get home. Wedged between two women and their grocery bags, I text Eddie, **why did you even encourage me to come out here**

Ellory doesn't ask why my car isn't parked outside of our apartment, so I don't tell her. I take a fifty-four-dollar Uber to the tow yard, where I'm told I need to pay $381 to get my car back.

"What about three hundred?" I offer. "You know how hard it is to find parking on the PCH."

"It's just PCH," he says. "And it's $381 or the car goes to auction."

The next day, I sit at a café in Los Feliz, laptop open but dead. Pretending to work, just staring at Hillhurst Avenue. Watching the people, like deer in the forest, waiting for a rare animal to appear.

"Excuse me, sir?" A server gestures to the remains of my sandwich. "Are you finished?"

"All set," I tell him. And then I remember what Eddie said in Las Vegas about his valet job. *And these paparazzi are approaching me, giving me their numbers, wanting me to hit them up whenever someone famous comes in.* I consider how much cash I have on me. "Actually," I say to the server. "Can I ask you something?"

chapter fourteen

After scaring a housekeeper by trailing too closely in a hotel hallway, getting threatened by a nightclub bouncer, barked at by a dog walker's cavalcade of purebreds, then kicked out of a high-end hair salon, I finally meet a production assistant who knows exactly what I'm looking for. He believes my fake confidence—*say no more, bro, I got you*—which gives me actual confidence. I spend the next few days giving out my number, promising money, acting like I've been doing this for years.

I call Ellory from my car. "I just pretended to be this person and they believed me." I scan the parking signs, mumbling their instructions. "Two-hour parking on Wednesdays, permit parking on weekdays, no overnight parking, no parking between noon and three on Thursdays. What . . . ?"

"But how do you know they're not also pretending?" Ellory asks.

It's a good question, and I suspect most of them are, but if at least one or two are well-connected, that'll be a start.

A server at a sushi restaurant in Studio City is the first to be useful, her text concise and articulate, telling me about an actress and a basketball player who will leave out the back entrance of the restaurant.

I'm not the only person who got this tip. There are four of us in the darkened alleyway, watching the gate for a sign of movement. On the other side, the famous couple's driver is supposed to be waiting. Once they're done with their dinner, they'll climb into the car and the gate will open. There won't be much time. What I'm hoping is that the gate will open before they get in the car; that way I can get a photo of them outside. Their bodies, their facial expressions. I see more shots like that in the magazines and on the websites, which leads me to believe that photos taken through the glass of a vehicle are not as valuable.

The other men wait and don't speak. This behavior is easy to imitate, familiar to me. I scan for a restaurant employee or security guard or combination of the two, someone who might spot us and tell us to leave. It's dark, nearly midnight. The restaurant closed to the public an hour ago, but I'm sure the famous couple can stay as long as they like. *Give them good service*, the restaurant manager probably informed the staff through clenched teeth, just like my boss at the Bluebird used to tell me whenever a high roller stumbled out of a casino and into the diner.

When the gate finally opens, they are already in the back seat of the car. I breathe out, disappointed but still high on pretend swagger. And then I start snapping. We all do. I can barely see the actress and the basketball player through the window. The collective flash of the cameras creates a glare. Through breaks in the chaos, I make out their sunglasses, their hair, their expressionless faces.

An employee in a black vest and an enormous security guard wave them through, working together to keep us away.

The driver rolls down his window. "Hey!" he says. "Hey! I can't see with all these flashes."

The car rolls forward and I follow, pressing my camera against the glass, trying to get a photo of the couple in the back seat. The noise and the lights. I am outside of my body. I'm really doing this. I'm really this person. The couple remains still as the driver and security guard and restaurant employee yell, *Get out of the way get out of the way get out of the way*. I am right at the passenger-side door, taking photo after photo, willing them to roll their windows down, but they don't. Camera lights flash off the windows, the mirrors.

"I'm serious, guys," the driver calls out to us. The others back off, but I stay where I am. I'm not just going to do this; I'm going to be fucking good at this. Just as I take another step forward, the car accelerates. I'm knocked off my feet, a sharp pain in my shin, and all I'm thinking about as I fall is my camera, my camera, my camera. I hold it above myself like I'm crossing a river and I do not let it strike the surface, even as the back of my head connects with the pavement.

I'm sprawled on my back, still holding my camera high, and I sit up and look at my leg, hot and radiating like an emergency. What does a broken leg look like? What does a broken leg feel like? What am I supposed to do? I fall back down. The sharp crack of pain softens to a pulsing throb, and maybe it's not so bad.

The camera lights keep flashing. My vision blurs, refocuses.

The security guard tells the other guys to leave, to stop taking pictures, but they ignore him and keep going. These pictures now include me, I realize, and I'm the subject, not the photographer.

"See?" the driver says through his open window. "You see what happens?" And I don't know who he's talking to, if he's talking to me or the other guys or the famous couple or all of us. He just keeps going, "See? You see?"

And then I roll out of the way and find my feet. The driver hits the gas and they're gone. I'm okay, I'm okay.

"You could sue them," one paparazzo says to me, and his lack of hostility is as good as kindness.

My photos are useless, and I don't know who to sell them to anyway. Not yet. But a few days later, the ones the other guys got are discussed on the news. A journalist interviews the driver. He's adamant he did nothing wrong.

"Should the celebrity couple have gotten out to check on him?" the journalist asks the driver.

"No. Legally, they were not obligated to do anything."

"You could have been killed," Ellory says, watching the clip on her phone. She's not calling me adventurous, but she's not calling me stupid either.

"These paparazzi create dangerous situations," I hear the driver say from her screen. "They're so aggressive that someone getting hurt is an inevitability."

These paparazzi, I repeat it to myself. A category that now includes me.

I try it again, outside a restaurant in West Hollywood. Another spot from the *places where celebrities hang out in LA* list. I am too early. I was nervous and expecting traffic, difficult parking, but the drive took twenty-five minutes and there were plenty of spots on a side street when I arrived. I am still learning the city's rhythms, figuring out when it is easy, when it is difficult.

The sun has not set yet. The hostess looks bored. Empty tables inside. I try not to look like I'm loitering. I look at my phone, pretending to be engrossed with email, social media.

Ellory has an audition tonight for a burlesque and variety show. A onetime thing for charity. This was the only opportunity the manager from Giggle Water could produce. It's not a surprise to me that he isn't very well-connected in Los Angeles, but I don't say this to Ellory. **Good luck**, I text her.

Just got here, she says. **Strange vibe.**

What do you mean, I type, and then delete.

The sun goes down, and out from the shadows, a man with a backpack appears. Then another and another. They stand beside one another, not speaking, as if afraid to spook an animal. They don't acknowledge me. It's either a mercy or they don't remember. No sign of Eddie. I try to think of cold nights in the high desert, waiting with the others for Ghost.

A security guard steps out from the restaurant and eyes us. Or rather, eyes them. I'm not a threat. Not yet. I realize then that this is a finite resource I can't squander, this nothingness. To the other paparazzi, it's a vulnerability. But when I think about the people on the other side, it's a strength. I step forward, closer to the restaurant. I keep looking at my phone, my nonexistent watch, like I'm waiting for a date to arrive. The security guard may be fooled, but the other men on the sidewalk know what I'm doing.

A Mercedes at the valet. Black shoes, black pants. My pulse quickens, willing it to be Jack Whitlock, but I know, somehow I just know, that I won't get to him yet.

It's a different actor. A man who does a lot of romantic comedies. I can't remember his name, but I've been looking at enough paparazzi photos to know this at least. He steps onto the sidewalk. He smiles, says something to the valet. He is shorter in person.

It's now.

Breathe in. Breathe out. I picture pronghorn antelope, bighorn sheep, wild burros. Ghost. His white mane, his blue eyes. Steady. I approach with my camera.

This is the same this is the same this is the same.

The men from the shadows are behind me, hollering and jostling and suddenly transformed from inert to kinetic. But I am first. I hit the shutter release again and again. The camera flashes.

"Hey," the actor says. He points at me. I keep taking pictures. "I didn't come here to have my picture taken. Don't you have something better to do?"

I say nothing. I just keep taking pictures. His face is angry through the viewfinder. His mouth forms into curse words as he tells me to leave him alone. I can sense that the other guys have backed off. I keep going.

"I mean it. Leave me alone."

"Please follow me, sir," the security guard tells him, putting an arm between us. An employee opens the door to the restaurant. The actor moves toward it, shaking his head and saying, *Unbelievable.* The security guard keeps telling him, *I know, I know, I agree, what they do is pathetic.*

But the actor turns and looks at me one last time before he enters the restaurant. With his hands down by his sides, he flashes me a nearly imperceptible thumbs-up. I think he does, anyway.

Did he?

"That fucking guy," one of the men on the street says. "It's like, if you want to be left alone, don't eat at the most popular restaurant in LA."

"Are you talking to me?" I ask.

"Yeah, you. What's your name?"

"Ben," I say. I am dizzy, out of breath. I step backward and nearly trip off the sidewalk. My fingers are buzzing. I hold my camera like it's the only thing tethering me to earth. What I want to do is ask the men how to sell the photo, where to go tomorrow. But to do that would ruin the temporary illusion that I might actually know.

I drive home with the windows rolled up. No music. Air-conditioning until I can't feel my hands on the steering wheel.

At the apartment, I sit on the couch in the dark, looking at the images of the actor. The room smells like sweet chili sauce.

I got my first shot, I text Ellory.

Her phone dings from the bedroom. I get up and find her there.

"Hey," I say. "You're home?"

"It wasn't really an audition."

I sit on the edge of the bed. "What do you mean?"

"They were looking for something else," Ellory says.

"Like what?"

She threads her fingers through mine. "Just . . . I don't know. I'm not feeling well. Can we talk tomorrow?"

"Shit, I'm sorry. But hey, I got my first shot. That rom-com guy."

Her eyes are closed. "That's really good, Ben. Sorry, can we—"

"Yeah. Of course. I'll let you rest."

"I'm happy for you," I hear her say as I close the bedroom door.

I go through the photos again, start editing them.

This I can do.

Two weeks later, the actor dies and the photos triple in value. That's what the agency I sell them to says.

You're green, they keep telling me, now that they've finally started talking to me. When I get sunburnt standing on Rodeo Drive all day. When I wait at the front of a hotel where celebrities are known to leave from the back. When I pump the wrong restaurant manager for information and get kicked off the property. When I take photo after photo of someone who isn't famous instead of the very famous person standing right beside her.

You're green, they keep telling me, because it is so obvious that I do not move like they move, do not dress like they dress, am not prepared like they are prepared.

You think you're hot shit because you got one shot, they say.

And they're right. It isn't enough to have one shot. It isn't enough to have googled *places in Los Angeles where celebrities are* or *where to sell celebrity photos*. It isn't enough to have gone to a few celebrity hot spots and been right about the assumption, the hope, that there might be paparazzi there. It isn't enough to playact, to dabble; I have to actually do it.

You're green, they keep telling me. So I retreat. I step back. I watch. Some people are good at performing; some people are good at observing. I have always been good at observing. I study the paparazzi. The way they communicate with celebrities and the people around celebrities, the places they hide, how fast they run. Everything.

And there is the other work too. The work of following the celebrity narratives, knowing who is famous and why. Who is dating, who is feuding. Rumored scandals and actual scandals. Every week, I walk to the grocery store on Glendale and buy all the celebrity gossip magazines, and then I go home and read them at our table. And when I'm done I go on the internet and read more. I buy us a TV and a cable subscription so that I can watch the entertainment news channels. And one day, the landlord comes over to fix a leak and he looks at the spread of magazines, the muted channel on the TV, all of the botoxed faces and breast augmentations and who-wore-it-bests, and he makes a comment, like, *Women, am I right?* And I say, *Those are mine, actually*, and he smirks and goes, *Oh, okay, fella.*

I don't care. These things matter. A photo of a reality star is worth more if that reality star has recently thrown a drink on someone at a nightclub. A photo of a basketball player is worth more if the basketball player's son is very funny on social media.

I can see Ellory's eyes drift and then refocus as I explain this all to her. But these things matter.

You're green, they keep telling me.

Until they stop.

Eddie was right. He may not want to help me now, may not ever acknowledge that we knew each other before this, but he did do something for me when he said, *It's just like wildlife photography.*

The similarities are everywhere: a subject who doesn't stand still, doesn't pose. No control over the light. No ability to redo the shot if it isn't perfect the first time. Carrying all the equipment in a backpack. Constantly on the move.

And though I am not photographing animals in the wilderness, the gear and the instincts still apply. My hiking boots are ideal for this work—lightweight, supportive. Good for standing. Good for sprinting. I wear breathable wool socks, moisture-wicking T-shirts, polarized sunglasses. I keep a lightweight rain jacket rolled up in the bottom of my backpack just in case. I know how important it is to actively hydrate. Not just water, electrolytes too. I prefer coconut water over sports drinks, which have too much sugar. And salt. You have to consume salt, especially when it's hot. Salted pretzels, salted almonds, little packets of salt from restaurants if you're desperate. If you're hydrating, you have to maintain your sodium levels.

People say Los Angeles isn't walkable, but not me. I treat it like it's the wilderness, like I'm carrying my camera into the mountains, across the desert, through the forest. Ten miles a day, no problem.

"It's just like wildlife photography." I repeat Eddie's words to Ellory.

She makes a face I haven't seen before, somewhere between a laugh and a wince.

"I don't know if you realize what you're saying," she says.

Sometimes when I tell her about the things I've seen other paparazzi do—the fistfights, the high-speed chases, the crying child stars—she starts to speak and stops. I can see her in those moments recalibrating, like she's listening to a description of a movie instead of a story from real life. I wonder if she ever thinks about the napkin where I wrote the list of things I wouldn't do.

There was this guy, I tell her, who really wanted a shot of this model who'd recently gained weight. When he finally tracked her down and got it, the model fell to the floor crying, pulling on the hem of his jeans, clawing at his legs, begging him. *Please please please delete it.*

"But you'd never do that," Ellory says, even though the story was about me.

chapter fifteen

Nothing comes from the auditions, so Ellory starts working gig jobs instead. She downloads the apps on her phone, receives messages from onboarding teams she will never meet, gets tasks assigned to her by an algorithm. Delivering food, walking dogs. The apps promote themselves as a *work when you want to work* solution. They promise twenty dollars an hour. Most days, she makes ten. At night, her phone lights up on the bedside table with cheery robotic messages from the apps, telling her that if she works right now she'll be eligible for a 60 percent bonus, if she accepts this last-minute delivery her star rating will go up.

We walk to Echo Park Lake and rent paddleboats shaped like swans. She buys a book about the city's hidden staircases and we find every single one in our neighborhood. We go to old movie theaters and watch thirty-five-millimeter screenings. We make out in a dark hotel bar and then charge a room to my credit card. She straddles me on a velvet couch, says *I love you* when she fucks me. After, we order ice cream from the room-service menu.

We go hiking in the Angeles National Forest and there's no cell service. Ellory sees me checking my phone, searching fruitlessly for the calls and texts I might be missing. She knows what I'm doing but doesn't say. After that, we only hike together in places with coverage, places close to the action. If she wants to go somewhere farther, she goes with her new friends or by herself. She seems happy spending time with the people she's met, but I know she misses her old roommates, and I can't ignore the disappointment on her face each time she asks me if I want to join and I say that I can't. She goes to Las Vegas to perform, to see friends. When she's gone, I look at her Instagram, from most recent all the way back to the beginning, again and again. Somehow, the photos feel more permanent than her presence in Los Angeles.

When she returns and I hold her, it's like I'm hanging on to her.

Her existence in California is delicate to me, like she could delete the apps from her phone and no longer be here at all.

They're showing *Double or Nothing* at the Hollywood Forever Cemetery, so we buy tickets and arrive early. It's lush and blue at dusk. We spread a blanket out on the grass in front of a granite mausoleum. We buy popcorn and wine and look up at the Mexican fan palms, the tallest palm trees on earth.

The movie starts and there's Jack Whitlock, smiling in the booth at the Bluebird. I imagine myself approaching the table with champagne. I can see it so clearly it's almost a real memory.

"You still got that tuxedo?" I ask Ellory.

"I do."

We watch him navigate a high-limit poker room. We watch him in a showroom, flanked by girls in feathers and sequins. He puts a cigarette to his lips and a redhead with big eyelashes lights it for him. The air tonight is honey sweet, like the perfumed air of a casino.

The audience in the cemetery laughs in places where a Las Vegas audience wouldn't laugh. Ellory looks around at them, unsettled. I am looking at Jack, who on the screen is thirty feet tall, his palms pressed against the window, like he is trying to reach for us.

He is somewhere in this city, I keep thinking.

After the movie, after the traffic leaving the movie, we are on a mercifully empty stretch of the 101, listening to scratchy mariachi music on the radio.

"If you could get a picture of any celebrity," Ellory asks, "who would it be?"

I think about Eddie's words from that night at the wedding: *A celebrity you really, really want to take a picture of. Do you have someone like that?* And then I think about Jack Whitlock. What he's doing right now, what he eats for dinner, the music he listens to when he is alone in his house.

"I don't know," I lie.

"Jack Whitlock would be cool," she says.

We pass a billboard for a new streaming service, a billboard for an existing streaming service.

"That Las Vegas connection," Ellory says. "I've seen *Double or Nothing* so many times that he seems to belong in Las Vegas to me. Crazy to think we actually live in the same city as him."

I put my hand on her thigh. I say it casually, like I'm just thinking of it too for the first time: "Yeah. Crazy."

"Do you think you'll ever get it? A photo of him?"

"Maybe."

"You have to *manifest it*," she says. "Isn't that what people here say?"

I laugh. "I think they do, yeah."

We drive past Dodger Stadium, quiet and dark. A sign reads *love fades but Dodgers are forever.*

Ellory says, "I always associate Jack Whitlock with the night we met."

"That and other things," I say.

"Like what?"

I think of watching his mouth move at the drive-in theater, seeing his movies at my parents' house, at my apartment alone, at parties where I didn't know how to talk to anyone. The comfort of his presence turning into something I couldn't identify, though I could feel it settling beneath my skin. I take her hand and kiss it. "Nothing."

I say it cautiously: "I think that would be a good end point, getting a photo of him. I think if I got that, I'd be done. There wouldn't be anywhere else to go."

I catch a glimpse of her face in the headlights of another car. Her expression appears concerned, but the light passes before I can be sure. "What do you mean?" she asks.

"Just that he's very famous. If I took his picture, I would stop. What do you think?"

"You know I don't make the rules," she says.

That night, I dream that I'm in the same room as him. There is a crowd and I'm at the front. And then the crowd is gone and it's just me and him. There is something wrong with my hands. There is something wrong with my camera. He is waiting for me to take the picture, but I'm not taking it. *I'm not going to stand here forever*, he says, and moves on.

When I wake, there are parrots in the trees outside our window. Our apartment is so beautiful, I think. The potted jade, the string lights, the yellow rug. I can no longer remember the layout of my apartment in Las Vegas. I look up the building, and it has changed management companies, changed names.

Ellory wants to go to Las Vegas for Thanksgiving. Her friends don't give a shit about the actual holiday, but they're throwing this party. Potluck style, a makeshift bar in a dusty desert backyard, live music from a local band.

"It's this big, all-day thing"—she says it with her hands. "You should come. And you could see your parents while you're home."

"They're probably busy," I say.

"Come to the party, then. It'll be fun."

"I don't know. There might be stuff going on here."

"What stuff?"

"Work stuff. But you can go without me."

"If that's what you want."

I have not been back to Las Vegas since we left. It hasn't been that long, I say, whenever she tells me her friends and family think I no longer exist. But we have different definitions of what a long time is. There have been opportunities for work there—a music festival I could have shot, a lesser socialite's birthday party at a lesser casino's nightclub—but I don't want to do that.

"There's supposed to be record traffic this year," Ellory says. "Multi-hour backups at Cajon Pass on the way to Las Vegas and at Jean on the way out."

"How can they know that?"

"I don't know. But it's what they're predicting."

I'm going through photos on my laptop. A teen model giving

me the finger. Her mother, the reality TV star, scolding her, smiling at me, mouthing *sorry*.

"So you'll stay here?" I ask Ellory. "Because of the traffic?"

"No, I was saying that I think I'll leave Tuesday instead of Wednesday."

What she actually ends up doing is leaving Monday. On Thanksgiving, I call her and she answers on speakerphone. She's in her car with her friends, headed to the store to get champagne for the party. "Hi, Ben," they all say.

"I miss you," Ellory says. Her voice is happy. I can hear Las Vegas through the phone. It isn't the repetitive one-note sound of a machine cashing out or a piano player at a jazz lounge or the thunder of the Bellagio fountains. It's just something in the air, in people's voices. All morning long, I've been sitting on the bed, typing the word *saw* into Twitter followed by various celebrity names. Sometimes, random people will tweet sightings: *saw Bella Lawrence at the grove just now* or *Saw Alexis Kingston and Vincent Broder on Abbot Kinney*. If you catch these seconds after they appear and drive fast enough, they can be useful.

"I miss you too," I tell Ellory.

I type *saw Jack Whitlock* and every tweet that comes up is just *saw Jack Whitlock's movie*.

"What are you doing today?" she asks.

"Headed downtown, I think. There's some charity event." I pull it up on my computer. *Event-goers can expect some familiar faces*, the copy teases. "It might be something."

Someone in Ellory's car says something about paparazzi like *Wait that's seriously what he does?* and the others laugh.

"I should let you go," I say to Ellory.

Later, she texts me a photo of the party. A yard full of people in the sun. Furniture from the house brought outside so people can eat together.

I text her: **send me some pictures of you**

what kind of pictures?

Just pictures, I say, and she doesn't respond.

At the charity event, there are no familiar faces, just a Pilates instructor with ten thousand YouTube subscribers.

"It's enough to monetize it," she says. She's dressed in white leggings and has a practiced cheeriness. She makes direct eye contact as she hands out discount codes for an online fitness program she's launching. I take her picture, but I know it's worth nothing. I can tell she knows this too. She puts her hand on her hip—the skinny-arm pose—and stays that way even after I lower my camera.

I email my contact at the photo agency and get an auto-response telling me she's enjoying the holiday with her husband and their three basset hounds. I drive to a boutique pie shop in West Hollywood and hang around outside. One of the entertainment news channels said it was popular with celebrities last year. But this year, it seems they've all either moved on or sent assistants. The pie shop is open but empty.

Another paparazzo has the same idea. "This town is dead today," he says to me.

The woman working at the pie shop sees us from behind the glass. She shakes her head, motions for us to leave.

"Well, she's friendly," the paparazzo says.

I consider the Hollywood Hills above us. The mansions

where there are no cameras. And somewhere beyond that, in Bel Air, Jack Whitlock.

"Seen anybody today?" I ask.

"It's a bust like every year," he says.

"So why are you out?"

"Believe me, if I had somewhere else to go, I'd be there."

A single cloud covers the sun for a moment. The air cools. The woman from the pie shop opens the door. "We're closing soon, so you assholes can go away now." The bells jingle, followed by the sound of the lock clicking. I text a few waiters, a few valet drivers. None of them respond.

"I really don't know where else to go today," I say.

"Might as well go home and be with your family," he says. The neon *open* sign goes dark.

"How long have you been doing this?" I ask him.

"Forever. I started back when it was good. We were making real money then. It wasn't like this."

Someone passes in a car and hollers out the window. A tour bus follows with no one inside.

"I think I'm going to go to Beverly Hills," I say.

"Waste of time. I'm telling you, the golden age has ended."

"I just got here. How can that be possible?"

"Bad timing. Sorry."

"I don't believe that."

He lights a cigarette. "Believe what you want. You'll see."

"I'm only going to do this for, like, six months."

"No shame in that. Not everyone can handle it. Most people, they've only got a year—"

"It's not that. I can handle it. It's just, I told my girlfriend—"

"Girlfriend. There it is. Did no one tell you about that? You can't really do this shit and have a girlfriend. They either think you're gay for following around famous people or they can't stand what you do." He holds up a ringless finger. "My ex-wife thought it was both."

"I think I'm going to go to Beverly Hills," I say again.

"I'll tag along. If you don't mind."

"No problem," I tell him, but after I get in my car, I drive to Bel Air. I hold my breath as I pass the gated entrance to Jack Whitlock's neighborhood. There is a guard outside, and he looks up when I pass. I take this as a sign that he's home.

Ellory decides to stay through the weekend. I pretend not to be disappointed. I go to Venice Beach, where a big-budget superhero movie is filming. Only one other paparazzo.

"Come for dinner," he says. He's been around for a while—he counts the years that he's been doing this on his fingers and it's close to ten—recognizes I might be around for a while too.

"I'm good," I say. "But I appreciate it."

"Come on," he says. "I bet you're looking at an hour in traffic. My house is practically walking distance from here. Marina del Rey."

"Really?"

"Yeah, really. What's wrong with Marina del Rey?"

"Nothing. And again, I appreciate the offer, but I'm fine."

"I bet you think we all live in Hollywood," he says. "That where you live?"

"Echo Park."

"You'll be in Hollywood eventually, like most of those young and hungry guys. But hey, when you get older like me, you'll want a slower pace. I can see boats from my living room."

On Abbot Kinney, the restaurants are opening up for happy hour. I can smell fried oysters, grilled swordfish. My phone buzzes to let me know about a slowdown on the 10. He catches me looking. "Come have a beer. Wait it out."

I think of the empty apartment in Echo Park. "Okay. A beer."

I follow him to where he lives in Marina del Rey, but when I get there it's not what I imagined. I pictured a set designer's idea of a one-bedroom bachelor pad. Neon beer sign, futon, fridge containing only condiments. But he has a two-story condo, a small yard. And there is a woman and a child there. All of this is his, it turns out. He owns the condo. He is married to the woman. The child is his daughter. She just learned to walk, he tells me. He holds her hands and she tests the ground with her feet. She is wearing pink socks, a pink onesie. She grins at me and laughs.

"Oh," I say, like, oh, maybe he's brought me to the wrong house somehow. Or, oh, maybe he's not really a paparazzo. He can't be that and a husband and a father. If he is, he must be miserable, dreaming of leaving the industry or leaving his family. *Six months tops*, I told Ellory. Relief in her eyes after I said it.

"Let's get you a beer," he says, clapping me on the back.

We go to the living room and indeed there is a view of boats from the window.

"Boats!" the baby announces.

"It was her first word," he tells me.

His wife smiles, rolls her eyes kind of playfully. "It's her only word."

On the wall there are photos of them at Disney in matching mouse ears, on a towel at the beach, kissing in wedding clothes.

They cook together and I stand dumbly in the kitchen answering their questions about my life.

"Wait until you try this risotto," he says. "She makes the *best* risotto."

"You made the bread," she says, setting it on the table.

"You bake bread?" I ask.

"It's a hobby I picked up."

At the table, the baby watches us eat with her big googly eyes, her big smile. She is a happy baby, they keep saying. The happiest baby. She never cries. They say grace before we eat, an act so impossibly good I start to wonder if this man is living a double life, telling his family he works at an insurance company or something. But no. His camera is on a nearby credenza. When I comment on a framed wedding photo, his wife mentions the drunken heiress whose picture paid for the rehearsal dinner.

"We've been very lucky," she says. "Are you married?"

"I have a girlfriend."

"Hopefully we're not keeping you from her."

"She's not in Los Angeles right now," I say. "She went to see her family and her friends."

"You didn't want to go with her?"

I look down at my plate. "I thought there would be stuff going on here. Work."

He laughs. "Thanksgiving week? LA is always dead this week. Today was a total fluke. Sorry no one told you that. You could have gone with her. Next year you'll know."

"Yeah," I say. It's a nice thought, next year. "I don't know if she wants to be here, though. I don't know how long she'll tolerate what I'm doing."

They smile politely, chewing their food.

I force a laugh. "Sorry. That was . . ."

He clears his throat. "Well, you're young. You're a good-looking guy. It'll all work out. Most of the young guys like you are single, having fun, you know? Running around Hollywood."

I check my phone for text messages and there are none. "She'll be back in town soon."

"Good," he says, gesturing with a forkful of risotto. "She can join us next time."

When I bring up celebrities I've shot, tried to shoot, would like to shoot, he steers the conversation away. Back to Los Angeles chatter—talk of freeways and grocery stores and farmers' markets and restaurants.

After dinner, when it's just me and him out on the balcony, looking at the lights in the harbor, I try again. I mention a famous couple, the rumors of a breakup they're hiding until the press cycle for their movie ends.

"I hate talking about celebrities when I'm not at work," he says. "I don't read the magazines I sell my photos to either."

"But if you don't know what's going on, you're going to be worse at your job."

He drinks his beer. "That's a price I'm willing to pay." He sets the bottle down on the railing. "I was only out on that beach today because it's close to home. This work, it's not my whole life. And there are other ways to make money—easier ways to make money, especially now. But even if this business was still lucrative, I'd feel the same. If I have to choose between being here with my wife and my daughter and chasing the latest twentysomething around with a camera, well, it's not even a choice. I'm here."

"And your wife, she isn't bothered by what you do for work?"

"She's always supported it. Wholehearted support."

I look at the water in the dark. "Always?"

"Always. Believe me, I know how lucky I am. You can't make someone get on board with this."

On the drive home, I decide he was lying. A lot of people are. His wife isn't really okay with his work and he isn't really okay doing a mediocre job at it for her sake. Someday they'll both realize the truth.

But I feel uneasy as I drive east, the lights of empty buildings downtown burning for no one, the road uncharacteristically free of traffic.

I will avoid him, I decide. I will make excuses if he offers dinner again. When we are in crowds together, I will stand away from him. I won't think about that baby saying *boats* and her mother smiling and saying, *Yes, that's right, boats.*

At the apartment, I call Ellory. I want to ask her if she is really okay with what I'm doing, if she could continue to be okay with it. If she can imagine a life built around it. But she doesn't answer. She texts, **call you later it's really loud here**. I wait, watching Jack Whitlock on TV. I try to focus on that. There is no such thing as wholehearted support. Not for me or for anyone doing what I'm doing. Ambivalence is the best any of us can hope for.

But I can't change the fact that I've seen it. Their house with all their stuff. Their baby's big wet eyes. Their hands touching as they said grace.

chapter sixteen

A longtime paparazzo quits after a famous comedian offers him a job taking photos for social media. *The defector*, we keep calling him, some of us jealous, others genuinely betrayed.

"It's like a Democrat voting for a Republican," one paparazzo says.

"I *am* a Republican," the defector says.

The last day I see him, I'm at the Santa Monica Pier. A bunch of us are trying to get photos of a sitcom that's filming a scene. Eddie isn't here, and I have this nagging sensation he knows of somewhere better to be.

"It's my last hurrah," the defector tells us. "One last week of papping before the easy life starts."

The crew from the show spots us. A production assistant waves over security. A lead actress in a terry-cloth robe is hustled out of our collective eyeline.

"I'll tell you how it happened," the defector says. "It was pretty simple. I posted some pics of him on my Instagram and tagged him, so he messages me and says, hey, I like your style." He pauses, waiting for us to say, *That's crazy*, but none of us do. We're focused on the set, which he isn't even looking at.

"Are you just here to brag?" someone finally asks him. "Because the rest of us have to earn money so we can eat."

I know why he's here. It is for the same reason we're all here: because he can't let go. Even though he has a way out, he is here.

"It sounds boring," I say. "What you're talking about doing."

He ignores me. "This time next week I'll be flying around on his private jet. It's an international tour. We're going to Europe. And I'll be his behind-the-scenes guy, taking photos of him backstage, at the hotel, getting ready."

"What are you, in love with him?" someone asks.

"Yeah, I'm in love with him. In love with his money."

The security guard is speaking to the production assistant. Then he's looking at us. Then he's making his way through the sand, waving his hands at us and motioning for us to leave.

One paparazzo cups his hands over his mouth. "It's a public beach."

Another goes down to the water and wades into the surf, holding his camera up and shouting, "No laws in the ocean."

On the pier, several crew members have begun to prop up a massive mirror.

"Shit," I say. "They're mirroring us." The ray of light hits me before I can look away, burning my eyes, my face. The heat on my skin takes me back to a canyon in the desert, holding my camera up to capture a bighorn sheep on a cliff above, the setting sun making my vision go blurry and red for a moment. Was I ever good at wildlife photography?

I retreat. The others follow. I got one decent shot, I think. My pulse spikes. The body high of it. I want to beat the traffic, go home and edit the photo set, see what it's worth.

We head to our cars, leaving the defector behind. He kicks at sand as he tries to catch up with us. "Let's keep in touch" is what it sounds like he's saying, but it's drowned out by ocean, music, carnival sounds.

A wave of paparazzi leave to drive for Uber.

"It's more reliable," one of them tells me when I see him outside my new gym. Jack Whitlock was spotted at this gym once, on a Tuesday in May with a black bag and a green juice.

The paparazzo turned Uber driver holds a gallon of generic-brand laundry detergent. "You must be doing well if you can afford a membership at this place," he says.

"I thought it would be a good way to pick up information, meet sources, run into famous people."

"Is it?" he asks.

"Eventually, I'm sure it will be."

He laughs. "Good luck with *eventually*. If you get tired of it, consider Uber."

I look at the pavement, his bare feet in his sandals, his too-long toenails. "Yeah, okay."

"You can work when you want to work. And there are always people requesting rides. I'm not chasing celebrities up and down Hollywood Boulevard anymore." He taps at his phone. "It's just right there now. Stable money, can you imagine?"

"I can imagine."

"If it stays this good, I'll be doing it forever." He goes inside the laundromat and I go inside the gym. I run on the treadmill for sixty-one minutes without stopping, which is longer than I've ever gone for. I picture the final scene of *Double or Nothing*. Jack Whitlock running away from the neon of Las Vegas, into the dark.

* * *

"She is famous," he keeps telling me. "Extremely famous. No one ever told me she would get to be this famous. I had every chance to shoot her before but I didn't ever think she'd be famous. And now she's famous. God, she's so, so, so famous."

He is a paparazzo who will soon be leaving the industry; he just doesn't know it yet. He is in the death throes of it, the final stage of grief, the last days before the end. There he is like the rest of us, outside restaurants and shops and hotels and hair salons and gyms, but he is nothing like the rest of us, I decide. He is nothing like me. He is weak. He is a zombie, staggering around in circles while I am so alert, so ready with my camera, ready to run, to chase, to shoot. I've decided it doesn't matter that people keep telling me this is no longer a viable career. They're just not as good as me.

"Damn, he is just absolutely fixated on that Lily Prince," another pap says. "Yeah, I'm talking about you. Give it up, bro."

"You don't understand. No one ever told me she would get to be this famous. Last year she was everywhere I went. I didn't take a single picture of her. No one knew her name. Now she's . . ." He gestures to something invisible in the air. That ineffable quality we all understand.

He continues muttering to himself. He doesn't even bother to take a picture when the tattooed bassist we're all waiting for appears from the hotel. After the bassist leaves, the paparazzo remains in place, still muttering, just looking at the ground. The other paparazzi distance themselves from him as if he's contagious.

The next time I see him, he's drunk and his eyes are red. "I would have made so much money."

"There's still money," I say.

Eddie is there, smirking like he knows something.

"What do you think?" I ask him.

"I'm making it work," he says, but doesn't elaborate.

Lily Prince is above us on a billboard, draped in gauzy fabric and sitting in a field of poppies. *New Album This Spring*. In the clouds above her, the words *In Your Dreamz*.

"Bitch," the drunk paparazzo says when he sees it. He turns to me. "She was everywhere before. And now I can't find her."

"Some people get famous for no reason," I say.

"Bullshit. There's always a reason."

I leave him there on the sidewalk, snapping photos of the billboard with his phone camera, murmuring about the chance he didn't take.

At home, I look at Jack Whitlock on the internet. I make lists of the restaurants where he eats, the hotels where he stays, the islands where he vacations with his wife. I am looking for a correlation, a sign, anything.

Months later I'm at LAX, following a basketball player's wife across the terminal, when my phone buzzes in my pocket. I don't stop to look at it.

The basketball player's wife does not want to be papped. She does not want her picture included in an article about the rumors that her husband has been sending illicit texts to his coach's daughter. In the photos I've seen of her, she is glamorous in a specific *Top Ten Hottest Basketball Wives* way. Today, she is tired and wearing a wrinkled gray T-shirt. This will sell.

When she sees my camera, she puts on a pair of mirrored gold sunglasses and holds up her hand. "Please, please. Not right now."

"Just a few," I say. "Just a few and I'll leave you alone." A trick I learned from watching other paparazzi. It placates the subject because it is a bargain. It gives them agency. They think, Okay, I'll just let him do this and then he'll go away.

"I said no."

I start taking pictures. Through the lens she looks upset. I can imagine the headlines. *Spotted! Alone and distraught at LAX amid her husband's flirty text scandal . . .*

I am good at this, or at least getting good at this.

My phone buzzes in my pocket.

The basketball player's wife has a plastic bag of snacks from Hudson News. This is an interesting detail, the little package of pretzels, the candy. It is humanizing in a way people will like. I zoom in on it.

"Where are you coming back from?" I ask, still looking through my camera, still taking pictures. "Why are you alone?"

She says nothing.

"This isn't a video," I tell her. "You can talk."

The goal is to get a reaction out of her. A change in facial expression. The sunglasses are no help. It's clear she's had training on this. She knows not to look at me, not to give me anything. I follow her a few minutes longer and keep taking photos, determined to get something. But she is resolute. And when I realize that what I have is the best I will get, I tell her thank you and turn back. A short buzz from my phone, indicating a voicemail. A Los Angeles number I don't know.

Each time this happens I think of Jack Whitlock. Of course,

that's never what it is, but still, I love the faint possibility that it might be. I suck in some air, readying myself. This must be what people who play slot machines experience while the reel is spinning, the red sevens and blue diamonds settling into place.

I press play on the message and hold the phone up to my ear. Just as the voice on the recording begins to speak, there's a loud announcement overhead about a gate change. I can't tell who is speaking or what they're saying over the noise of the airport. The only word I catch is *emergency*.

I rush to the parking garage, hitting play and trying to listen again, my own breath louder than the recording as I run. I don't know what the message is, just that it is important and I have to go wherever it is sending me. I imagine an actor causing a car crash, a rock star overdosing at a hotel.

Mentally, I calculate the distance to various hospitals, bumping up against my own shortcoming, which is that I still don't know this city perfectly, no matter how hard I've been trying to. But I will, I will, I will. One day, I will know this city like I knew the trails of the Spring Mountains, the secret caves along the Colorado River, the canyons of Death Valley. Every time I get there first, I am one step closer.

There's a long line of cars. I honk futilely. The person in front of me puts their hand out the window and gives me the middle finger. I play the message again, this time on speakerphone, with my windows up, so I can finally hear it. The voice belongs to a man. "Uh, yeah, I'm looking for Ben? I'm calling to let you know your girlfriend, Ellory, has been in an accident. And . . . anyway, I'm bringing her to the emergency room. I think the nearest one is in Silver Lake?"

An invisible blow to the sternum. I'm sweating through my

shirt. I didn't put deodorant on today and I'm just realizing it now. The smell of my own body; it makes me sick.

The message is from forty minutes ago. Forty fucking minutes. I call back and call back and call back as I drive to the hospital, but he doesn't answer. I call Ellory again and again and again, and it goes straight to voicemail. The recording of her voice is still playing when I park in a tow-away zone, when someone in scrubs yells at me to move my car, and so I go to the parking garage and I cannot find a spot but finally I do at the very, very top. I look out at the smoggy city. I don't know why I stop to do that.

Ellory is not in the emergency room. She is nowhere in the hospital, at least nowhere that I go, nowhere that I am allowed to go. *Sir, you can't be in here*, people keep saying to me, and I am finding myself in all sorts of places where people are bleeding and weeping and screaming, being born and dying. And it's sick that I can't stop myself from wondering if any of them are famous. When I go back outside, I am alone and it is quiet, quieter than it has ever been. And she is not there, she is not there. So there is nothing for me to do but go home, and when I get to the apartment, she is lying on the bed with her eyes open and I tell her that someone left me the craziest voicemail saying that she was in an accident but obviously she's fine, and then I see her leg. Her thigh, her entire thigh, is deep, dark purple and black at the edges. In the center, four red puncture wounds in the shape of teeth.

"Oh god, oh god." I fall to my knees, my voice as desperate as the model's was, begging for the photos to be deleted. I put my hands around her foot. I kiss her ankle, her shin. "Oh god, what happened?"

I crawl into the bed with my shoes on, getting the new, nice sheets dirty. "What happened, what bit you?" I am crying now. I am crying, and she is not.

"You didn't answer your phone," she says.

"It was loud at the airport. I'm so sorry. What happened?"

She speaks to the ceiling. "I was delivering food. There was a dog—"

"Jesus. Holy shit. Fuck, I'm so sorry."

"The owner called you. You didn't answer."

I touch her hair, and she turns her head away.

"Why were you at the airport?" she asks.

"I was at LAX because this basketball player's wife—"

"You should have answered your phone. Don't you know that when someone calls you repeatedly it's important?"

I kiss her face, her neck, her shoulders. "I didn't recognize the number. If you had called from yours—"

"Mine broke when I fell."

"I'll get you a new one—"

"You answer your phone all the time for these complete strangers who call you about celebrities," she says. "You jump out of bed when it rings in the middle of the night."

I ask her what I can do, what I can get her. Water, food, medicine, money, a ride somewhere, anything. I sit up and look at the black bruise on her leg, shiny with antiseptic, a glossy black hole between us.

"I don't need anything."

She closes her eyes.

"Do you just need to rest?" I ask. She says nothing, so I get up to close the curtains.

"I don't need you right now. I needed you earlier, but you weren't there. You were at the airport, taking pictures of someone. Because that's what you do. And I've been cool with it, even though you're just, like, not doing the wildlife photography thing anymore, which is what I thought—"

"I can't go into nature. There's no cell service. And if I get a tip—"

"That's not it. You like this better. And you said we'd go hiking together here, but we don't."

"You have your hiking friends."

"That's not the point."

I kneel by the bed. "What can I do, Ellory? What can I do?"

I sit on the floor, looking at her bruise, watching her sleep. It gets dark outside. I glance at my phone, thinking of the valet driver I'm expecting to hear from, the rumors of a secret concert in Santa Monica, a pop star revealing her new boyfriend. Ellory's eyes are open, watching me. "Just go," she says. "Just go if you want."

"No. I'm staying with you."

Later, I order Indian food for us both and put a movie on my laptop. A biopic from a few years ago about a scientist in the Arctic. Jack Whitlock navigates the frozen coast, passing by ice floes on a ship. Harp seals look back at him with their black doll eyes. Ellory takes a few bites of naan and then lies back down again, leaving the styrofoam container on the nightstand. I watch the movie until the end, until he finds out why the seals are all dying. I look at him, alone on the tundra, the camera panning out farther and farther to show how lost he is.

los angeles, amid scandal

chapter seventeen

A rumor among paparazzi: Jack boarded a flight to Colorado from the celebrity terminal at LAX. Supposedly, he's headed to a luxurious treatment center with mineral baths, mountain views, and one Michelin star. The photo agency wants to know what my plan is. They're not going to pay for any travel, but they'd still like to know. My plan, I tell them, is to find Jack Whitlock.

"You can't get within a mile of that treatment center," a paparazzo tells me in the parking lot of a grocery store. He's waiting for a folk musician to come out. I'm waiting for anyone who might be connected to Jack.

"I heard some people are flying out to try," I say.

"Good luck to them. Sounds like a fool's errand."

The folk musician appears, deliberately vintage in his little round sunglasses and Beatles shirt. He flashes us a peace sign. "Good to see you, friends."

"Cool haircut," the other paparazzo says, taking his picture.

"Keep it real," the folk singer says, then crosses the too-small parking lot to his car. As I watch him, I see the awards-show photographer getting out of an Uber.

"This fucking guy," I say.

The awards-show photographer approaches, grinning. He

offers us both high fives. "Look at you two. Still at it, huh? Good for you. Keeping the dream alive."

The other paparazzo indulges him while I look at flights to Denver on my phone.

"Not so talkative today, huh, Ben?" the awards-show photographer says. "You're so tough over text, but in person, not so much."

I ignore him, looking up car rentals from the Denver airport. Everything is too expensive.

"What's wrong?" he asks with fake concern. "Money problems? Everybody hates you?" He squeezes my shoulder.

I shake off his hand. "Don't touch me."

"Well, when you're ready for real, respectable, stable work, let me know. I can hook it up." He offers a business card. I don't take it. "You got a problem, Ben?"

"Nope. No problem."

He puts the business card back in his pocket. "I have pride in what I do. And I'm not some fucking leech. And I'm really talking about you specifically, Ben."

"At least I'm not a sellout," I say.

"What'd you call me?"

"A sellout."

"Can I have one of those cards?" the other paparazzo asks.

"No," the awards-show photographer says. "Fuck you guys. Have fun in Colorado chasing around Jack Whitlock."

"What do you know about that?" I ask.

"Wish I could tell you," he says, winking. "But I'm just a sellout."

He gives us a stupid little salute and goes into the store.

At my apartment, I comb the reviews of the Colorado treatment center, looking for hints of Jack's presence. There is nothing but quail egg omelets on porcelain, snowy mountains. I don't believe he is there.

Ellory has gained about a thousand new followers since her last post was shared by the hotel she performed at. They flood her comments with happy face emojis, yellow stars.

A well-known magician writes: *Congrats on joining THE BEST SHOW ON THE STRIP!!!!*

you've really earned this babe, one of her roommates comments.

The man from her photos leaves a single red heart. His profile is set to private.

I go to Erewhon and take pictures of a TV actress buying cilantro. Her red-faced child toddles behind her, reaching for her hand.

"Dada," he says, pointing at me.

The actress sees me. "Not Dada." She abandons her shopping cart and walks toward me. "Pedophile, pedophile, pedophile." She says the word louder each time, shaking her finger at me. "Pedophile," she says again.

I lower my camera. "I deliberately kept the kid out of frame."

"Pedophile," she says again, pausing as if she's waiting for an audience reaction. I can see her desire to be perceived, to perform. She hasn't worked much since she married a tech titan. A man whose company is *pioneering automation.* Their *Architectural Digest* Open Door home tour did big numbers on YouTube. *A serene and sustainable farmhouse in the heart of Los Angeles.*

"I didn't take any photos of Louie," I tell her.

She steps back like I've spit on her. "Excuse me? *Louie?* You know my kid's name?"

"It's my job."

"What job is that? Professional pedophile?"

"I'm a pap—"

"Get a new job, loser."

"You're out in public," I say. "This is fair game."

The other shoppers are looking, surreptitiously removing headphones, holding up phones to record.

"Excuse me." A teenage girl approaches her nervously. "Excuse me, but I loved you in the Coco Chanel movie. Can I get a selfie with you?"

The actress looks from me to the girl. Her kid starts crying silently, tears running down his cheeks.

"Fuck no," she says. "Why can't you people leave me alone?"

A manager appears. "Is everything okay?"

"I was just leaving," I tell him. And then to the actress: "I won't take your picture again."

"I don't believe you."

There is no way to tell her that I was just doing it for the money, which isn't enough anyway. I turn and go, her voice still echoing *pedophile* behind me, even after I get into my car, even after I call the agency and find out they're not interested in the photo set at all because she isn't famous enough, which I explain to them is her fault, really, not mine. That's not how it works, they say.

At Lake Hollywood Park, I walk behind rescue dogs, people in athleisure. They talk about writers' rooms and open mics and apartment applications. Regional accents filter into conversations, even though everyone is trying so hard to sound like they're from California.

A group of young people with indeterminate careers talk about Jack, making jokes about him and then arguing about the offensiveness of the jokes. Is it funny to joke about his sex life if he is actually a sex addict? Is it funny to joke about his infidelity if his daughter might one day hear the joke? Is it funny to joke about any of this, to treat him as a punch line when he is, in fact, a person?

Maybe they're workshopping material, I think. Or maybe, for some reason, they're just people, having a conversation.

There's a man leaning against the driver's side of my car. Baseball cap, jogging clothes, looking at his phone.

"I think you've got the wrong car," I say.

He doesn't look up at me, just keeps scrolling his phone.

"Would you mind moving?" I say. "This is my car."

His face is blank, inscrutable as a text message with no punctuation.

My breath catches in my throat as I inhale. I exhale uneasily. Breathwork exercises, I tell myself, do your breathwork exercises. The man is my height, my weight—less than six feet tall, slight frame.

"Whatever you're here to do," I say, "just do it."

He puts up his hands.

"I know you're one of those people—"

"What people?" he says, smiling now. "What people?"

I can still feel the photo agency's smile through the phone.

The taste in my mouth when I got the money, like metal, like wine. I can still see Ellory's eyes.

He moves aside, presenting my car like it's a gift. His sunglasses are mirrored. All I can see is myself. And then he lifts his phone and points the camera at me.

"Are you recording me?" I ask. I drop my keys and then pick them up.

"How do you like it?" he asks. "You should be thrown off a bridge for what you did to her."

"It was business," I say. I try to swallow but there's no saliva in my mouth.

I see him in my rearview mirror as I pull away. The phone is still raised.

On the drive home, I brace myself for a car accident, imagining he's following me. I can see myself hurtling toward the guardrail, tearing the chain-link fence like it's a spiderweb, careening into the traffic below, dissolving in a cloud of fire.

You have to manifest it, Ellory said.

The email arrives just after I've stepped inside my apartment and locked the door: a photo of my license plate. Subject line: *it was personal*

I double-check the lock. I watch the security camera. A deliveryman, carrying flowers for someone. A different deliveryman with a pizza. I listen to the footsteps above me, as if there might be a pattern to them.

On Jessica's Instagram, puffy white blossoms, which I identify as beargrass. Native to Montana. *Grateful*, the caption reads.

All the comments ask the same question: *grateful for what?!?*

She hasn't responded to anyone. It's unlike her—this vagueness, this teasing. But it's a move I've seen before: Let the narrative play out in public before making a statement, a decision.

On TV, they're rehashing what few images exist of Sasha, who appears to have vanished completely. *Before moving to LA, she was a teenage model in New York*. They interview the heir of a shipping fortune, who was once treated at the same Colorado rehab that Jack Whitlock is rumored to be at. The interviewer asks: *Do you think it's possible Jack is staying in the very same suite you had?* The shipping heir grins. *Absolutely!*

The next few days will be crucial.

I can focus on that.

My phone rings. I can't tell if the surge of energy I get is excitement or fear. At this point, they feel the same.

A 702 number. Las Vegas. No one calls me from that area code anymore. I look at the number on the phone, realizing I know it. I deleted the contact after I quit, but it's the Bluebird. My stomach turns in on itself, as if being kneaded by a set of invisible hands. I don't want to think about the people I knew there. A missed-call notification, and then a minute later, a voicemail. I delete it without listening. I press a finger into the spot below my wrist that's supposed to alleviate anxiety. It doesn't do anything. I need a cigarette, even though I don't want to leave my apartment, even though it's been years since I had one. *I only smoke when I'm on break at the restaurant*, I told Eddie.

Double or Nothing on TV. Jack out in the desert by Lake Mead. The water, bluer than the sky. Bright red blood blooming at the shoreline. Jack tries to turn away from it, but he can't. He has to look.

* * *

I'm in the bath drinking a seltzer. No alcohol right now; I need to keep my head clear. The local news is on mute. The subtitles tell the story of car accidents on highways, bears swimming in Pasadena pools, homeless encampments, a café in Hollywood where the servers do a choreographed dance if you order cake. The news anchor smiles.

The phone is on the bath mat beside the tub. I shake the moisture off my hands and reach for it, feeling the familiar swell of a really good tip coming in. Like fate, the news shows a photo of Jack. I know the shot; it's from 2015, the premiere of a movie in which he played a disgraced Wall Street executive living off the grid in the Sonoran Desert. Red carpet, step and repeat, bright lights. Kelly-green suit that all the fashion blogs agreed was *a bold departure from the traditional black tux*.

A message from a dating app: *Would you be interested in going for a hike tomorrow?*

I unmute the news and listen to the anchors talk about Jack.

"What's so crazy," one of them says, "is that he seemed like such a family man."

A photo of Jack, Jessica, and their daughter outside a ski chalet. Sundance 2016.

My phone reminds me of the message again. The woman is a yoga instructor who enjoys camping, kayaking, and tacos. She wears pastel workout clothes in all her photos. She has a lotus flower tattoo on her forearm, a diamond nose piercing. I flip through her photos, all taken in nature. I imagine a camera on self-timer, poised on the branch of a tree.

We did that too, Ellory and I. Before the thunderstorm in the Tushar Mountains, we took a photo together, just like that.

Maybe the yoga instructor will be from a Beverly Hills studio that costs fifty dollars a class. The kind of place where single actresses and married producers make eyes at each other from their mats. The kind of place where Jessica might have worked out, or at least someone who knows her, knows Jack.

God, it is a long shot. Long shot of long shots. I look at a photo of Jack, as if he could tell me what to do.

I text Eddie, **I'm really lost here.**

And then, because there is nothing else to do, I message the yoga instructor: *Runyon?*

She responds quickly. *Meet at the entrance on Fuller? 11?*

And if she doesn't turn out to be useful, at least Runyon Canyon is a good place to spot celebrities.

The blond dirt, the dry hills, the outline of the city through the smog.

I know he isn't here, but I can't stop seeing him.

Jack behind the tinted windows of luxury cars with their wheels turned toward the curb. Jack with his head down, a little farther along the trail, moving at a faster pace than I can, out of reach. Jack disappearing into the Hollywood Hills, preparing to live off the land, feasting on rattlesnakes, drinking cold water from secret springs.

When I mention Jack to the yoga instructor, she says, "I hope he's okay," like she's talking about a coworker with the flu, someone from another department on a separate floor of the office.

She is not judgmental about what I do.

"I think it's really interesting," she says. "So LA!"

"Being a yoga instructor is also very LA," I say, already thinking of my next sentence, and the one after that, how I'll slowly guide her toward telling me what she knows.

"I've never really thought about it like that."

"Really?"

"I just love it. That's why I do it. And I guess I'm very lucky to live in a place where it's popular."

"Where do you teach?" I ask.

"The 24 Hour Fitness in Glendale. The ashtanga class is very popular if you ever want to check it out."

"Oh," I say, thinking of ten-dollar memberships, aqua aerobics for seniors. "Yeah, maybe. I don't know. I don't really do yoga."

"The class I teach is good for all skill levels." She laughs. She has a nervous laugh. "You can get a free three-day trial membership if you do want to check it out. But no pressure."

We're on the steep part of the trail, almost to the place where it flattens out before descending. The dirt is soft and fine, coating the backs of her taut calves as she leads the way. She is in running shorts, a tank top referencing a half-marathon in San Diego. I am in jeans and a cotton T-shirt. *Cotton kills*, the hiking books always say. Cotton gets soaked with sweat during the day, then stays wet after dark, gives you hypothermia. *Cotton kills*, I thought in the mountains high above Las Vegas, Death Valley. *Cotton kills*. But not here it doesn't.

The yoga instructor tells me about a book she just read, a music venue out in the desert she likes to go to, a Vietnamese restaurant near her apartment. I try to come up with reasons for being here, things I might ask her, information she might give me.

We pass a woman in yellow leggings, talking into her front-facing camera, perhaps to an audience of one, perhaps to an audience of several thousand. "Imagine yourself getting over that last hurdle," she says, "because on the other side, life becomes amazing."

People around us are walking dogs, talking to their dogs, talking to one another about their dogs.

"She's got some Australian shepherd in her. Lot of energy."

"He's hypoallergenic, but I still feel like I'm allergic."

A man on a bench has his arm around a gray pit bull. He looks happy. I have never had a pet. Caring for an animal seems impossible, an experience that inevitably ends in grief.

The yoga instructor is talking about a trip to Yosemite, the John Muir Trail, the Pacific Crest Trail, even.

"Are you pretty into hiking?" she asks.

"Not so much anymore."

"What happened? Sorry, I'm prying."

"I just . . . can't be out of cell service."

I think about Ghost. I haven't thought about Ghost in a while. I used to think about him every day. I almost tell her about him, but I don't.

We reach the viewpoint at Cloud's Rest and pause to look at the city. A peek of powder blue from the gray sky. A ray of light, turning Hollywood into gold. It is quiet up here. Below, sirens and honking. "Look," the yoga instructor says, touching my forearm. A cottontail rabbit. Nervous eyes, twitching nose. There and then not.

I want to disassociate from her kindness; it hurts too much to receive it. I want to turn this into a daytime fuck. I want to descend the trail alone, back to my apartment.

Up ahead, there's a group of people taking a photo with a celebrity chef. He's known for his Italian fusion restaurant in Culver City and his show where he cooks alongside famous guests. The famous guests can never cook, but everyone laughs and learns a lot at the end of the day. On the show, the celebrity chef is winsome and twinkly-eyed. *Look at how perfect your meringue is*, he'll say to a doe-eyed underwear model. *This demi-glace is much better*, he'll say to a tween influencer.

"Am I about to see a real-life paparazzi in action?" the yoga instructor asks.

"He punched me in the face last time, so I don't think so."

"Really? Sorry, I don't mean to laugh. I hope you're okay."

"It's okay. It happens."

"You've been punched in the face more than once?"

"Yes," I say, remembering each time, the specifics of the pain.

"I had fun," she tells me when we're back at the park entrance. She waits for me to say something, to ask her to have lunch or drinks or to come back to my apartment. The possibility of conversation about things in common, future plans that might be mutually exciting.

There is a green bench with a sign beside it that says: *Smile, say hello and spark a conversation with the persons sitting on this bench. This is a dedicated space to combat social isolation and loneliness.*

"Are you hungry at all?" she asks.

"Not really," I say. "I should get home."

Later, when I am back at my apartment, I take out my phone, open up my contact list, and block her. I shower off the dust from the Hollywood Hills. I have a headache from the sun. It's still light outside, but I get into bed. I dream of Yosemite. The blank face of El Capitan rising from the meadow below. Jack at the top, looking down on me. I put my hands on the rock. It's warm from the sun. But it's too smooth to climb. I can't get to him.

chapter eighteen

A text from Sherry, whose name is saved in my phone under a pseudonym: **How's my favorite pap? Got some news for you xoxoxo.**

Dice emoji.

I think of Jack Whitlock in *Double or Nothing*. Walking through a casino. Pausing at a craps table and smiling.

I order a Shirley Temple and put the money under the glass.

"My two favorite things," Sherry says.

She plucks a cherry from the ice and chews it contemplatively. As a teenager in Wisconsin, she told me once, she pictured Los Angeles as one great big Playboy Mansion. A land of limestone castles, tennis courts, and artificial waterfalls. When she finally moved to California, she spent years ripening in the sun by Hef's pool, waiting to be plucked from a row of beauties and invited into the house. But by then she was considered too old to be anything more than a party guest.

Sherry holds up a French-manicured finger. The bartender sees this and places a silver saucer of maraschinos in front of her.

"How's business?" she asks me.

"We'll see," I say.

She smells cartoonishly feminine, like the beauty counter at a mall, like Ellory's dressing room full of flowers. She performed better with me there in the audience, she said once. She liked the feeling of me watching.

"Ask me where I was today," Sherry says.

"Where were you today?"

"Linden House."

"Linden House. Really?"

"Ever been inside?"

"Never," I say. No paparazzo has penetrated the ivied West Hollywood walls of Linden House. It's members only; no phones allowed. Millions of dollars' worth of photos—famous exes reuniting, embattled directors hiding out, beloved TV hosts stepping out on spouses—hidden beneath the waxy leaves of banana trees. All-knowing bartenders with NDAs serve frozen drinks. The pool shimmers with secrets. Or so I imagine.

"Sherry," I say, "you texted a dice emoji."

She smiles. "And what does that mean to you, Vegas?"

"Is it him?"

She waits for me to say his name out loud, but I don't want to. I don't want her to tell me I'm wrong. I'm drunk on the hope of it, the promise of it. I don't want to move on to the moment where she says the name of some second-tier reality-show guy.

I put my palms on the bar, focusing on the cool veneer of the wood against my skin.

"Everyone wants this," she says. "It's killing you."

"Was it Jack?"

"It was."

I shudder involuntarily. "What can you tell me?"

"He was there alone. He was drinking a lot but didn't seem

drunk. Servers kept bringing over food but he didn't eat it. He took a phone call at one point." She stops to eat a cherry, her taffy-pink lipstick still in place.

"Was he . . . How was he?"

"I don't know. He was just there."

"So he's not in Colorado."

"Don't tell me you believed that one."

"It didn't feel right to me."

"You have good instincts," she says. "Better than the other guys."

"Thank you," I say. "Really, thank you."

She eats another cherry, the delicate Playboy bunny charm on her wrist catching the light. "Are you sure you're okay?"

"Yeah. No. I don't know. What was it like? Seeing him."

"Every time I see you, you ask about him. What is it? What's so special?"

I don't know how to describe his face on my parents' TV, on bus stop ads, in my mind each time I questioned as a teenager, an adult, what a man was supposed to be like. All the nights I closed my eyes and listened to his voice from a video on my phone, as if I'd called him and he'd picked up.

"He's Jack Whitlock," I say.

Sherry finishes her drink. She stirs the ice. "I don't know if that kind of magic works on me anymore." She looks at me sadly for a moment and then smiles again. "Walk me to valet?"

She takes my arm and we pass through the crowded bar, out into the chilled hotel lobby, and then through the heavy glass doors to the canopied valet. The driveway is made of polished black stone, a river at night. The young valet attendant looks at Sherry longingly as he delivers her pink car.

"Nice color," I say.

"It's what all the girls are driving these days."

From the driver's seat, she pulls a slip of paper from her bag and dangles it out the window. I take it. An *X*, written in drips of candle wax. A handwritten address.

"Don't lose that," Sherry says. "You'll need it when you get there."

She wiggles her fingers goodbye, rolls up the window, and drives away. Across the street, there he is again, on a billboard, looking directly at me.

I turn the slip of paper over in my hand, the waxy *X* warm and pliable against my thumb. *X* for eXit. The address is in Hollywood.

The world's most elite sex club, says Page Six.

A roving erotic theater, says the *Los Angeles Times*.

Invite-only, incredibly decadent, and maybe a brothel, says Vice.

The thing about eXit is that it's exclusive, but it is not a secret. This is the point, with places like eXit—it exists to be dangled in your face, to remind you each and every day that you cannot have it. Or perhaps you could, if you were more successful, more beautiful, more charismatic, more connected—more something. But you are not. You are not enough. So you can google it, watch the thirty-second promotional video for it, which features women in satin lingerie—so many you can't count them—crawling on the floor of a mansion toward a man who is not you.

The attendees are actors, producers, musicians, models,

politicians. NDAs at the door, no cameras, no cell phones allowed inside. I have never even gotten close.

There's no set location, but there is a website. A black page with a white serif font. An illustration of a hand being punctured with a key. A drop of blood—vaguely Catholic. A single word: *Curious?* You click it and it takes you to an application with a $750 fee. I start to calculate how much of my total net worth that is and then stop myself because I know the answer will remind me how dire things are. The application asks for income, occupation, references from at least three current eXit members. Three photos are required, *one face, one full body, one intimate*. Then a question, requiring a three-hundred-to-five-hundred-word answer: *What do you want?*

Application does not guarantee membership. Most people are refused. If admitted, a basic membership is twenty-five thousand dollars annually for men, free for women. There's a higher tier that grants you access to an ultra-exclusive sister club in Dubai.

I think of an employee at a high-end lingerie store who's been obsessed with eXit since helping someone famous pick out panties for it.

"I make most of my monthly commission in the days leading up to their events," she tells me when I call her. "Today is going to cover my share of the rent. You know, I once helped someone really, really famous find the perfect—"

"I know," I say, "but that's not who I'm calling about."

"It was a huge celebrity. I can't tell you who."

"You've told me before."

"I have? Well, whatever. There's nothing you can do with that information anyway. The people who run that place will straight-up murder you. I'm not kidding." Classical music, someone asking her a question. "I'm sorry, we don't carry that size," she tells someone. "Ben?"

"I'm here."

"Why are you asking about this?"

"No reason."

"Are you trying to get into tonight's event?"

I stare at the bleeding hand on the website. The application says that lack of response should be taken as a rejection. *Accepted members will be contacted in person.*

"You can't possibly be making enough money to afford a membership. And even if you are, you can't tell them what you do for a living. I guarantee everyone there hates you."

"I'm just gathering information," I say. "Happy to pay for it, as you know."

"Okay, okay. Here's something. A few months ago, I helped this singer shop for one of those events. Not exactly a household name, but pretty famous. You'd know her. It doesn't matter. I'm not going to say who. She'd been waiting to get her application approved for sixteen months. At a certain point, you've got to take the hint, right? She said she'd gotten something called a referral slip from a member and was going to plead her case in person. Said she was tired of auditioning. She *really* wanted in."

"A referral slip?"

"She showed it to me. It was a piece of paper with an *X* on it in red wax. It had the address of the party—or, I'm sorry, apparently they call it a soiree."

eXit welcomes attractive, intriguing guests on select occasions, the website reads.

"Thanks," I say. "This is helpful."

"It's not worth trying. I don't know what you're trying to do, but you can't do it. If you walk in there with your camera, they will, like, dismember you. Ritual sacrifice. Can you imagine an unseen mob of people monitoring your every move, torturing you with threats until you're so tired of living in a perpetual state of fear that you're almost begging them to get it over with?"

"Plenty of people want to hurt me."

"Then you should already know better," she says.

Almost immediately after she hangs up, my phone pings with a threatening email, as if underlining her point.

We're never going to forget you. We're going to destroy you.

A photo of the door to my apartment, the unit number clearly visible, a gloved hand on the door.

Subject line: *any day now*

I follow the rules.

I dress in all black and leave my camera at home. I call a cab and give the driver an address several streets away from the one on the slip of paper. We coast through the velvety night, past the glow of stores selling cigarettes, lottery tickets. It all seems prescient.

An alert on my phone. New leaked text messages. Jack and Sasha.

Send me a picture of your pussy

why

So I can lick it through the phone

"Jesus Christ, dude," I murmur, as if Jack is sitting beside me in the back seat. And for a moment, he is. What if it was just us, on the way to some party together? Would he try to explain himself? Would he shrug it off like, *Hey, man, you get it?* Or would he sit with me in comfortable silence?

I pay cash and tell the driver to keep the change.

"You sure?"

"Have a good night," I say.

Once, I brought an energy healer home from a bar. Her cousin was a director, but she wouldn't talk about him. *Good karma can be achieved through generosity*, she said. *Say it: If I am generous, good things will come.*

If I am generous good things will come if I am generous good things will come if I am generous good things will come.

I repeat the mantra to myself as I walk to the sex club. Each passing car is a threat, a prophet, a sign, or nothing at all.

The fluorescent center of Hollywood Boulevard, where tourists spill soda on Walk of Fame stars and buy *I Love LA* T-shirts, is a mile away, but it seems like a long way down from this neighborhood. Up here, it's cool and quiet. No sidewalks, no lights. I pass Spanish-style houses, smelling jasmine in the dark. Another turn, another hill, and then the final street dead-ends at the base of a narrow tower rising a hundred feet or so, like a misplaced section of castle. There's a door at the bottom and a man beside it with his arms at his sides, alert and waiting. I approach him like this is a reality I inhabit too and not a hallucination. I pull the slip of paper from my pocket, stop my hands from shaking just long enough to offer it to him, and he takes it, withdraws a gold key from inside his jacket, and unlocks the door, revealing an elevator. I get in.

It creaks as it rises, opening at the top to a pathway. I follow it through a garden of agave to a house where another man waits. He holds a black tray containing masks and I am guessing that a person who has been here before would take one, so I do.

"Indulge," he says, and opens the door.

I don't know if I'm early or late or right on time. This is the only party in Los Angeles where punctuality matters, I've heard, where you don't want to miss the show. The interior is dark, lit with red. Essential oils in the air—bergamot, orange, ylang-ylang. A hallway stretches toward an opening. I hear organ music. The silhouette of a horned figure appears, disappears. When I reach the other side of the hallway, a woman wearing only a garter approaches with a basket.

"Surrender your phone," she says, and when I hesitate, she adds, "It's easier to indulge, if you do." And then her smile falters. She looks at me very deliberately. "You have to."

I give her my phone and she withdraws a set of tarot cards from her garter. Her eyes are the eyes of a cat, wide and yellow in the dim red light. "Select a card."

I draw the Hanged Man.

"You are trapped," she says. "Stop struggling. The answer will come to you when it's time."

It's the card I have always drawn, every time a deck has been presented to me, but I don't tell her this.

"Go forth," she says. "You'll find others waiting to satisfy your needs."

In the room behind her, there's a collection of beautiful people, some sitting on furniture, others standing. A man in a wolf mask grazing a naked woman's torso lazily with his fingertips, like it's the surface of a lake. A man in a tuxedo giving head to another man in a tuxedo. A woman with a birdcage on her head touching herself. There's a mattress at the center of the room, but it is empty. Some people have dispensed of masks—*the choice to reveal your face is yours and yours alone*, the sign in the hallway said—and I recognize actors, talent agents, real estate moguls. I lean against a wall, looking for signs of Jack. Outside of the faces I can identify, it's difficult to tell who is a guest and who is staff. I've heard that sex workers get jobs at eXit as a way to find whales. In another room, there's a woman in a bunny mask being tied up by an anchor from CNN. He finishes with the knots and stands in front of her, touching himself. A couple approaches—a TV star and his wife—holding peacock feathers. "Oh, please tickle me," the woman in the bunny mask says. "I *love* to be tickled." They descend upon her with the feathers, teasing her inner thighs, her shoulders, the soles of her feet. She giggles, asks for more. I go to another room, where there's a California king bed draped in silk. A man and a woman fucking on one side, two girls taking turns going down on each other on the other. Both parties ignoring one another at first, and then merging, recoupling, recoupling again, until they're a tangle of bodies. In the hallway, men on all fours crawl toward a woman in a chair, rising to their feet one at a time and then urinating into her open mouth.

In the final room, a producer is gagged and whipped by a woman in pearls. The muscles on her back flex and release as she hits him. She looks at me, "You want a turn?" The producer's eyes bulge, communicating *yes yes yes*.

I shake my head. It's better not to speak, better to avoid someone recognizing my voice, that same voice that has begged for just one more shot, just turn around, just roll down the window, just be cool, please just be cool.

A line has already formed behind me, men and women eager to whip the producer, the same man whose housekeeper once told me about how he used to scream at his children, how his dog would shake and cower in his presence.

Back in the main room, I take a seat on a velvet couch, where a nepotism hire at a talent agency sips a whiskey on the rocks and tells me that at nineteen, he's the youngest member of this club. "My dad ponied up the money for the membership after I agreed to do the dumb internship."

I point to the empty mattress. "What's going to happen there?"

"Oh, you'll see."

A tall woman stalks the room, her underwear made of diamonds, her wrists dripping with gold bracelets. The words *fuck me* spelled out in what looks like blood on her breasts. A happy face painted on her stomach. Her black eyes watch me from behind a lace mask.

"You have to ask to touch," the nepotism hire tells me. "It's all about consent here. It's not like out there where you have to guess if it's okay and then you get in trouble for, like, hugging someone."

I stare at the red paint, thinking of the bleeding hand on the website.

"Can I touch you?" he asks the woman. She says yes, and a few minutes later, she's unzipping his pants and sliding down to her knees. As she takes him in her mouth she looks up at me with a trace of recognition before closing her eyes.

On the floor, there's a woman on all fours balancing glasses of whiskey on her back. I get up and take one. I find a new place to sit.

The music changes. It is slower and louder. A new woman enters the room. Everyone turns to look at her. She's wearing flesh-colored lingerie and a mask made of mirrors. She circles, stopping before each of us, one at a time. Slowly. She stands in front of me and waits, motioning for me to get up. When I do, her mirrored face is close to mine. I look into my own eyes, reflected in her. I can see how terrified I appear. I see the reflections of other people behind me, watching me watch myself. Any one of them could recognize me, could connect my fear to the things I've done.

Breathe in. Breathe out. Breathe in. Hold it.

Mercifully, she lets me go. She moves to the mattress. The crowd gathers. A man wearing wings is lowered from the ceiling. He lands and undresses her, pushes her down on the bed, climbs on top of her. He looks at himself reflected on her face when he fucks her, keeping his eyes open the whole time. She sounds like Ellory when she comes. I never thought I'd hear that again. My heart breaks and then hardens on instinct. For a moment, I'm sure I'm going to die.

The man with wings pulls out of her before he comes, finishes on her breasts just like porn, and then he reaches for a towel and cleans her tenderly, lovingly.

By this time, everyone around me is turned on, moving in on each other. No one approaches me. The woman in the mirrored mask stands, and it is then that I notice the tattoos on her hips. Roses.

Jack Whitlock's sidepiece, the TMZ story said.

Roses. Just like the photos from her deleted Instagram.

The Hanged Man in my pocket. *The answer will come to you when it's time.*

She takes off her heels and walks barefoot through the writhing bodies. I think of her surprised laughter in the video with the statue, the laconic tone of her last text message: why

I follow her out of the room, down the hall to the bedroom with the big mattress, which is now empty. The music is pulsating and she doesn't hear me. From the doorway, I watch her remove the mirrored mask. It's her face. I know it from the photos. Still naked, she opens a dresser drawer and finds a silk robe, puts it on. Her hair is dark and ropy with sweat.

"Excuse me," I say. She startles, turns.

Her face is bare. She looks younger, shorter. A face from a university lecture hall. I almost want to tell her never mind. But I know now why Sherry sent me here. I have to see where this leads. Sasha is not the end, but she is a means to it.

"You're lost," she tells me.

"No, I'm not."

"You should go back to the party. Were you not enjoying it?"

"There are parts of it I like," I say.

She moves toward me, feet in a straight line, an impression of how models on runways move. "You were watching me earlier."

"Everyone was watching you."

She puts a finger on my chest, and I imagine her touching him, being touched by him. She traces the center of my chest in a straight line and then stabs at me with her pointed nail—again I think of the key, the hand, the blood. "You like to watch," she says. "You like to watch more than most people do."

She slides her hands down my torso, asks if it's okay to keep touching me, and I say yes. I hear myself groan; I feel myself go hard. I am outside myself. To fuck her would be to feel what he has felt. What he feels.

"This club is not about sex," she says, pressing her mouth to my ear.

"It's not?"

Her fingers travel farther down my body.

"It's about a higher consciousness." She undoes my belt. I think of the texts, the photos, Jack's face in the movies. Her hand is around my dick. I'm him, I tell myself, being touched by her.

I close my eyes. "Tell me about him."

Her hand moves up and down. "About who?"

"Jack."

"What did you say?"

She lets go, backs away, pulling the robe tighter around herself.

"I didn't know you'd be here," I say. "I wasn't sure what to expect."

Fear in her eyes. She touches the mask on the bed as if she's considering putting it back on, slipping into the anonymous woman with the mirrored face. "Who are you?"

I put my hands up. "It's okay, it's okay. I'm not some crazy stalker or something."

"Get away from me." She makes her way to the door.

"Wait. I'm really not. I'm Ben. I'm . . . a photographer. I'm trying to get information about Jack Whitlock. I'm not trying to get information about you." I refasten my belt.

"Fuck," she says, slipping her feet into sandals.

"I'm not going to hurt you."

“Just . . . stay back.”

“Okay. I’m not moving. I’m not coming near you.”

“I don’t know anything about Jack Whitlock.” Her voice shakes.

“I know it’s you. Sasha.”

“I can’t talk about it. Get away from me. Who are you?”

“You’re scared. I get that. He probably had you sign something—”

“No, I didn’t sign anything. I just . . .” She puts her hands over her face, not speaking. “You let me touch you. Why did you do that?”

“If you could just give me something. I swear it won’t come back to you.”

“No.”

“Please.”

“Why would I ever do that? I don’t know how Kendra got it, how it got leaked. If there were other people who . . . and we were just . . . I was just . . .”

“I’ll leave you out of it. I’m only trying to get to him, I promise.”

“You’re a liar,” she says.

“Here,” I say. I reach for my mask and take it off. “This is what I look like. You’re right. I am a liar. You can see.”

I want to ask her what it is like, being with him. If he talks in his sleep, if he lies on his back or on his side.

“I’m supposed to be safe here,” she says.

“I’m sorry.”

“Is this what it’s going to be like now? Are people going to recognize me? Are people like you going to look for me?” She sits on the edge of the bed. “After it came out I went to the grocery store and bought cheese. Cheese. Fucking cheese. I don't . . . I don't even know why. I'm lactose intolerant. And I thought, is this it? Is this the last time I get to just go to the grocery store without being tied to this?"

"It'll pass."

"I can see how it looks that way to someone like you," she says.

"I think if I can get to him. Just him. If I can take photos of just him, talk to just him, that'll shift things away from you."

"I didn't want this," she keeps saying. "I didn't want this."

Down the hall, the moans and screams crescendo in unison. It is almost beautiful.

Sasha looks up at me. "I'm never going back to my life. Not the way it was before him."

I move closer to her but do not sit down next to her. "Would you really want to?"

"Fuck you. You don't know anything."

"Is he in Los Angeles right now?" I ask. "Can you at least tell me that?"

"I said *fuck you.*"

"He's not in Los Angeles?" I ask.

Her eyes are hard. "Pay me."

"And you'll tell me?"

"Maybe."

"How much?"

"Five hundred. To start."

I have enough to pay rent in my checking account, and that's it. But I can be late this month; I can pay those fees; I can risk it if she can lead me to him.

"Okay," I say.

She leaves the room and returns with the basket of phones. Every screen is lit up with a sea of text messages:

I love you

I miss you

I hate you

Come home

She pulls out her own and then watches me fish for mine. I transfer the money. Once it goes through, she says, "He was in town, but he's not anymore."

Down the hallway, a man grunts, telling another person, *Take it, take it, take it all.*

"Do I get another question?" I ask.

She taps her long nail to the screen of my phone. "Again."

Another five hundred.

"Did you meet him here?" I ask.

"Does it matter? I said he's not in Los Angeles. He's not here."

"I just want to know, I guess."

She laughs, that same laugh from the video. "Oh," she says. "I get it."

"Get what?"

"The way you feel about him."

"It's just my job," I say.

She looks at me with pity. "No, that's not true."

I don't say anything.

"Yes, I met him here." She wipes her nose. "He never fucked any of the other girls. That was what he said. He had only ever watched before. But he said he felt like he could trust me."

My heart pounds. I can't believe I'm hearing this. I have to sit down. I sit on the floor. She looks down at me. "We were together here. And other places after that. I took him to my apartment. You already know that from my old roommate's video. I can't live there anymore because of this."

"I'm sorry," I say.

She pats her cheeks with her hands. "Stop saying that. If you were sorry, you wouldn't have let me touch your dick. You wouldn't be here. You wouldn't be doing any of this."

"Where is he?" I ask.

"I don't ever want to see you here again," Sasha says. She begins braiding her long dark hair, unbraiding it. She picks up the mask, holds it up, looks at her own reflection in the mirror. She makes eye contact with herself, watching her own tears fall. "How much money do you have?"

"Not much."

"Get up. Show me."

I stand and pass her my phone. "Oh," she says. "You're not lying."

"I wasn't."

"I knew it wasn't just your job. If you were only doing it for the money, you'd have quit by now." She passes my phone back. "I want all of it."

"I gave you a thousand. Where is he?"

She says nothing. I send her the money.

I ask again, "Where is he?"

"At a friend's house."

"Where?"

"Palm Springs."

"Palm Springs," I repeat.

"I'm going to tell them you touched me," Sasha says. "After that, you can never come back."

"Okay."

"Right after I tell you the address, I'm going to scream that you touched me. They'll throw you out."

I nod. She says it. I say it back to her.

She moves closer. For a second, I think she's going to kiss me. But then she says, "I hope you never find him. I hope you ruin your life trying."

She spits in my face. And then she screams.

The doorman and four others just like him appear almost immediately. They pull me back to the hallway, and I can hear cries of pleasure all around me as they pummel me. They beat me until I can barely walk, toss me back out into the night. I crawl down the path on my hands and knees and then force myself to stand. This time, I know there will be no elevator ride. A stone staircase instead, and then another, and another. I stumble down the steps, falling and landing on the street. I repeat the address out loud as I run, all the way to the front desk of a chain motel, and when I enter I must be bleeding, because the teenager working there says, "Uh, should I call 911?" And I am still repeating the address and I say, "No, don't call 911. Give me a pen."

"Give me a pen," I say, and when he does I write the address on my arm, pressing so hard I draw blood.

Maybe I walk home. Maybe someone drives me. Maybe I descend the stairs at Hollywood and Highland and take the train—even though I never take the train—and stare at the bruised reflection of my face in the dirty window, thinking that I belong here, beneath the city.

And then I'm at my building, in the elevator, with no memory of pressing any buttons, but it takes me to my floor.

I see it from the hallway. The door to my apartment is propped open. My chest tightens, the air suddenly hot and thick and difficult to draw into my lungs.

Maybe it was a simple mistake. I left the door open. But I know, I know, deep down I *know*, I wouldn't do that, I have never done that.

The breathing exercises don't work. My heart pounds, my head hurts. Double vision, turning the single open doorway into two: one leading to the apartment I live in now and one leading to the apartment I can never go back to, not because it was taken from me but because I gave it up when I did what I did.

los angeles, two years
and four months earlier

chapter nineteen

Later, I will say I had no choice.

There is this pop singer, Mia Luna. She is having a party for her twenty-eighth birthday. A small restaurant inside a boutique hotel. Given that she rarely hosts or attends parties, this seems strange.

There is this feeling I get. It's an instinct I've developed. Is this what believing in a higher power is like? A whisper inside that tells you to go and you listen?

It's the easiest thing in the world, listening to that voice. And when I do, I can't hear the cries of paparazzi leaving the industry, leaving Los Angeles, broke and humiliated. I can only hear the voice that will one day lead me to Jack.

Mia Luna's public image is intensely calculated. Every song and music video and interview and brand partnership has the rehearsed quality of a decision made based on focus groups and data. When she appears in public, it is with a stylist, a publicist, or her mother. She does not write her own songs; therefore, there is no clue into her inner life. Her only political endorsement is a cheery reminder to vote.

She is kind and boring and I don't care about her at all, but millions of people do and I can sense that, I can feel the money materializing in my bank account like gray-scale text becoming black. This faith is a mathematical certainty. It is something I've tapped into, the ability to know what leads to follow, where I need to be.

This, I know, is what will one day lead me to him.

I have papped Mia Luna before in very controlled settings. Inoffensive outings designed to make headlines (*At the 7th Annual Jingle Bells Home for the Holidays Concert Presented by EnergyLyfe Mineral Water, Mia Luna brought one lucky fan onstage . . . click here for the heartwarming pics!).* Mia Luna is known for being gracious to paparazzi, waving at us before she disappears into a waiting car, remembering our names, asking about our families, girlfriends, dogs, summer plans. At a breast cancer gala, she smiled at me and said, *Good to see you.*

All her features communicate warmth and relatability. Pretty but not so pretty that you feel overwhelmed with jealousy, desire. The freckled skin (*Mia Luna is the ultimate girl next door in makeup-free photos*), the jeans and T-shirt wardrobe (*Mia Luna steps out in a look you can *actually* afford!).* Her estimated net worth is $300 million, but you can imagine running into her at Target, in the candle aisle.

"I'm going to find a way to take pictures at that party," I tell Ellory.

We're at a Thai restaurant on Sunset, eating green curry at an orange table. Ellory is in shorts, the bruise on her thigh faded to vomit yellow, the puncture wounds silver-white scars.

"You shouldn't mess with her fans," Ellory says. "You know why they call themselves Lunatics, right?"

"It's just a cute nickname they came up with."

"I don't know about that." A bus roars by and she follows it with her eyes. She hasn't worked since the accident, not in Los Angeles, not in Las Vegas. Driving, bicycling, walking—it all hurts. *It's okay*, I told her when she realized how long it would take to feel better. *Take all the time you need. I can cover rent. And in Los Angeles that's really saying something.*

Uh-huh, she said. *That's really saying something.*

"There has to be something Mia Luna is hiding," I say.

"I think she's probably just not that interesting," Ellory says distantly. The sun crouches below the buildings.

"How can you be boring and have crazy fans?" I ask.

She leans back in her chair, folds her arms. "I don't know. You're the expert."

"I hear she left a waiter at the Cheesecake Factory a thousand-dollar tip last week."

"So she's nice. And she eats at chain restaurants."

"Maybe that's an intentional choice. Part of an artificially constructed—"

"Can we talk about something else?" she asks, but when I say sure, pick a topic, she goes silent.

How hard would it be, I wonder, to get into that party?

"Pretty hard," a bartender at the venue tells me when I ask. "And I like my job, so don't bother asking me to help with this."

"How much do you like it?"

She scoffs at the question, but eventually, I do find her price. The next day, she tells me where security will be stationed, about a gap between the bushes and the wall by the pool.

Sometimes, she says, staff use this gap as a shortcut to the street where they take their smoke breaks. That's how she knows. I ask her to describe it again, trying to visualize it.

I explain to Ellory that I won't technically be on the property, so nothing illegal, nothing bad. It's a hotel anyway, I say. It's not like it's someone's house. I put on my black hoodie, my new sneakers. It's 9 p.m. and Ellory is already in bed, her eyes closed. I sit on the edge of the mattress, wanting, suddenly, for her to come with me. But that's not possible.

"Maybe this weekend we can drive to Joshua Tree," I say. "Go for a hike."

"Okay," she says.

"Or the Eastern Sierra. Get up into the mountains."

"Don't you need cell service?"

I wait. For what, I don't know. For her to touch me, I guess. I wish she'd touch me, but she doesn't. And I can tell she doesn't want me to touch her.

On my way out, she asks me to turn the lights off. I close the door silently, like she's already asleep.

I park at the bottom of the hill and walk up. The boutique hotel is isolated, tucked away in a residential neighborhood. It looks just like a house. The bartender's directions are accurate, and I'm able to find the place where the bushes meet the gate. The restaurant's patio backs up against a pool with an artificial waterfall. Star-shaped pendant lights hang on wires. There are a few bungalows, which I think are vacant, but their curtains are drawn, making it impossible to tell. Candles flicker on the stone terrace and lilies bob on the surface of the water. There is a small group gathered—people I recognize from Mia Luna's Instagram—but there is no sign of her. I take my camera out of my backpack and wait.

The people at the edge of the pool wear summer colors and drink white wine. I can't hear what they're saying, but I can feel the tone of their conversation, which is soft and ordinary. A lesser paparazzo might think this scene is the whole story, but that's not me.

I'm crouched between the bushes and the wall, my legs shaking from holding the position. There is an actual ache in my chest, a bruise that appears when I think of Ellory. What would I be doing if I had stayed home with her? If I had taken a few days off? If I had meant it when I suggested the mountains? We could be driving there now. We could get there after midnight, rumble onto some dirt road. We could camp among the boulders. We could climb a mountain at sunrise.

There is a crevice growing between us. An earthquake fault line threatening destruction.

I'm thinking about applying to grad school, Ellory said in bed the other night.

For what? I asked. *I've never heard you mention grad school before.*

I'm just thinking about it, she said. And when I asked if she meant in Los Angeles, she said nothing.

A waiter appears carrying a white slab of granite. Through my camera, I see water chestnuts and radishes.

And then the small crowd parts, and there is Mia Luna. She's dressed in silk and smiling warmly. Shimmer on her cheekbones catches the light. A woman with blunt black bangs and a septum piercing, whom I recognize as her childhood best friend turned assistant, hands her a glass of wine. A different waiter passes through the small crowd with a bottle, refilling glasses. Mia Luna makes a toast, smiling, tears in her eyes. What is special about this night? This birthday? Her voice is low and honeyed and I try to read her lips, but all I can pick up is *this year has meant a lot to me*.

Something tells me that the moment—*some* moment—is imminent.

When Mia Luna finishes speaking, the others raise their glasses and drink. A few models, a child actor, her mother, her sister, her stylist, her manager. Mia Luna finishes her wine and taps the side of her glass, indicating to her assistant that she is going to get another. The assistant follows her. But instead of going to the table where there are bottles chilling on ice, they make their way toward me. I crouch down even lower, knees in the dirt, the scent of the plant life around me familiar, but I can't place it. I watch them through the lens of my camera. I do not put it down for a second. My hands are sweaty like I'm on the summit of a mountain, discovering I'm too high, too exposed. The assistant opens up her purse and looks inside. I hold my breath, waiting for the drugs to come out. But the assistant merely withdraws a phone, as if to check a text. Mia Luna looks at the flowers, the pool, the sky. She is looking right at me but she doesn't know it. No one knows I'm here. No one but the bartender who isn't working tonight, who seemed so disgusted with herself for giving me any information at all. No one but Ellory, who would perhaps also like to forget.

And there it is: That whispered intuition in me goes wild with *nownownownownow* and the assistant reaches for Mia

Luna, cupping her heart-shaped face in her hands and kissing her. Both of their eyes are closed as they hold each other and press their mouths together. Mia Luna kisses the assistant's cheeks, her neck, her collarbones. The assistant leans back, mouth slightly open, her eyes closed, her face catching the moonlight. And it's this. This is what I was waiting for. I'm getting all of it. I'm taking photo after photo of them kissing, their hands clasped, their foreheads together.

And then I'm gone. I get out of there, tripping down the hill, my chest heaving. In the darkness of my car, I look at the photos. They are perfect.

Ellory is still awake when I get home, watching a documentary about insects on her laptop. *They consume everything in sight before moving on to a new habitat*, a deep voice says. *Meet* Melanoplus devastator. *The devastating grasshopper.*

"She's gay," I say breathlessly.

Ellory looks up. The documentary keeps playing. The sound of buzzing in the sky.

"Mia Luna is gay," I tell her. "She was kissing her assistant. Like, they were really kissing. Fuck, I think they might be a couple. Maybe they've been a couple for a while. Maybe for this whole time? Even though she's had boyfriends. She's always had boyfriends. But I think she's gay." I pace back and forth. I can't believe my luck.

Ellory meets my eyes. "What did you do?"

"What?"

"What will you do?"

"I'm going to call the photo agency."

In the antique mirror by the bed, I see my skin, beaded with sweat, my smile, wide and crazy.

"Let's go on a trip," I say. "I mean it. For the weekend. With this money, we could—"

"You would be outing her, you realize," Ellory says. I take my camera out. I sit down on the bed to show her the photos. She says, "I don't want to see them."

"People are more accepting than they used to be. It's not a big deal."

"It must be a big deal," Ellory says. "It must be a big fucking deal because you are so excited. It must be a big deal, because you're going to get paid."

"This is how I make money. I don't have a choice."

"Bullshit."

"Ellory, I'm doing this for both of us."

"No," she says. "You're doing this for you. I thought you wanted to be a photographer."

I hold up the camera. "I am a photographer."

"You know it's not about the art or the quality of the photos when they're of someone famous. It doesn't matter if they're good."

"So, what? You're saying I'm a bad photographer?"

The buzzing of the insects on the screen gets louder. "Can you turn that off?" I ask, but she doesn't. "I don't want us to fight. I'm going to the other room."

In the kitchen, I pour a splash of vodka into a glass. Through the window, the city sparkles in celebration. I take out my phone to make the call.

Ellory appears in the doorway in a white tank top and black underwear, arms crossed. Her voice is soft. "Think about what you're doing. Even if you don't care about what happens to her, you should think about her fans. They're really, really intense, Ben. They'll come after you."

The vodka is cold and good. "It'll be okay," I say.

"Sit with it for a minute. Really think about the gravity of this."

I try to, but all I can feel is joy. "It's going to be a good thing, I promise."

She puts up her hands, turns, and goes back into the bedroom. The light turns off.

I don't know why, but I text Eddie. **I took some photos tonight of someone and they're going to be a big deal**

Maybe I send that message to the version of him who told me to come to Los Angeles, to do this. The Eddie from that night would care, would be happy for me, would say it's okay to do what I'm doing, it's part of the job, actually it's a good thing, a victory. Or maybe I just want to talk to someone. Anyone. I set the phone on the counter.

It buzzes: **who was it?**

Mia Luna, I tell him.

interesting, he says, and I read the word about a hundred different ways. He's being sarcastic, polite, patronizing. He knows something, the same thing that I now know. He got there first somehow.

But when I call the photo agency, it's news to them too. I close my eyes and smile.

After I hang up, I go to bed and hold Ellory. I tell her about the money, not just this money but the promise of more money. I talk about paying off her student loans, a vacation to Hawaii, a house.

I want to do it again. I want to feel that terror and elation.

"I can't believe you did that," she says. This is what her voice sounds like when she's talking to someone she doesn't like.

When the money hits my account, I tell her it's all for us. "It's ours. And I swear I'll never do anything like that again."

"It's yours," she says.

The photos are everywhere. First, there are the celebrity gossip websites and magazines with varying degrees of respectability. *MIA LUNA GAY LOVE AFFAIR REVEALED*. Next, the legacy media publications. *The Ultra-Private Pop Star and the Assistant*. Then there are her fans, who swirl tornado-like on the internet with usernames like lunatic_forever, assembling into a singular organism with a singular goal: find the person who took these pictures.

A well-known pop culture blog does it for them. Headline: *Here's the Guy Who Outed Mia Luna*

Ellory sits cross-legged on the bed with her laptop, not blinking. When she looks at me, I can tell she's read it.

My full name in the second line of the article. A photo of me that I can't place at first, smiling uncomfortably in jeans and a white T-shirt, holding a brand of beer I don't like, other arm at my side, too straight like I didn't know what to do with it, like I still don't.

The photo is cropped. There were other people in it but they weren't standing with me. A party at an apartment with sand-colored carpet and white walls. Just like every stucco apartment in Las Vegas. A party, I remember it now, for someone's last day of work. Eddie.

I go outside to make the call. Straight to voicemail. "Eddie, I know it was you. Why did you do this?"

I read his last text again: **interesting**

I call him four, five, six more times, as if that could change anything. My shirt is soaked with sweat, pressure gathering in my temples, sun in my eyes like the headlights of a car that's going to hit me.

I leave another voicemail. "What did I do to you, huh? That's right. Nothing. I've never done anything to you and you do this. It's so stupid that you would do this. It doesn't make sense. We're from the same city. We worked at the same restaurant. You were supposed to be cool to me. But you act like you don't even know me and now this." I'm half laughing, half crying, and I know he's going to play the message for whoever he's with, so I try to think of something tough to say, but I can't, so I just hang up.

The door opens behind me.

"Who are you talking to?" Ellory asks.

I sit down on the front step and put my head in my hands. "Eddie," I say, too exhausted to lie.

She sits down next to me. "Vegas Eddie?"

"I can explain."

"Ben," she says, her voice quiet like she's going to comfort me. "It's all over the internet now."

The next part happens fast.

Soon, every social media account I have is flooded with comments and messages.

ur evil

Piece of shit paparazzi!!!!!

everyone hates you

Moon emoji after moon emoji, metastasizing into a viral hashtag: #breakhiscamera

The next day, a woman grabs it out of my hands and starts sprinting. I buy a new one and two men push me onto the sidewalk, take it from me, throw it to the ground, and stomp on it. The third ends up at the bottom of a pool. I know this because I am repeatedly tagged in the video of it sinking into the water.

"You should hang back for a minute," a paparazzo tells me. "Unless you want to keep replacing your camera every time they destroy it."

"You're jealous," I say.

"Of the money, yeah. But not of how fucked up your life is going to be now."

Then emails, text messages, phone calls. More threats. Specific details about my life. I change my phone number, but they find the new one.

Go back to waiting tables in Vegas, loser.

BEN WE KNOW YOUR ADDRESS

It's not long before they find Ellory.

cant believe you have a girlfriend . . . does she know what a bad person you are?

Each photo on Ellory's Instagram contains an endless scroll of strangers demanding she break up with me. She says nothing about this. One morning when she's in the shower, her phone chimes with a text message. Her mother, asking **what on earth**

is going on with all of these comments on your Instagram honey. And then a message from one of her old roommates: **heard about Ben, what the fuck.**

We keep our phones on silent at night; otherwise the calls and texts would make it impossible to sleep. But I can't sleep anyway, and I can tell she is only pretending to. I pace the kitchen and living room, lifting the blinds and looking out into the darkness. I go back to bed and try to spoon her. She's so stiff I think for a moment she's dead, that maybe they—whoever they are—have poisoned her or something.

"Are you awake?" I ask, shaking her by her shoulder.

She turns onto her stomach.

"We should talk about it," I say.

She shifts even farther from me. "We did."

There is the feeling that soon there will be a knock at the door, and then one night there is a knock at the door, and human shit on the doormat, the one with peonies on it that Ellory bought from a boutique in Highland Park. She throws it away. We don't replace it.

Our mailbox fills with drawings of moons. Someone approaches Ellory at the laundromat, tells her she must be as bad as me, because how else could she be with me? After that, we don't leave the house for a while. We cook food but don't eat it. She takes phone calls in the bedroom with the door closed. I check my bank account again and again, looking at the number. It comforts me. It seems to imply that this was worth something.

I ask our landlord to change the locks.

"There was a break-in," I tell him.

"Oh yeah? What was stolen?"

"I just need you to change the locks. Please."

"I'll consider it," he says.

"What the fuck? Why can't you just do it?"

"I said I'll consider it."

I buy a little white box that lights up red and beeps when it senses motion. I mount a camera outside and the next day it's gone.

I text Eddie: **if something happens to me, it's on you**

After ten days of isolation, Ellory says, "I can't be in here anymore. I'm going to the farmers' market."

"That's a good idea. I'll come with you."

"I don't know."

"Please," I say. "Let's have a normal day."

"I think we're past that. But fine."

She puts a green dress on and gets a tote bag from the closet, this one bearing the name of a bookstore in Las Vegas. I triple-check the locks on our way out. Mercifully, there is no one on the sidewalk waiting. It could be dying down, I think, but I don't say it, because the last note in the mailbox said *this is never going to stop*.

It's late morning, and the magnolia trees all have white flowers.

"I've never noticed that before," I say.

"Pretty," Ellory responds, and it's the nicest thing she's said to me since the photo. Her voice is flat when she adds, "You should take a picture."

Our sandals slap the pavement as we make our way down the hill. The farmers' market is busy. People fill wicker baskets with leafy greens, sample pear juice from a local orchard. Somewhere, a banjo is playing.

"Remember that time we made a whole dinner with stuff

from the farmers' market?" I ask. "You want to do that again?" I feel like an absentee parent, overdoing a birthday after several months away.

"Okay," she says.

"Yeah?"

"Yeah."

We fill the tote bag with French bread, radicchio, heirloom tomatoes, peaches, feta. I pay for everything. At home, I make the meal. I'm so transactional it's transparent.

I put my hand on hers at the little dinner table, the one we only just bought, which feels too late now. "Hey," I say. "I'm sorry. Ellory. I'm so sorry."

She nods.

We finish eating. She starts to clear the plates and I stand, following her to the kitchen.

"Let me do the dishes," I say.

"No. I'm going to do them."

She runs the water, and I put my hands on her waist from behind. I kiss the back of her head. I feel like crying, but I don't let myself, because I know she'd see it as a ploy for sympathy. And maybe it would be. Even I don't know. Does she still love me? Has anyone ever?

She pauses, as if she's waiting for me to say something. When I don't, she says, "I can't wash the dishes with your arms around me."

She goes to bed without me. I stay up, watching TV in the dark.

It's late, but I call the landlord anyway. "Are you going to change the locks or not?"

"That's not in my budget," he says.

"I'll pay for it."

"If you're so uncomfortable, you should just move."

"I said I'll pay for it."

"From what I've heard, it sounds like you brought this problem on yourself."

"You know what? Fuck you."

The local news asks, *Have paparazzi gone too far?* There is that picture of me again, and I wonder, just for a second, if Jack Whitlock is watching, if he sees me.

chapter twenty

In *Backcountry*, Jack Whitlock is the head of a tiger-poaching operation in India. When his girlfriend finds out, she leaves him immediately.

How could you do this, the girlfriend says, pulling coats from a closet. *How could you keep this from me?*

I love you, he says. *No matter what, I'm the man who loves you.*

She wipes her tears with the back of her hand. *You're a stranger to me now.*

It is a perfect Tuesday in Hollywood, and the theater is almost empty. Smell of popcorn in the dark, gold sunburst on the ceiling. Everyone in Los Angeles is sitting on some patio somewhere, talking about going to the beach but not actually going to the beach. My phone buzzes with death threats. I turn it off. On the big screen, tigers flex their claws and bare their teeth, their fur so orange and smooth I want to put my bare feet on it, wear it, run my hands over it. I want what Jack's character wants, even if he is the bad guy.

When I get home, Ellory tells me, "I don't feel safe here."

"Did something happen today?"

"Nothing that hasn't happened before."

"It has to stop eventually," I say. "It's only been three weeks."

She looks up at the ceiling. "I can't live here anymore."

"You're right," I say. "I've been thinking it too. We should move."

She reaches for my hand, which is a surprise. "That wouldn't be enough."

"Yes, it would. We can move to a completely different neighborhood, a completely different part of the city. Maybe even the Westside. Live by the ocean."

"Ben," she says, "I have to go back to Las Vegas."

"No," I say. "This is all going to go away. And Los Angeles is enormous. We can find somewhere to live. Somewhere with a doorman and better security."

"I'm sorry, but I have to go."

"What if I made some sort of public apology? Maybe that would make things better."

"You don't have to do that."

"But I could."

"You're not hearing me," she says, but her voice isn't angry.

"This is just a shitty excuse," I say. "You've been looking for a reason to go and now you've got one."

She doesn't deny it.

I kneel in front of her. I put my head on her lap. "Please."

She puts her fingers in my hair. Her touch is comforting but vacant.

Her face is bare and she hasn't been crying. She looks so calm, sitting on the couch. I know that's what I'm going to remember, how calm she looked.

* * *

She begins separating her items from mine. She offers me the plants, the plates, the bookshelf.

"Take it all," I say, again and again.

"You bought most of this."

"For us."

What I don't say is that I'm going to discard everything she leaves behind, everything that smells like her, looks like her, feels like her. I will buy new things.

"Where are you going to live in Las Vegas?" I ask.

"The same place. My roommates never rented out that room."

"I guess they knew."

"Knew what?"

"That you'd hate it here. That you'd hate being with me."

She looks up from the floor where she's sitting. Her voice is soft. "I didn't hate it."

"Yeah, right."

"I gave it a chance."

"Barely."

She stands and faces me. "Despite what you may think, you did not force me to move here. I did it because I wanted to. You project so much onto me out of your own insecurity. I do not hate LA. I hate that you hurt a total stranger and feel no remorse."

She spends the rest of the day packing in silence. My DMs on social media are filled with messages from accounts like Mia's Angel and xoxoLUNATIC telling me to kill myself.

I text Eddie: **you didn't even consider the repercussions did you**

Ellory and I continue to share a bed and eat meals together. We go to a concert we bought tickets to months earlier.

On her last night in Los Angeles, we walk to an Italian restaurant and order a bottle of wine. We drink it too fast. The pasta tastes like lemon and nothing else. Our server doesn't offer a dessert menu; there is a line at the door and she needs our table for someone else. On the walk back to the apartment, the city is as blue and beautiful as ever.

"I could come to Las Vegas and see you," I say. "We could try to make it work living in two different places."

"Ben."

"What? Is it so dangerous to just be associated with me?"

A text from a cocktail server, telling me about an actor who just sat in her section.

"What is it?" Ellory asks, looking at me looking at my phone.

"Nothing."

"At this point, why lie?" she says. There's no malice in her voice.

I stop and face her. "I would have done anything to keep you safe. A gated neighborhood, thousands of dollars on a security system. I would bankrupt myself hiring you your own personal bodyguard. Anything."

"I know that."

"So tell me it's not about that, then. Tell me safety has nothing to do with it."

"Ben. Stop."

"Tell me that it's me."

We look at each other in the city light, both of us just breathing.

"You're right," she finally says.

"What if I hadn't sold the photo?"

"I don't want to get into hypotheticals."

"But what if?"

"Then there would have been something else," she says.

"Please," I say. "Please don't go."

When we get to the apartment, she hesitates at the threshold. I unlock the door and turn on the light and it looks bare, so bare. The potted succulents are still on the windowsill, but only because they do better in this climate. I'm going to leave them for the next tenant.

We sit on the couch and drink the last bottle of wine in the apartment. When it's gone, we find ourselves on the floor, taking off each other's clothes.

"Let's go to the bedroom," I say.

She shakes her head. And I know she's never going to sleep there again. My jeans are still partway on when we have sex, our foreheads pressed together, neither one of us saying anything. I want to make her come again and again. I need to fill up on that sound. But she can't get there at all. Not tonight, not ever again with me.

I fall asleep with the cool laminate against my skin. I wake up alone.

A few hours later, I join a crowd of paparazzi outside a restaurant. We elbow one another, jostling for the best angle of the beautiful couple eating brunch.

I am heartsick, hungover, but I get the shot.

After she's gone, an email from the Forest Service arrives, sandwiched between messages from strangers containing photos of my car.

Months earlier, Ellory applied for a permit to climb Mount

Whitney, the tallest mountain in the lower forty-eight. She wanted to do it together. *I really can't be out of cell service*, I said at the time. *But maybe*.

The email contains a permit for July.

I text Ellory: **Did you see the Whitney permit email? We could still do it together if you wanted.**

The dots indicating she's typing, then nothing. A few days of silence and then: **I think it's better if we don't talk.**

I keep the permit because it is all I have left of her.

On her Instagram, she posts a photo from the dressing room of Giggle Water. A vanity mirror framed by soft yellow light bulbs. Her reflection, applying red lipstick. Caption: *home again*

I type *this is cruel* and start to delete it but instead leave it as a comment.

I train at the gym, walking on the treadmill at an incline until I can barely stand. I could build the same muscles climbing the hills in Echo Park, walking up the 32 percent grade on Baxter Street again and again, but every stranger in the neighborhood seems to recognize me and every scent in the passing wind reminds me of Ellory.

She posts a photo from a venue I don't recognize in a pink feathered outfit I've never seen before.

Where is this, I write.

And then I find myself going backward on her feed, like I used to when she would go to Las Vegas for the weekend, liking and commenting on old posts.

One of her roommates messages me: *stop being a creep*

I text Ellory: **super mature of you to have your roommate communicating for you**

And then: **sorry I just really miss you and i'm just really hurt**

I buy a Mount Whitney guidebook and read it, checking Ellory's Instagram in between chapters, liking and unliking posts.

She texts me: **Ben, I'm going to have to block you if you keep doing this.**

I call her and she doesn't answer.

I text her: **I don't understand why we can't talk**

She blocks me.

I get drunk and delete all my social media accounts.

I create a fake one with a fake name and a fake picture. It's just for work. It's just so these Mia Luna fans leave me alone.

When the time comes, I drive to the Eastern Sierra and camp at the trailhead. No cell service. For once, I am grateful for it. No voicemail recordings of Mia Luna's songs, no texts telling me I deserve to die in a fire. Outside my tent, black bears as docile as labradors approach, retreat, approach, retreat. At night, I can hear them huffing in the alpine air.

I really miss her.

The guidebook calls for hikers to be on the trail before daybreak. Hiking in the dark, the author says, is *an inner voyage*.

Early on the trail, I see the silhouette of Jack Whitlock, a specter haunting the trees, a god pretending to be an ordinary hiker.

Now that Ellory is gone, he is all I have left.

My body doesn't count the predawn miles. I don't exist until the sun comes up, touching my skin long after it has touched the ocean, the city, the Echo Park apartment I'll be leaving soon, the new one in West Hollywood I haven't moved into yet. *Furnished units available*, the sign outside the leasing office said. It is what I want: a sterile, gray, one-bedroom life I can fit myself inside. The rent is high, but I have the money—for now at least. I don't think about the future.

The sky is blue when I reach the switchbacks above Consultation Lake. I am moving slower than I want to, drawing the thin air into my lungs. It doesn't fill me up. The talus at Trail Crest is glazed with ice. I hold tight to the cables and traverse the spine of the mountain, picking my way across slabs of granite, and when I am above fourteen thousand feet, I crouch down and try to vomit, but nothing comes out. My brain swells in my skull. My limbs are numb. I grab a handful of unsalted pretzels from my backpack and force myself to chew, to swallow the tasteless mush. The guidebook said it might be this bad, but I can't accept it.

When I reach the top, there are three other hikers there. They wave their trekking poles at me and cheer, *Woooo, you did it.*

We are so lucky to have such perfect weather, they say. *No afternoon thunderstorms today.*

California, our benevolent, cloudless god.

The other hikers grin at me and talk about this big accomplishment, the highest thing in the Golden State. They are delirious with joy. *Come sit with us*, they say, *you're all alone.*

I stay on the summit for five minutes. I take one picture.

Weeks later, at my new apartment in West Hollywood, I find the image sandwiched between two separate photo sets of the same famous siblings. Pinnacles and spines and endless ridgelines of ancient mountains. Clear views into the Owens Valley, the White Mountains on the other side. The ghost playa where a lake used to be before William Mulholland, architect of the Los Angeles Aqueduct, said, *There it is, take it*, and did exactly that, just as I have done, just as I will do.

chapter twenty-one

I meet the aura photographer at a bar in Koreatown. An event for the public. A rarity. She usually caters to high-end clients. *A gift to the community*, the flyer read, *$89.75 includes a one-on-one aura photography session, an interpretation, a photo to take home, and a signature cocktail that coincides with the colors of your unique electromagnetic field.*

She leads me by my hand to the back room, looking back at me in the twilight of the bar to say how sorry she is.

"For what?" I ask.

"You don't need me to tell you."

She instructs me to sit on a stool. The room is empty. "Your aura can only be captured in a dark room," she says. She takes out an old Polaroid camera from the eighties. A real one from before everyone started buying them at Urban Outfitters.

"Is that a Supercolor 635CL?" I ask.

The aura photographer nods. "You can look at it for as long as you like, but I know that's not why you're here."

"So you know why I'm here," I say.

"Yes."

"Anything you could tell me about your clients would be—"

"Place your hands on the sensors."

"I can pay you for—"

"Please. Your hands. Just lightly, rest them here."

I do. The sensor is cold and metal.

"Are you ready?" she asks. She holds up the camera.

"I'm not used to being on this end of it."

"Relax."

The camera flashes.

She holds the photo as the image materializes, waiting patiently and not speaking. When it finishes, she does not react; she just hands it to me, intentionally not making eye contact. The composition is beautiful. Me, surrounded by a void. I am wearing a black shirt, per the email confirmation's suggestion, and my face is floating in the center of the photograph, flattened by the flash. On the aura photographer's Instagram page, there was post after post of photos like mine, but each one contained a kaleidoscope of colors. Some burned orange and pink; others glowed purple or turquoise. Some contained famous faces. Others just beautiful hopefuls.

I tap the photo. "Mine doesn't have any color. How'd you do that?"

"It's nothing I did," she says.

"The ad said something about an interpretation?"

"I have another appointment. And you don't really care about an interpretation anyway." Before, her voice was a meditation app. Now it is a DMV employee, a TSA agent.

"I paid you," I say. "You're supposed to tell me what it means." I hold up the photo, forcing her to look at it.

"It's obvious," she says. "You don't have an aura."

"So take another picture."

"No."

"Why don't I have an aura?"

She takes out a bottle of hand sanitizer and rubs it on her palms, cleansing herself of me. Her eyes flicker up. "It's something you've done. Something you do."

"I'll pay for another appointment, another photo," I say.

"Money won't change it," she says, and waves me away.

I throw the photo away. I walk until I'm not shaking, until I'm at a grocery store in Laurel Canyon. People in Los Angeles lovingly refer to it as *the country store*, which sounds folksy and wholesome. Like the kind of place with a wooden porch and a barrel of pickles. Big amethyst chunks of rock candy on a stick, the same kind I used to crush and scatter on hiking trails as a kid, believing I could trick people into thinking they'd found gemstones in the desert.

But the country store does not have rocking chairs and Vermont cheddar wrapped in cellophane. It is bright and clean and stocked with water-lily-seed granola, parsley matcha powder, and twelve different types of nondairy yogurt. There is an entire aisle of small-batch sea moss in different colors. I pick up a jar, surprised by the weight of it. The sea moss is bright blue and sourced from the Caribbean. *The sea moss inside this jar is still alive*, the label says. *Consume within a month.*

Yesterday, I found myself at a park I'd never been to before. In the shade of an oak tree, a small group of Hare Krishnas chanted in a circle. I sat on a bench and watched them for a while, until one of them stood and approached me. He was bald, the crown of his head pink with the start of a sunburn. He said his name was Nabendu. *The chanting cleanses you*, he said. And then: *Have a meal with us. Krishna tells us that when we eat, we consume the consciousness of those who prepare our food.* I stood, told him I had somewhere to be. I sat in traffic after that, thinking about the uni I'd eaten while surreptitiously photographing a model at Sushi Park, the meals I made for myself, the takeout I ordered, all the things I would consume alone.

I buy the sea moss. Benefits, the label says, include cleaner blood, fewer colds, and protection from radiation poisoning.

"This is the best brand of sea moss," the cashier says, and this feels good, this nod to the fact that I am performing the part correctly, doing what everyone else here is doing, buying this expensive, obscure product and believing in its impossible promises.

"I love it," I tell her.

She has gold bracelets on her wrists and she makes deliberate eye contact, and when I ask her if she wants to come over to my new apartment she says yes. And I don't even know why I fuck her. I guess I am single now and I am young and I am decent-looking and it's what I'm supposed to do. But the choreography I know is paired with a partner who isn't here anymore. The cashier from the country store doesn't lift up her hips when I unbutton her jeans like Ellory did. When I kiss her neck she turns away, says, *Don't do that, it tickles*. She doesn't want to get on top, wants to be on her stomach. She smells like the country store smells, which unsettles me, makes me feel like I'm fucking the country store. I think of more lost choreography: taking the 101 to Echo Park, reaching for a hand to hold. *Come on my back*, the cashier from the country store says. There is something like Vaseline on her lips and she gets it all over my new sheets when she is pressed face down on the mattress. She gets dressed as soon as we're done, takes a nectarine from the fridge, and leaves. There were so many things I could have asked her, I realize, about the rich and famous clientele who shop at the country store. About Jack Whitlock, even.

There is an oily imprint of her mouth on the bed that I can't get out no matter how hard I scrub.

No more relationships, I decide—not even casual ones—where there is nothing to be gained.

On Instagram, Ellory performs at Giggle Water. She is draped in silk. She is dusted with glitter. She is smiling. And then she is doing karaoke with her friends. She is hiking at Red Rock with a dog I do not recognize.

On TV, Jack Whitlock accepts an award. "The moment I stepped onto the set of this movie, I found a home. But there's someone in this room who was an even bigger champion of this film than I was." The camera cuts to his wife, standing in a pale blue gown with her hands clasped at her chest, pear-shaped diamond ring sparkling. "Jessica, honey," Jack says. "You read this script and told me to take the role. Without your instincts and your love, I am nothing. And it is you and our daughter who make me everything. Thank you. I love you."

A text message from an unknown number: **you're going to die alone.**

The jacaranda trees are blooming, blanketing sidewalks and parked cars with purple, and everywhere I go I'm brushing petals off my shoulders. This feels like a special kind of Los Angeles magic, and it would be so nice to share it with someone else. I pass a long line outside a Korean coffee shop and overhear someone say, *This is a good jacaranda season.* Later, I repeat this to a bartender, and she says, *Okay, did you want to order something . . . ?* At home, I peel crushed flowers from the soles of my sneakers. The blossoms are gummy and brown, unrecognizable.

I tell myself it's better being on my own. Sometimes, I believe my own lie. I can watch the celebrity news without feeling like it's the kind of hard-core pornography you'd switch off at the sound of keys in the door. Though the truth is, she never judged me for watching celebrity news.

Still, every time there is a call or a text or a handwritten note telling me *we haven't forgotten what you did*, every time there is a stranger waiting to get buzzed into my apartment building, I am glad there is no one but me at risk. It isn't safe for anyone to be in a relationship with me.

I text Eddie. **i still want an explanation**

When I see him, he is waiting in the same places I wait, other paparazzi around him, such convenient armor.

"Come talk to me," I say. "Fucking coward."

Some actress's cousin calls me and tells me where the actress is having lunch, and when I get there she's just leaving and I follow her, taking photos as she tells me to go away.

"I'm going to call the police," she says.

I take out my phone and pretend to start dialing. "Here, let me do it for you."

"Just stop. Can't you just stop?"

"No, I can't."

I drive by Jack's neighborhood so many times in one day that the guard at the gate stands up and says something into a walkie-talkie. For a second I panic and start thinking of lies I'd tell Ellory in the event of an arrest. But then I remember that it doesn't matter.

I tell myself that this is good. I don't have to soften the details of my life to anyone anymore. When asked what I did that day, I don't have to say *took pictures of an actress* when what I really did was chase that actress down the street. In fact, I don't have to say anything about my day, because there is no one asking me about it.

I watch Jack Whitlock movies every night, but never *Double or Nothing.*

There are still reminders of Las Vegas as a concept, as a cautionary tale.

A thirty-three-year-old actor who is finally too old to play a teenager on TV leaves Los Angeles for Las Vegas. A retired football player best known for beating his girlfriend with a twelve-pound dumbbell does the same. As does a comedian with dated jokes about breast implants. And a gossip columnist turned mommy blogger. D-listers, no longer getting jobs or invitations, no longer getting photographed by me. On social media, they write screeds about why they're leaving. *Los Angeles is too artificial. Los Angeles is too crowded. I've realized the city's values don't align with mine. I don't want to raise a family here. This is not the place it was when I came here twenty years ago. It's changed for the worse.*

Anything but *I have failed.*

When they move to Las Vegas, they're hired for residencies at middling casinos. Three nights a week at the Galaxy

Showroom, the Coco Lounge, the Versailles Club. *Best bang for your buck in Las Vegas*, the ads say. They appear as celebrity guests at nightclubs with one-word names. They pour cocktails to hawk their signature tequila brands. *This Memorial Day weekend, Abscond Nightclub and Dayclub is proud to welcome . . .*

Las Vegas is the afterlife of their careers. They are invited to ribbon-cutting ceremonies, restaurant openings, graduations. They light Christmas trees at outdoor malls, host off-Strip pool parties. Local news anchors fawn over them on cable TV. Eventually, they are offered keys to the city.

Las Vegas has a dearth of celebrities. Los Angeles has too many. The former has always been grateful for the scraps of the latter.

Las Vegas is a backup plan, a safety net. But it will not be that for me.

Ellory doesn't have to worry about running into me in Las Vegas, because I'm not going back.

chapter twenty-two

I park on Westerly Terrace and walk to the Silver Lake Reservoir. I find myself here some nights now, looking for coyotes. The water is black and impartial, reflecting the gaze of the city back on itself like a front-facing camera. The dirt path is empty, too late even for the late-night runners. I look up through the branches of a coast live oak at the houses on the bluff, trying to picture Jack Whitlock inside one of them, at a dinner party maybe. Where is Ellory tonight? Is she in her bed, three hundred miles away? Is she alone?

A car with its high beams on passes, window down, a Mia Luna song playing. The radio, a coincidence. A smile full of metal in the front seat. Just a teenager with braces. But still, I shield my face, thinking of an email from earlier in the day. An unknown sender: *you shouldn't exist.*

I pinch my left thumb between my right thumb and forefinger. I breathe. I am here, I keep telling myself. It isn't much of a mantra.

I don't usually walk through the neighborhoods, but tonight I do, maybe because of the car with the high beams, maybe for some other reason, maybe for no reason at all.

Silence, and then a bird's scream. Two notes, one short and one long and echoing. I used to hear that sound as a kid, coming from the house of a man who got rich playing poker and imported an ostentation of peacocks from India. When his hot streak cooled off and he lost everything, he drowned himself in his own pool—though I didn't hear about that part until high school—tied weights to his arms and his legs and dove into the glistening water in his backyard, while the peacocks looked on from the artificial grass. After that, they roosted in trees, chased stray cats, and shrieked on top of cars. By the time I got into photography, they'd been rounded up by the city and placed in some sort of government holding pen that I was never able to find.

The houses on the hill appear modest, but I know the real glamour is hidden. Sprawling patios with staircases climbing greedily to even bigger, higher patios. Heavy glass doors leading to plunge pools. Bedrooms with skyline views and clean white pillows, fluffed and waiting.

There is a man at the end of a driveway, trying to look inconspicuous. I know that posture. I learned it too, practiced appearing confident and undetectable until it became instinctual. I used to feel so unsure of my place in the throng of men jockeying for the shot, but then I thought of ravens riding warm currents of air—thermal soaring is what it's called—the way they tap into something invisible and just glide.

The man is in a hoodie and jeans, just like me, with a backpack. I know there is a camera inside. And I know that he is here because of some tip I didn't receive, at the house of someone I don't know but should. It makes me angry, not knowing these things, and when I approach him, he turns to look at me, but I already know who he is before I even see his face. Because it's Eddie, it has to be. His eyes widen as he recognizes we're alone. There's no wall of paparazzi between us, no one pushing me away, no one saying, *Just let it go, Ben, it's over.*

"You," I say, and lunge at him, because after everything, what else is there to do?

He turns and runs, away from the house and down the hill, and I follow, sprinting after him down the middle of the street. His backpack bounces and his arms pump and he isn't as fast as me. I can hear him breathing as I gain on him, both of us careening down the hill toward the reservoir.

"Hey," I call after him, and he ignores me and keeps going.

"Talk to me like a man," I say, like I know what that is, like I'm not just playing a part: the hero of the story seeking vengeance, sweaty in the street at night, chasing a retreating figure into the shadows.

We pass the dog park and he is slowing down now. He stumbles on the dirt path and heads toward Silver Lake Meadow. We race across the grass and I'm close enough to touch him, so I do, grabbing him by the strap of his backpack and pulling him to the ground. His cologne smells like a Las Vegas bachelor party because that's who he is, that's where he's from. He is the one pretending to belong here—not me—and he is panting, trying to get words out, but none of those words are *sorry*, so I tell him to shut up, I don't want to hear it. I'm on top of him, pinning him down, both of us breathing hard.

"If you broke," he wheezes, "my camera . . ."

My hands are on the collar of his hoodie. He won't make eye contact with me. "Look at me," I say. And then louder, "Fucking look at me. My girlfriend left me. The only person who's ever loved me and that's it, she's just gone, she doesn't want to have anything to do with me. And there are all of these people, I don't even know how many, harassing me, and they're going to follow me forever. These news stories with my name in them are forever too. These people, they might actually follow through with their death threats. They're crazy."

Eddie laughs. "*They're* crazy? You're the one who's crazy. The line cooks at the Bluebird used to joke that you were a serial killer. Everyone thinks you're a freak."

"So is that why you did it? Gave my name to—"

"I sold the information for money. It didn't mean anything. I don't have some, like, vendetta against you." He wriggles beneath me, frees one of his arms, and shoves me off him. I land on my back, the grass cool, even through my clothes. I shiver. It can be cold here at night; no one tells you that.

Eddie sits up, facing away from me.

The sound of a siren from far away. I study the back of his head, the starless sky above us, the water so incredibly still, off-limits. Last week, a man jumped in and swam to the center. Videos on the internet taken with cell phones showed him naked and on his knees, crying as the police handcuffed him. Hypothermic, the news said, but it seemed like something more than that.

"Look," Eddie says. "It's not my fault that you took whatever I said when I was fucked up in Vegas so seriously that you decided to come out here."

"You destroyed me."

He shakes his head. "You're gonna believe what you're gonna believe, I guess." He climbs to his feet and brushes the grass from his jeans.

I stand and face him. "I at least want an apology."

"For what? Giving that website your name? People do that kind of thing all the time. I needed the cash. I'm not sorry."

"For ruining my life."

"Ruining your life?" His mouth hangs open. "I didn't ruin your life. You went to her party. You took those pictures. You sold them. And you even texted me about it, like an idiot. If you want to know who is responsible for your girlfriend dumping you and those people following you and whatever else happens, I'll tell you. It's not me. It's you."

Across the water, the lights in the windows are off now. Families sleeping, children comforted and cared for. And I think of one of the last conversations with Ellory. *You're not someone I'd ever want to have a baby with*, she told me. Before then I hadn't realized a baby was an option, that it was something either of us might want. Suddenly, I wanted it more than I'd ever wanted anything. But I didn't say so, because it was too late. So I just said, *Fuck you*, which seemed to hurt her, because I'd never said that before either.

I'm not going to tell Eddie that he's right, even though I know he is.

"Are you seriously crying?" he asks.

I touch my face and realize I am, just like the man who went swimming that day. I wonder what he saw beneath the surface, what he felt before his limbs went numb.

"You know they don't use this for drinking water anymore," I say.

"What?"

"The reservoir. It's just for show."

"I'm going to get out of here," Eddie says. He opens his

backpack and inspects the contents. "The good news is you didn't break my camera."

He slides the straps over his shoulders, puts the hood of his sweatshirt up, and doubles back on the dirt path he took to get here. His clothes are black—an advantage or occupational hazard, depending on the circumstances—and alongside the dark reservoir, he seems to dissolve.

At the edge of the water, there are five coyotes, skinny and spectral as ghosts. They look right at me, impartial as the Silver Lake Reservoir, eyes containing all the knowledge of the city.

the desert

chapter twenty-three

Inside my apartment, the glass coffee table is shattered, pieces of it scattered across the floor like precious minerals. Large red letters on the gray living room wall: *SCUM*. The fridge door hangs open, the interior empty and white. Every trash can is overturned, embarrassing debris of my existence exposed. Uneaten takeout ground into an overpriced rug. Torn pages from magazines screaming *scorned mistress tells all, baby number three on the way, country singer in dive bar brawl, child actor now homeless, stars they're just like us.*

I crunch across a carpet of glass to the bathroom. The shower curtain is shredded, the tub filled with trash. Not my trash, but from some anonymous dumpster, the same as all the other dumpsters I've waited beside, hoping for someone beautiful and beloved to tumble out of a nightclub like scraps tossed to a dog.

Smell of sulfur from the bedroom. Sheets wet with urine.

I find my phone and text Eddie. **I got my ass kicked but I think you'd be proud. I think you'd say it was worth it.**

And then I slide down to the floor. A hurt animal sound comes out of me.

I turn off my phone, turn it back on, open the camera app, lens on me. My mouth is crusted with blood, my right eyelid swollen, a crescent moon of purple forming around it. I press record.

"To whoever broke into my apartment," I say, split lip cracking open as I speak, "and to all the people who have emailed, called, messaged, found me in person. I just want to say . . ."

I look up at the ceiling, squeeze my eyes shut for a second, and then return to the camera. "I just want to say, I know why you're doing this and you're not wrong. I took those photos of Mia Luna. I sold them. You hate me and you should. Everyone does. There's no one . . . there's nothing left. And you've been doing this for such a long time and so have I and I am begging you, please stop. I know you think I deserve to be tortured forever and maybe you're right, but I'm human like you and . . . and . . . and, I don't know, just"—my voice breaks—"just do what you're threatening to do or leave me alone. Please. Stop trying to ruin my life. I have nothing."

I touch the red button and the video ends. I send it out in response to the emails, the texts. To as many of them as I can. The air is stagnant in the dark bedroom, the scent of urine making me sick. I go to the living room, slide open the balcony door, and collapse on the couch. I swear I can still smell the perfume of the background artist who just wanted me to look at her while I fucked her, which was such a simple thing I could have given her, and now there is no one here to touch or be touched by, just the address on my arm, which might lead to him.

I look at Ellory's Instagram.

Her showgirl smile on the Las Vegas Strip. A large crowd. *I'm so grateful for you all*, she writes, and it is easy to include myself in her acknowledgments.

I keep myself awake in case I have a concussion, because the movies taught me to do that. I refresh the celebrity news sites, will myself to go to the kitchen for water, for coffee, but I can't get there so I just imagine it. I drift off before dawn and am awakened by a single coyote, barking frantically below my balcony. They've been producing larger litters lately, reproducing for their own sake, for the same reason every living thing does. To exist.

My phone is face down on my chest. I lift it slowly, preparing for the Greek chorus.

A text from another paparazzo: **is this you?!?** And a link to a tweet. I click on it and the video starts playing automatically, my own voice begging *please just stop*.

Is this what I wanted?

Two hundred and one shares, two hundred and two, two hundred and twenty. The numbers grow in real time. People react to it with crying-laughing emojis, with *sorry but I don't recognize the paparazzi as human*, with *THE GUY WHO SPENDS HIS LIFE HARASSING PEOPLE WANTS TO BE LEFT ALONE DO YOU SEE THE IRONY?!?!?*

And then a screenshot of purple text from a verified account appears: *To my fans: You're my friends, my family, my everything. Your support during my darkest times has meant more than you could ever know. I ask that you please do not threaten or hurt anyone on my behalf, including the man who took those pictures. That is NOT what it means to be a Lunatic. Sending love, positivity, and forgiveness.*

I curl up on the couch like a child. The notifications stop, replaced with a palpable silence. A gift from this famous stranger who should only feel hatred toward me. Forgiveness, the last thing I deserve. Forgiveness, from someone who shouldn't forgive me. Of all the strange and awful things I've seen and done, imparted and received, this gesture of kindness is unfathomable. I can't wrap my hands around it. I lie still, looking at the writing on my arm, memorizing the address Sasha gave me, waiting for the intruders to return, but they don't.

I watch videos of Jack speaking in press junkets. I smile back at him when he smiles. I mouth the words to the answers he gives.

I watch one of his early movies. He's twenty-five and barely famous—just one villain in a movie full of villains—and although his character holds a woman hostage in her own bedroom, he is charming and funny as he ties her up. There's a wink in his smile that says, *Lighten up*. Her body heaves against the restraints, her eyes gazing up at him. She is afraid of him; she is in love with him. When he cuts her loose, she kisses him and the shock on his face betrays his previous swagger. Of course, I think of the woman being tied up at eXit. I try to imagine him watching, just watching, as he told Sasha. I try to imagine him leaning back on a couch with a girl on her knees before him. I try to imagine him wrapping the length of a rope around someone, and even though there are images to suggest this is all possible—the movie, the photo, the text messages—it doesn't seem real, not yet.

I read Jack's interviews. Every word he says I've already memorized. Every joke he makes I know. This feeling of knowing is a friendship, a brotherhood. The deepest kind of intimacy, the longest relationship of my life.

I hobble to the bedroom, day-after-a-car-accident ache reverberating down my spine. The autographed photo from the

Bluebird is still in the nightstand drawer. I run my index finger across the glass, tracing the curves of his signature. They didn't find it. They didn't take it away.

In the bathroom, I strip down and cover myself in CBD cream. It smells like mint and lemon and something just a little bit rotten, or maybe that's the trash decaying in the bathtub, maybe that's me. I turn the lights off, not wanting to look at myself while I wait for the cream to absorb. In the dark I see Mia Luna's purple letters spelling out *forgiveness*. Absolution, a rite of passage for what comes next.

I take five ibuprofen and pack my backpack for Palm Springs. I have zero dollars in my bank account. Two credit cards. One is thirty-two dollars away from being maxed out. The other is eight hundred away. That's the line. Eight hundred and thirty-two dollars.

I need this photo. I need this money. I need to feel that rush again. And I need it to be Jack.

All around me, there are reminders of Las Vegas. A man on Hollywood Boulevard wearing a black silk jacket with a casino logo on the back. A new billboard rising from the smog with the face of a DJ, the name of a Las Vegas day-club. And then as I drive to Palm Springs, the Bluebird calls again. The white lettering on the black screen a ghost. I let it ring. No voicemail. I pull over at a gas station in Riverside and pace back and forth, delete the number from my missed-call log. Another call, just as I'm entering Palm Springs, the white wind turbines turning in the purple-brown mountains. I pass through the downtown area—mid-century antique shops, martini bars, ice cream parlors advertising date shakes—and turn left into a quiet, manicured neighborhood where every home looks like a movie about a dissatisfied couple in 1963. Every block is a time capsule. No gates to stop me. These houses are meant to be admired. I find the street and then the house. I park discreetly—close enough to see it, but far enough from it to not arouse suspicion. Golden barrel cacti line the walkway to a turquoise door. On either side, white breeze blocks sheltering the windows from view. Palm trees like sentinels. Green grass, trimmed as short and uniform as Astroturf. There is no car in the driveway, but that doesn't mean he isn't here. I imagine the owner, this friend, picking him up in Bel Air and taking him to this house.

I turn off the engine and sit in the hot car. Turn it back on and run the air-conditioning. Repeat. An old real estate listing tells me this house sold in 2013 for $3.4 million. *Swanky sunken living room, saltwater pool, outdoor shower.* A slideshow of professional photos shows a stone wall, a fireplace, a bedroom facing a wall of sliding glass doors. There's a whiff of investment property to the place, and when I track down the name of the owner, that's exactly who he is. A real estate developer named Albert Alden. Jessica follows him on Instagram, which confirms the connection to Jack. His own account is a stream of Southern California homes he has acquired, remodeled, and sold or is renting as luxury vacation homes. There is a single photo of the house in Palm Springs, the one I'm looking at now. A comment from Jessica: *Gorgeous! When can we move in?!? Haha*

Has she been here? Have they been here? Could she be here now?

On her own Instagram account, there's a new photo. A picnic table draped with linen, a huckleberry pie. Caption: *When in Montana.*

Someone says: *damage control*

why did u abandon Jack when he obviously needs u

Where is he??????

I imagine Jessica waiting at her parents' ranch, taking calls from a crisis PR agent, watching public opinion shape and transform, weighing whatever love she feels for him against how bad it would look to stay, how good it would look to leave. The paparazzi who flew to Montana are still there, but not for much longer. They're hoping to catch her looking sad or angry or tired. Ugly enough to justify his cheating or so beautiful it's impossible to understand why he'd ever fuck someone else. *If she can't keep a man, nobody can*, the internet will say, because they don't know that it has nothing to do with how pretty or kind or smart or adventurous she is. It is about what he wants.

Looking at the Palm Springs house, I say it in my head: Jack, I understand. I know what it is like to want, to be hated for wanting.

The hours pass. In the desert, it is warmest later in the day. I think of 4 p.m., summertime in Las Vegas. Another call from the Bluebird, as if someone knows something.

I'm prepared. My backpack is in the seat next to me and it is filled with everything I need. Hiking food: granola bars and jerky. High-protein stuff that won't spoil. Sunscreen and ibuprofen and spare layers of clothing. And mini binoculars, a birthday gift from Ellory. Good for looking for wildlife. Good for monitoring a house in Palm Springs when you don't want to take out your camera. Not yet.

Other paparazzi bring books and magazines and tablets with TV shows downloaded for long stakeouts like these, but I can get into the same state I got in while waiting in the sagebrush for Ghost. I can do better than that, now that I've learned some meditation techniques. That's all this is. Meditation. I drink water and control my breath. My eyes are always on the house, waiting for movement. My hand on my backpack, hovering above my camera.

A dull pain vibrates the length of my spine. Still the pain from eXit, a line of bruises forming. I take another handful of ibuprofen but I know it won't do much. What I really need is to get out of the car and stretch and twist. Or to lie flat on my back. Or to see a doctor. But I can't do that. There is no choice but to endure this.

Ellory's Instagram is flooded with new followers, new comments:

Saw your show last night and you literally took my breath away!

an absolute angel

QUEEN OF VEGAS

She is performing on the Strip again. The lounge at the top of the casino, a jewel box. Her costume embroidered with diamonds.

A car passes and I put the key in the ignition, acting like I live in one of these houses and am just leaving. The car drives away, up the road that curves and stretches into the aubergine mountains. I imagine I am above this scene, on the nearby white-domed summit of Mount San Jacinto. The air is cool and smells like pine and it heals me.

Down here in Palm Springs, elevation just a few hundred feet above sea level, the late afternoon heat roils. I turn on the engine and allow myself the pleasure of a blast of air-conditioning again. I shut it off, keep the windows down, drink my water, try to put myself back up on Mount San Jacinto, and for a moment I am there, but then I'm pulled back down to the desert again by the pressure in my bladder. I really, really need to piss. And I've prepared for this. I have an empty water bottle in my backpack. I take it out and unzip my pants. It feels good, the release as I fill the bottle.

"Hey, you." Knuckles rapping on the windshield. A wrinkled face with glasses.

"Shit," I say. The bottle is hot in my hand.

"I'm going to call the cops if you don't get out of here."

I cover myself, put the bottle in the cup holder of my car. The liquid inside is amber. I'm dehydrated.

The knuckles again. "I said to get out of here. Did you hear me?"

"I'm sorry. I'm just waiting for—"

"You've been waiting all day. Don't think I haven't seen you out here, with your binoculars and your . . . your . . . Whatever this is, you go do it somewhere else, okay?"

I put my hands on the steering wheel, like I've just pulled over for directions. "Can I ask you something? Have you seen anyone come in or out of that house in the last few days?"

"What is wrong with you? I said to get out of here or I'll call the cops."

When I don't respond, the knuckles become a fist slamming down on the windshield, punctuating the words, "Get. The. Hell. Off. My. Street."

And then a crack in the glass.

"Fuck," I say. "I'm going."

I drive a few blocks and wait there, watching the small crack in the windshield splinter and spread. By golden hour, the crack has spiderwebbed several inches. It's the heat that causes the glass to expand. I learned that in Las Vegas.

I call a windshield repair shop in Los Angeles and they quote me $370. It's too much. It would put me too close. I google *safe to drive with cracked windshield* and learn that it's either dangerous, illegal, or both. *But would it kill me?* I ask the internet, ask Eddie. When it's finally night, I can't see the crack anymore. A small comfort.

I put on a hoodie and keep the hood up. Dark shirt, dark pants, dark shoes. I walk back to the house. No lights on, not even exterior ones. Still no car in the driveway. My phone is full of text messages from other paparazzi asking me about Colorado, Montana, places in Los Angeles.

I stay low to the ground as I cross the manicured lawn. I palm the sides of the house, moving across the perimeter in the dark until I am at a door. And when I push down on the handle, it opens. Of course it does. This was meant to happen. I go inside. I hold my breath, because maybe Jack is careless too, waiting in the dark with the door open.

I say it in my head: Jack, are you here?

And then out loud: "Jack?"

It's such a fucking thrill to say his name, to know that he might hear it.

I don't turn any lights on. I let my eyes adjust, scanning for movement in the shadows.

I feel him in each room, in each piece of furniture, in the weight of the glass bookend I lift up and put down. He was here. I know it. I see him in the painting above the couch. I taste him in the cold white wine from the refrigerator that is halfway finished, maybe by him. Definitely by him, I think, as I drink it from the bottle. I take it with me to the backyard, where there is a kidney-shaped pool, a row of lounge chairs, an unlit fire pit, and the silhouette of Mexican fence post cacti against breeze blocks. After finishing the wine, I take off my clothes and get into the pool. It's warm and tastes like salt. I dive to the bottom and I can feel him holding me there. It's not that he's in the water beside me, but that he is the water itself. I get out and sit on the edge of the pool, looking up at the stars. And then I go back inside, leaving wet footprints on the hardwood floor as I make my way to the master bathroom. I flick the light switch on and look at the cool sapphire tile, a marble greyhound guarding a soaking tub. A rain shower. I turn the water on and get in, squeezing greedily from the seaweed shampoo, the conditioner with the French name. I dip my fingers into crystal-infused body scrub, rubbing it all over my skin, slowly at first and then faster, until my hands are his hands, anointing me.

Jack, I think. Touch me.

When I'm clean, I go to the bedroom and lie down. I smell him on the white sheets. My back doesn't hurt in this bed. This is a sign. A sign that I am close. That it has to be me. It *has* to. And although he is not there, I feel him lying in bed beside me, just as he has always been beside me. In the booth at the Bluebird, on movie screens and televisions, and even in Ellory, in the tuxedo she wore the night we met.

I close my eyes. I turn over onto my stomach. I am hot and the bed is cool. I push my hips against the mattress, grinding against the sheets where he has slept, a fistful of pillow in each hand. When I'm done, I find a pair of black briefs in the dresser and put them on. I like the way I feel inside them.

I fall asleep.

In the morning, no one throws me out. I drive back to Los Angeles.

From here on out, everything will mean something. It is important to pay attention.

The crack grows on the windshield, fills with light on the highway.

Pay attention.

The next time the Bluebird calls, I answer.

chapter twenty-four

I can hear the restaurant through the phone. A server kicking open the swinging door that leads to the dining room, the clatter of plates, the kitchen language—*behind*, *corner*, *heard*—the score of *Double or Nothing*. Maybe that last one I imagine. I'm in the garage of my apartment complex, the engine off, the interior getting warmer.

"Do you remember me?" Julie asks.

"We were coworkers."

"At the Bluebird."

"A long time ago."

"It wasn't that long ago," she says. "You're a paparazzi now. That's what I heard."

"Yes."

"That's crazy."

"Why have you been calling me?" I ask.

Cooks yelling at each other.

"I heard something from someone," she says.

There it is, unmistakable. The feeling, the instinct, the higher power telling me to listen.

"What did you hear?"

"I don't even know if you're the right—"

"What did you hear?"

"I just want to say that I have a baby now," she says. "Or else I wouldn't be doing this."

"Okay."

"The father is not in the . . . he doesn't acknowledge . . . and I'm still bartending at the Bluebird. And sometimes I'm doing some shifts at a new locals spot in the southwest part of town. They're building a lot of houses over there, and things are going to pick up any day now." She laughs, like she's just told a joke.

"Is this about money?" I ask.

"I don't know how to do this. My friend's boyfriend is this real estate guy, and he got drunk and told me something, and my friend—well, it's Madeline from the restaurant, remember?"

"Uh-huh."

"It was her idea to tell you. She heard . . . we both heard . . . that you're this paparazzi or whatever in Hollywood, and Madeline said that when someone sees a celebrity, they can call the paparazzi and if the paparazzi find the celebrity and take a picture and sell it, you get a cut of the money? Right?" She laughs again. "This is embarrassing. You can tell me to fuck off, if you want. I don't even know if I'm doing this right."

The mechanical *beep beep* of someone clocking in.

"Julie, who is it? Who are you calling about? What do you know?"

"No offense, but you don't sound great," she says.

"I'm fine. I'm very good."

"Okay. So, um, Madeline's boyfriend is in this real estate business that was involved in this somehow. He wasn't supposed to say anything but he can't keep a secret. He loves to brag."

I close my eyes. Continue to breathe. I wait. I slide the quartz out of my pocket and into my mouth. I should have picked up the first time she called. But it's okay, I tell myself. I'm here now.

"There's a client of his, or of his company's. And it's . . . god, you won't believe this or maybe you will, I don't know. It's Jack Whitlock."

I spit the crystal into my palm. "You're sure?"

"People always say that when he shot *Double or Nothing* in Vegas, he really liked the city. I always thought they were making that up. But they weren't."

"Julie, are you sure?"

"Yes."

"Fuck." I clench my fist around the wet rock.

"So how does this work? If you find him and take the picture, how much do I get?"

"Where? Where is he?"

"The same house he rented when he shot *Double or Nothing*."

"In Las Vegas."

"Yes," she says. "In Las Vegas. Apparently he just got here. Madeline's boyfriend said he saw the helicopter land out in the desert. Or maybe he just heard about it."

My entire body floods with euphoria. "Of course," I say. "Of course this is how it happens."

"What do you mean?" she asks.

"Nothing. You wouldn't understand. It's just all coming together."

"You really don't seem like you're in a good place. Maybe I should call someone else."

I swallow. "Like who? Who would you call?"

"I would have called Eddie," she says. "He was doing what you do, or at least I think he was, before—"

"I'm the person to talk to," I say. "It's me. Some people can't handle this, but I can."

She makes a noise I don't understand. I pinch the bridge of my nose between my thumb and forefinger, massaging the cartilage. "This is a new number," I say. "How'd you get it?"

"I messaged Ellory. She had it."

"Ellory?"

"Is that okay?"

"Just text me the details of everything you have."

"And then what happens?" she asks.

I can taste bile in my throat. I swallow it. "I'll let you know."

Before we hang up, I ask, "What did Ellory say when you messaged her about me? Does she know I'm on my way to Las Vegas?"

"Wait—are you on your way to Las Vegas?"

"I have to go," I say.

I open up the car door and vomit on the ground.

I go upstairs to my apartment, the interior shadowy, festering, unrecognizable. I take what I need, which isn't much, and then go back to the car. I call the photo agency. "I'm close."

"What do you mean?"

"That's all I'm going to say right now."

The crack on my windshield is still there. Three hundred and seventy dollars. When I get this photo, I will replace it, replace the car entirely, move somewhere so nice I'll be untouchable.

It's Friday, the wrong day to be driving to Las Vegas.

I know these highways are organized, but today they appear as a tangle, like they weren't planned but instead grew organically, branching and spreading like weeds. From the 10, the oily Los Angeles River is green and brown at the edges, flowing shallow in concrete beside empty train tracks. Orange buses move slowly in the smog, maneuvering around Star Waggons. Suburbs become industrial outskirts, houses with billboards in backyards, chain-link fences facing the freeway. Traffic all the way to San Bernardino, and then just like that, the city releases me.

I hate how easy it is to leave, like I was never even there in the first place, like I'm not coming back.

Julie's voice: *I messaged Ellory. She had it.*

What did Ellory say when she responded? Is she thinking about me now? Does she ever?

I listen to the radio until it fades out at Cajon Pass. I try to locate the beginning of the desert, that place where the lushness of Los Angeles gives way to rocks and sand and clumps of trailers rusting in the sun, but I'm in it before I can identify it. In some unnamed town, there's a bleached white screen and an empty parking lot. A billboard, I think at first. No, a drive-in theater, just like the one where I used to watch him. In Barstow, I stop at a travel center that smells like mildew. They're selling Los Angeles T-shirts, Las Vegas magnets.

I drink a soda beside a bus station. Taciturn people waiting with luggage. A tuxedo cat crosses the parking lot, looks up at me, disappears beside a dumpster. On my phone, I watch the opening of *Double or Nothing*. The car moving across the desert, bringing Jack to Las Vegas. That drive, the one I'm doing now, is the same story. It's a pilgrimage. I am the movie now. I am playing the role Jack played.

I book a room at the Flamingo. One of the nice ones. I put it on my credit card. I want to touch the glass like he did. I want to feel the city beneath me as it was beneath him.

Baker becomes Primm becomes Jean and then there it is. It's daylight when I arrive. The city is sun washed and open. I see it as he saw it. Golden towers and silver clouds. Three-story photos of magicians stretching their white-gloved hands toward the crowds below. Billboards making overtures, threats, promises. All the cars coming from the west, the synchronized movements of their blinkers turning right on Las Vegas Boulevard.

chapter twenty-five

In a parking lot outside a liquor store, tourists gather around a pickup truck, drinking beer and hyping each other up. I look at them from my car, waiting for the traffic light to turn green. They're confident like everyone around them is confident; they're going to have the best night anyone has ever had.

I pull up to the valet, the cursive lettering of the Flamingo falling on my cracked windshield like a benediction. I pass my keys to the attendant.

And there she is, stretched out on a taxicab ad, wearing silk gloves and silver heels. *Ellory Fox Performing Nightly at Lillian.* Her legs are long and her smile is big and she looks back at me, frozen in someone else's photo. The pink and orange and white lights dance on her skin. The taxi moves to the front of the line, picks up its passengers, goes back to the Strip, taking her with it.

I enter the casino. The coconut smell, the lights, the laughter. Did Jack feel like he was on vacation too, when he stood where I am standing?

The line at the front desk is long. People drink plastic tubes of frozen daiquiris to pass the time. I look at Ellory's Instagram. There's a photo of a cactus garden, one I've never seen in person but have seen her post before. There are other things too I don't recognize from real life: Her hair is a little bit blonder; she's wearing a dress I don't remember. The amber scent of her, the sound of her voice—those things belong to a different person. Photos like the one from the taxicab ad. I look up Lillian, which didn't exist when I lived here. How quickly Las Vegas becomes unfamiliar. It's what I wanted when I left. Rose wallpaper and saffron booths. They serve cocktails and dessert. A picture of Ellory on their website, lounging in a giant champagne coupe. It is this woman, the one who wears red and performs on the Strip, who I know now. Maybe the person I lived with in Echo Park was the fantasy and it is *this* Ellory Fox who exists in the world. The woman at the front desk waves me forward. She reminds me of someone I went to high school with, or maybe she reminds me of an actress from a movie, a dancer in a music video.

My room is on the twenty-seventh floor, facing east. Toward the mountains, toward the house where he is staying.

I reread the old article about it: *See the jaw-dropping desert estate Jack Whitlock rented during the filming of his Las Vegas mobster movie.*

I scroll through the images quickly, hungry for the next, the next, the next. The house is built into the side of a cliff, but it doesn't look like part of the landscape. It's sterile. A modern-looking home, much different from the stucco of Las Vegas, built to look over the city from a distance. The interior is all mirrors and windows and dark, glossy countertops. Cool and smooth and liquid. Twenty thousand square feet. A wraparound terrace. An infinity pool, a meeting room, a billiard room, a gym, a tennis court, a guest house. Mountain views, golf course views, Las Vegas Strip views. The article doesn't give the address, but it's easy to figure it out. I know this city too well. The Stratosphere is on the right, which means it's on the east side. The position of Frenchman Mountain narrows it down. The nearby golf course narrows it down further. A single shot of the neighborhood below contains a familiar Mormon temple, and from there it's just a matter of following that street up into the mountains. There are very few homes up that high.

Of course I know, have always known, where it is.

I take a hot shower. I press my body against the room's floor-to-ceiling window. Pliable skin, hard surface. I am alive, more so now than ever. I flick my tongue against the glass, touching the point where the road curves into the desert. Jack, I think, can you feel me? The television is on. One of those channels that shows you things to do in Las Vegas. A restaurant that serves gold-encrusted rib eye. A dolphin show behind a casino. A secret jazz lounge inside an ice cream shop. I put it on mute. Silent images of shrimp cocktails, lazy rivers, blue flames licking the meringue of Baked Alaska, acrobats suspended in darkness.

This city is so much better experiencing it as he has, as a tourist.

The television shows the Bluebird. The booth. Jack Whitlock in *Double or Nothing*.

I order room service. Prime rib and potatoes just like in the movie.

"Are you enjoying your time in Las Vegas?" the room service attendant asks when she hands me the receipt for signature.

"Very much."

I give her an extra twenty on top of the auto gratuity.

She smiles. "Good tip means good luck."

I eat on the bed. I am so hungry. I pull off pieces of meat with my hands, staining the white duvet pink.

On the celebrity news channels, they're talking to a dog dentist who took acting classes with Jack when they were both nineteen. *He seemed nice*, the dog dentist offers. That's the best they can do. It's not enough and they know it. On the internet, people share the leaked photos, leaked video, leaked texts. They analyze them, beg for more.

I receive texts from other paparazzi, theorizing about places he could be. Santa Fe, Antibes, Berlin, somewhere in Indonesia. They are all either boarding flights or giving up.

If this doesn't work out I'm going to apply for a job at Whole Foods, one of them says.

We're all spread out. Each one of us, a separate beam probing the dark matter of the universe.

I go out onto the Strip. It's the blue hour. The sky is darkening but not dark. All around me, the lights are turning on. Ellory passes again, on the roof of another taxi. I think of what she said on the night we met when I asked her where she performed. *Shitty downtown venues you've probably never heard of*. I think of her freckles in the photo I took at the Bluebird, the same inscrutable constellation I tried to decipher on the day she told me she was leaving. The sound of her orgasm, a permanent memory I would cut out of my body with a pocketknife if I could. I walk north, past the wax museum containing figures that look exactly like famous people, toward the Bluebird. A server sits on the loading dock in his apron, not smoking, not scrolling his phone, just sitting. He looks through me, at the city where I used to live. I turn back. I walk south to the gardens outside Caesars Palace. The fountains go off at the Bellagio. The fir trees on the sidewalk are big and old, their branches dark against the white spray. Above me, the sky is pink. The fountains settle. The crowd disperses. A pair of green eyes watches from an LED screen at the top of a hotel.

My phone rings.

"Are you really here?" Ellory asks.

"I'm here," I say.

"It's been a long time since we . . ."

"Two and a half years, almost." How do I tell her that I've gotten used to her voice on the internet, the way she sounds in videos taken by her friends? Her smile when she thanks the crowd for their applause, how kind she sounds when she tells her followers where she's performing and says *I'd love to see you*, so different from the person I'm talking to now.

"Okay," she says. "So, how long are you in town?"

"I don't know."

"Well, if I know you, it won't be long."

"I'm here for as long as it takes," I say.

"Is that a line from a movie?"

A duck lands and settles on the now-still water of the fountains. *Lake Bellagio*, it says on maps, like it's real. I look up at the hotel where Ellory is performing tonight. The show is in two hours. She is probably there now, in a dressing room, the light yellow, her robe the color of champagne. I lean back against a fir tree. Its trunk is sturdy. I know someday someone will decide it's blocking the view and cut it down.

"I keep seeing you," I say to Ellory, "on taxi ads."

"That must be weird."

"It's not."

"Well, I haven't seen you anywhere," she says. "Maybe

that's on purpose. I saw your parents a few months ago, though, at the grocery store, but they didn't remember me."

"They didn't really know you."

"They could have."

"Why were you buying groceries in that part of town?"

"Someone I know lives over there," she says, and I am reminded of the first time I saw the man's forearm on her Instagram.

"Oh," I say.

"Your parents said they assumed you were still in California, that you were probably fine. They hadn't heard from you in a while, but that's normal."

"This is my first time back here," I say.

"I figured."

"You could have reached out to me, if you really wanted to know how I'm doing."

I hear her breathe in. "I didn't want to."

Another duck lands on the water. The two circle each other.

"Are you okay?" Ellory asks.

"I've got it under control."

"Do you?"

"Don't worry about me."

"I used to worry about you a lot."

"But you don't anymore."

I hear her close a door. She sighs. "It's not like that. It's just that I had to move on. A lot has happened since you and I were together. And honestly, when I think about that time with you, it's like a mirage."

"A pool of water in the desert?"

"An illusion."

"So what about your new boyfriend? Is he the real thing?"

"I'm not going to ask how you know about him."

"Is he better than me?"

She pauses for long enough that I think she's hung up. And then she says, "He's different."

I start walking toward the hotel where Lillian is.

"I was going to suggest we meet for a drink," Ellory says, "but now I'm not so sure."

"I could come to your show. I wouldn't talk to you. I'd just watch."

I hesitate at the threshold of the hotel. The security guard eyes me. Inside, a slot machine makes the sound of a red-tailed hawk.

"Why would you want that?" she asks.

"I'd just watch," I say again.

"Why would you come see me? Why wouldn't you go find Ghost or do something that would actually make you happy?"

I step into the casino, where the air is cool, and she is maybe thirty stories above me, the closest we've been in a long time.

"You should stop looking for Jack Whitlock," she says. "I know that's why you're here. But it isn't good. He doesn't want to be found."

"How do you know?"

"Because he's a human being," she says. "This is how people are."

"What information do you have?"

"Nothing, Ben. Nothing. I called you to see if you're okay, not to give you intel on a celebrity. You think everyone has got something that you can buy or take. I didn't see that in you when we first got together. I was too swept up in it—meeting you at the Bluebird, the coyotes on the Strip, your photos of Ghost, that night at the motel in Utah, all the other nights at each other's apartments, cooking, swimming, fucking, talking. But once I saw it, I couldn't unsee it. And then I realized it had always been there. It's a tragic way to move in the world. It makes me really, really sad for you."

I turn back to the open doorway, to the sidewalk. I start walking back to the Flamingo. "It's better if you and I don't know each other in real life."

"What does that mean?"

I pick up my pace. "It's getting dark now. I have to go."

"Ben—"

"Maybe this is the relationship you'd prefer to have with me. One where you don't see me in person."

"That's not a relationship," she says, and I hang up.

I pack my backpack. Headlamp, portable charger, spare batteries, electrolyte drink, and snacks. I hydrate.

I can see it now. It was always meant to end here, on the outskirts of Las Vegas, so dark away from the Strip. No highways, just surface streets. East until the road dead-ends in the desert without ceremony.

I park the car and look up at the silhouette of the rocky foothills. He is here because he has to be. And so am I. My backpack is heavy with camera equipment, with water. I have a quarter of a mile to scramble in the dark. It has to be like this; I can't walk on the streets. A lesser paparazzi would turn his ankle and spend the night thirsty in the rocks. That's what most accidents in nature are like; not dramatic falls from cliffs or drownings in rapids, but a simple sprain that makes it impossible to return home.

That's not me. I've been preparing for this my whole life.

I start walking. Soft earth giving way to deeper earth, like the whole world could disintegrate if I pushed hard enough. No headlamp yet. I don't want to be given away. I hike slowly, deliberately, avoiding cacti and rocks. Down below, cars pull in and out of driveways. Nights beginning, days ending. No one can see me as I climb this hill.

I visualize Jack. Photos I've seen from the *Double or Nothing* set. His hair pushed back, his mouth open, a pool behind him. A pink suit jacket, a smile, the great Mojave all around him. The autographed picture I stole from the Bluebird. It belonged to me. All of these images of him, like the images of a father, a best friend, a lover, a god.

There are lights on the hill now. It has to be the house.

I trip and catch myself. I keep going. The lights are closer.

He is here, I know it. He is here because I am here. He is not in Los Angeles, walking into a restaurant. He is not emerging from the lobby of a beautiful hotel. He is not in front of a crowd of paparazzi with his hands up in surrender. He is waiting for me.

Oh, all the places I have seen you, Jack. All the versions of you I have known. All the things I have done in pursuit of you.

Almost there now.

Forgive me, Jack, forgive me. For leaving the city that raised me, for betraying the rules I swore to follow, for what I did to Eddie.

A cliff band to climb. My hands on the sharp rock. It cuts

into my fingers. I keep going. If there was someone here with me, they might call this a violation.

No more false summits. I arrive at the top. The black of the desert night suddenly blunted by the glow of the house. And then I am there, standing even with the infinity pool. It's lit from within, inviting me to break the surface. The lights are on inside the house. I can feel his fingers on each switch, turning them on, moving from room to room. I breathe in. I breathe out. There is no need to crouch low in the darkness anymore. I can wait. I can present myself.

There is a large and beautiful window. And through that a cathedral of a kitchen. I don't see him, but he is inside. I can sense it. I unzip my backpack. I take out my camera.

Give me this, Jack. Let me take this simple thing.

For so long, it has been a possibility and nothing more. But now I am standing on this rocky hill alone, so far east of the city, in the dark desert where the ceaseless beam of the Luxor does not reach. The Las Vegas below me is quiet and sparkling, inviting and repelling.

My heart, my heart.

On the grid of lights, I can pinpoint each cross street I used to know. The apartments I've lived in. And here in front of me, the house where he is staying. There is no wall, no security. It is right there. It is right fucking there. There is no hard boundary between dream and delusion. It is the place where the edge of the pool meets the night.

The money will keep me going. This time, it will last.

And then he appears, behind the glass, in the dark marble kitchen. The cocktail of proximity. I am dizzy, scared, sad, sick, elated.

Jack, all these years that I've spoken to you, you've never spoken back. Everyone I've spoken to—Ellory in the tuxedo jacket, Eddie in the water—I was really just speaking to you. Did you hear me? Can you hear me?

Jack, take me into your house. Lead me from room to room and find the light. Tell me I can take as many photos as I want, say you'll do whatever I need. Promise me it will be enough. Let me take one, two, three, a thousand. Jack, tell me it's okay. Believe me when I tell you that it has to hurt, it has to degrade you, it has to be a sacrifice. Take off your clothes. In the living room, light a fire and put your hands in it. Find the glass dildo in the bedroom and fuck yourself in front of me. Take a knife and cut your torso, your face, your arms. Spread your blood on the pure white carpet. Fall to your knees and ask me if it's enough, if you should keep going.

I am standing beside the pool. I am walking toward the house. I am looking through the glass. He is on the other side. People always say celebrities are shorter or taller in real life, but he is exactly my height, just feet away. He sees me.

He opens the sliding glass door. He stands next to me at the water's edge.

The air is still. Above us, a line of helicopters traces an invisible route in the black sky. Dot after dot, each one equidistant from the last. I reach up and cover the space between with my hand. I tell him: They make the same trip every day. Sunset tours of the Grand Canyon, carrying passengers from Las Vegas to Arizona to watch the light go from white to yellow to pink to purple to blue in the chasm below.

His face does not fill with hatred or fear, but with something else that I have decided is love.

acknowledgments

Thank you to my agent, Danielle Bukowski, for believing in me (and Ben!). You saw this novel exactly the way I'd always hoped the right agent would. Thank you to my editor, Olivia Taylor Smith, for making this book better in ways I could have never imagined on my own, for referencing *In a Lonely Place* by Dorothy B. Hughes during our first meeting, and for guiding me through the wilderness of edits with such care. Thank you to Sean Manning, Brittany Adames, Emily Farebrother, Omesha Edwards, Martha Langford, Amanda Mulholland, Olivia Perrault, Yvette Grant, Carly Loman, Ritika Karnik, Mikaela Bielawski, Laura Petrella, Eileen Chetti, Jackie Seow, Matt Roeser, Michael Nardullo, Mabel Taveras, and Irene Kheradi at Simon & Schuster for making my lifelong dream a reality. Thank you to Ali Lefkowitz for seeing this cinematically.

Thank you to my husband, Rory, for loving me and this novel. I get my best ideas on walks with you and Presley. Without you, this book would not exist.

Thank you to every person who gave me feedback or encouragement as I revised, especially Maile Chapman's fall 2022 fiction workshop at UNLV, David Morris, Caralea Cole, Billy and Liam Lezra, Mike Hanson, Rachel Walker, Veronica Klash, Maggie Slepian, and Meg Bernhard. The anxiety I feel over accidentally leaving someone out is a blessing; it means there are so many of you.

Thank you to Shoshone Village, Black Mountain Institute, Tin House, Spitsbergen Artists Center, and the staff at Starboard Tack for giving me time, support, and champagne, not necessarily in that order.

Thank you to my family for taking me seriously when I was ten years old and said I wanted to write a novel.

Thank you to the national parks I was lucky to live and work in for so many years and all the people I met there. I didn't know it at the time, but you were helping me write this book. Parkies forever.

Thank you to the readers for reading.

And lastly, thank you, Las Vegas, for everything.

about the author

KRISTA DIAMOND'S writing has appeared in *The New York Times*, *The Paris Review*, *Cosmopolitan*, and elsewhere. She holds an MFA from the University of Nevada, Las Vegas, and her work has been supported by Bread Loaf, Tin House, and the Nevada Arts Council. She lives in Las Vegas. *Close Relationships with Strangers* is her debut novel.